Copyright ©

All rig

No part of this b
or used in any manner without the prior written
permission of the copyright owner,
except for the use of brief quotation in a book review.

ISBN: 9798703368534

Cover art by Nathen Solly and Russell Deamer

The right of A.S.George to be identified as the author
of this work has been asserted by her in accordance
with the Copyright, Designs & Patents Act 1988.

This book is fantasy and fiction - presented
solely for entertainment purposes.
Neither the author nor the publisher will be responsible for
psychological or emotional apprehension.
The characters and events in this book are entirely
fictitious, and except in the case of historical
fact, any resemblance to actual events or persons,
living or dead, is entirely coincidental.

Although the author and publisher have made every effort
to ensure that the information in this book was correct
at press time, the author and publisher do not assume
and hereby disclaim any liability to any party for any
loss, damage, or disruption caused by errors or omissions,
whether such errors or omissions result from negligence,
accident or any other cause. No part of this publication may
be reproduced, transmitted in any form- photocopying,
recording, mechanical or electronic - without the prior
written permission of the author or publisher.

This book is dedicated to Bianca, Brett-Yasmin, Danielle and Nathen - the most 'perfect' accomplishments of my entire life.

A Message From The Author - The Inspiration, The Journey and The Acknowledgements

So coming to this section of my book, where I knew I needed to acknowledge my amazing family, friends and colleagues for all their support during this process; I felt like I had hit a wall harder than the elaborate fantasy world of conspiracies, tunnels, treasure and giants inside of my head. I always read the acknowledgements in a book, I consider them to be like accepting one's very own mini Oscar which runs overtime into the adverts. The same question kept chipping away at me 'Do I make this a quick list of names or a drawn out speech?' I had absolutely no idea where or how to start acknowledging these wonderful beings in my life, so I decided to go with the flow, completely winging it and just see where it leads me.

The Inspiration

My very first thank you has to go out to my son Nathen. This book and its sequels would not even be 'a thing' if it wasn't for the incredible mind of my boy. The story transpired from a very casual conversation with him one evening when he said "What if one of the Nazi experiments had actually worked mum and nobody ever knew about it?" That was the lightbulb moment I had been waiting a very long time for. Nathen's amazing imagination led me to combining my medical knowledge with major historical events that sent me on this prodigious incredible journey, entwining and enmeshing several timelines together bringing an entirely unknown and forgotten race into the Millennium. He also proceeded to design the artwork for the book cover. So to you Nathen I am truly grateful, this is all down to you – Thank you darling. I absolutely have to give an enormous acknowledgement and praise to Russell Deamer for his hard work on setting the artwork to an acceptable standard for publishing. You're a lifesaver!

The Cheerleading Squad

Writing this has been an 'on and off' pastime for over five years. I am not a novelist, but to say this was a life dream would be an accurate confession. I started penning my characters immediately after my eldest daughter Bianca told me she was pregnant with my first grandchild. Such exciting news of a new life spurred me to get my backside into gear and something to give my grandchildren for them to remember their 'Grummy'. I have come to the self-realisation that I procrastinate very well – and by the time I completed this story – I now have the pleasure of three grandchildren! Bethany, Robyn and Conrad thank you for making your crinkly old grandma laugh and feel more love than I ever knew possible. During those years I hit many walls trying to fathom which way the story was going. I was extremely blessed that so many people had a lot of faith in me to finish the journey. These 'long-suffering' loved ones have literally been my cheerleader's right from the very beginning, and when I say 'cheerleaders' they really were. They pulled me constantly up from regular moments of self-doubt. I need to praise my daughters Bianca, Brett-Yasmin and Danielle. They gave me the much needed confidence and incentive to see this through to its completion. I want to thank them for their continual support, optimism, love and unbreakable faith in their Mumma. Without their morale boosting moments I may not have reached Cheerleading Squad Finals. I also owe my Brett-Yasmin enormous gratitude and recognition for her help and inspiration during a couple of incidents where I suffered a major case of writers block. She breezed me through my wall hitting moments with such ease and clarity. Additionally being the very first person to read the entire story on its completion.

Thank you also to my step-daughters Millie and Cleo, who likewise guided me through another blockade in the story with their tech-savvy generation know-how and help with satellite imagery.

Also to Hannah Piper who miraculously saved my skin during an awkward and sticky conspiracy theory. You are all legends.

I am eternally grateful to my mum Sandy who never for one moment doubted my ability. Her faith in me achieving this was phenomenal and she would often wonder why I even doubted myself, because she certainly never did. I love my sisters Julie and Stephanie dearly, for picking me up when I felt it was all falling apart. For taking the time to listen and give constructive advice on the synopsis. Huge recognition to Stephanie for helping me kickstart a website for my story.

To my mum's brothers, Uncle Bob and Uncle Rene, for always supporting me throughout my life no matter what insane ideas I might have had. You were always there for me... even if you were rolling your eyes or laughing at my lunacy. Thank you to Uncle Bob who tirelessly nagged me every single week for the entire five years, just to make sure I wouldn't give up on this project.

I must mention my beautiful friends Michelle Scarrett and Maria Newman. These two amazing ladies have had to listen to the many plot twists, my meltdowns and excitement on a weekly basis. They have consistently praised me and built me up.

Clare Terry, Ruth Pearcey and Sandie Roberts, you ladies all have the patience of saints. Your tireless efforts in helping me to recognise my consistent 'tense' errors and editing shortcomings were invaluable. I learnt so much, you have no idea the appreciation and admiration I possess for you all. Additionally my gratitude to Claire Reeves who read my whole novel in one day a week after its completion. You four are my guardian angels.

The Synopsis Advocates

This part is always onerous and difficult, because it's is not just a list of names. This is a list of an amazing network of people that share a precious and significant part of my life. A part that is profoundly special that my indebtedness to each and every one of them is immeasurable. When the book was completed I had this incredible task force of friends and loved ones who happily took their time to read the synopsis and gave me unbelievable feedback. Thank you, thank you, thank you - to each and every one of you for your encouragement and support:

Sandra Hinde, Geoffrey Hinde, Julie Mutter, Stephanie George, Tiffany Hinde, Daren Deamer, Wendy Deamer, Rene Piercey, Bob Piercey, Bianca Fenner, Brett-Yasmin Boucher, Danielle Solly, Nathen Solly, Ben Fenner, Patrick Swift, Maria Newman, Hollie Bowker, Philip Boucher, Hannah Piper, Michelle Scarrett, Ruth Pearcey, Karen Howe, Natalie Howe, Simon Cox, Sarah Cox, Claire Bahadoor, Maria Clarke, Amanda Brimicombe, Claire Trillwood, Julie Hall, Sally Brind, Clare Terry, Sharon Puttick, Michelle Goddard, Jo Glover, Helen Hayes, Anne Pickett, Clare Saunders, Emily Constable, Sandie Roberts and Yalah Kennaird

The Backbone

To say my better half has the patience of a saint would be the biggest and most distorted understatement ever. Daren Deamer, there are no words to eloquently describe my gratitude, appreciation and love for you during this process. You were quite literally thrown into my insane world of characters, conspiracy theories and even though you never asked to be, Daren you kindly indulged me. You were deeply enveloped into each of the characters development and endured their quest to discover an unknown civilisation. You just listened, engaged my fantasy world, supported me and I have never known anyone as long-suffering as you. It's been an incredible journey and I am blessed to have travelled every part of it with you. You are my backbone and you are awesome.

The Defining 'F' Words

In our current world of *fake* news and *fake* stories you have to discipline yourself not to be *fraught* psychologically. I am a story writer, I would never wish to make anyone *fall* or *falter* because of my words. There is an exquisite labyrinthine of *fine-fibres* in *folktales*.

'Facts, Faith and Fantasy' - when these three elements are blended together to create an adventure it is – **FICTION**.

The Readers Quest

Hidden amongst my story is a 'cipher'. Your quest, if you desire adventure, is to unravel and decode its secret. May the journey solve obstacles and the task brings you indiscriminate riches.

<u>The Puppeteers</u>

I have to acknowledge the truly inspirational Authors, Actors, Film-makers and Designers that some of my characters recognise along their journey – or at least my journey. Thank you for your incredible knowledge and your provoking motivation. I have been grabbed by your mind-blowing characters, storylines that they have become so ingrained into society that achievement is phenomenal. You truly are the puppeteers and I am humbly your marionette.

Chapter 30 - Against All Odds. Writing chapter 30 was undoubtedly out of my comfort zone. I have never written anything on this level or scale before. The power of music is invaluable. It has the ability to influence, transform and heal. For me it 'inspires'. To aid me through this chapter I had a special piece of music that I put on repeat. If I listened to this a thousand times I doubt that would be an exaggeration. Played repeatedly from 04:35mins onwards I would like to thank and acknowledge the incredibly talented score composer Ramin Djawadi - Against All Odds - Game of Thrones Season 7 (HBO Series/George.R.R.Martin). He would not even begin to realise how influential he has been.

The Ending

...And finally an enormous 'Thank you' to those of you who took the time to read my story and stayed on for the credits...I'm writing this acknowledgement in January 2021. We are still in the midst of a Global Pandemic during our 'Second Wave'... Make the most of everyday! Love and laugh and smile, these things are free and make every single day worth it. Cherish your family and friends, they are the air that you breathe. Is it cliché to say "Life is too short?" After the thousands and thousands that woke up at the beginning of 2020 but never got to see into another year, nope it's certainly not cliché. There are so many things to be grateful for, the fact that many of us are still here into this insane game of Jumanji is just one of them....we are truly the lucky ones. I look forward to you all coming back again to see the characters adventures continue in the sequel – 'Deluge'. Love to you all.

The Nephilim Assignment

A.S.George

Chapter 1

"Why the hell is that clown hanging upside down from the scaffolding?" Bryan says appearing at the door.
"He thinks he's Batman!!" Louise responds and looks admiringly at Steve. Lou is a vivacious girl that has spent the past few years doing a terrible job of hiding the fact that he is her crush and she somehow has this unique ability in name dropping a movie at every given opportunity.
So here he is hanging upside down from the scaffolding, just dangling, the literal office joker and Steve knows it, he loves it and he relishes in the attention.
"Well take the photo quick, my head feels like a swollen melon" a rather odd description of blood rushing to one's head.
"Done it? Cool shot."
Steve is 6'2". This, in itself makes him look amusing, all gangly and dangly, but the navy pinstripe suit, pale pink shirt and the silk Selfridge's tie flapping in his face adds to the amusement. He looks like a Stock Broker who has just lost his marbles & his client's million pound investment.

He takes a variety of upside down phone-selfies, none of them are going to be very flattering and by this time he is very flushed red in the face and straining like he's constipated.

The girls surrounding him all giggle as they snap away on their phones, more interested in their social media uploads to worry about Bryan's appearance at the back door. "Policies & Procedures do not cover juvenile antics or insurance pay-outs Mr Garrett."
Bryan, editor of the newspaper has worked for The Thames Charter most of his adult life, a stout man, with a very good sense of humour. He's balding, with a dry and sarcastic personality. Most of the staff often call him Danny DeVito, not in any puerile back biting way, but with real genuine endearment. Steve flips his body forward, grabs hold of the bar his legs dangle from and in one graceful movement flips his whole body back until he's on his feet again. The girls, giggle and continue to stare at him. Steve has piercing blue eyes, flecks of grey and the cheeky lines that crease in the outer corners knows that he is very much liked by everyone. He straightens his suit and then his tie, grinning proudly at himself. Hanging upside down by some scaffolding outside the office isn't exactly heroic or majorly acrobatic, but cheekily rebellious enough for a dragging Friday afternoon. The sun shines and every ones spirits run high, the weekend is coming.

Louise thrusts her arm forward and turns her mobile phone screen to Steve. As the glare of the sun catches and reflects off the screen, Steve cups his hands over it to see. She looks at him responsively and stares at his messed up dark brown hair, all spiky and poking in different directions from having been gloriously taken by the law of gravity some moments earlier and reaches up teases her fingers like a comb through his hair.

"You look a bit......well, hedge and backwards comes to mind" she says very boldly, trying a feeble attempt at making her spontaneous grooming look completely normal, and in no way intended to look seductive.

"Excellent pic Lou, can you send it to me?" Steve says looking up from the screen and sees his photo reflecting off Louise's sunglasses.

"Sure, text or email?" she replies quickly breaking his gaze.

"Mr Garrett, can I have five minutes? And grab us a cuppa on your way, mate" Bryan says as he goes back in through the door, followed by the rest of the staff, all still muttering and looking at each other's mobile photos.

Steve straightens out his clothes again, pays attention to his cufflinks and the sleeves of his suit jacket. Louise turns her attention to the back door, while taking a glance at her reflection in the window, she notices Steve subtly looking at her legs & she does her best impression of a 1950's Marilyn Monroe wiggle walk, promptly trips slightly on the mat at the doorstep, Steve hides a small smirk as Louise hurriedly tries to cover any error pretending to ignore it had happened.

The small office hosts an average looking décor and

from the layout it is obvious it isn't that of a National press room. A small local business which made a lot of its enterprise on the fact it is based in London; sometimes they were first on the scene at some of the capitals most infamous events and sold many famous stories to the paparazzi 'Premier League'.

Louise composes herself back at her desk, wiggles her mouse just a bit to bring up her computer screen. Steve stands by the kettle and peers down the corridor at her, smiles to himself as she ducks behind her computer screen with a compact mirror in her hand to reapply her lipstick. Louise is very attractive with shoulder length blonde hair, hazel eyes, perfect bow shape lips and a little dimple that just appears in her left cheek when she smiles. She applies more red lipstick, which she always favourably refers to as 'fire engine red' to which Steve would respond 'more like a letter box gob Lou'.
Every day she wears a snug fitting Body-Con dress, but then she did have the perfect curvy figure for it. Today's dress is a royal blue that came just above the knee. Steve always credits himself on 'noticing things' about women. It is his joy in being able to brag 'I'm totally in touch with my feminine side'.

He picks up the two mugs and heads towards Bryan's office at the end of the open plan area of desks. The door is already open "knock knock" he says as he pushes the rest of the door open with his knee.
"Steve" Bryan responds, as he leans forward over

his windowsill, watering the line of plants along it. Concentrating on his office gardening he continues "Steve I have an assignment for you, it's well, a little out of our normal kind of stuff."

"Not the Women's Institute knitting circle or cake fair then?" Steve jokes.

"Ermm, well we could always let the Women's Institute onto this one" Bryan laughs very loudly at his own joke, which completely passes Steve by.

"No, no, it's an odd one Steve. From what I can gather none of the biguns want to touch it."

Bryan's referral to 'Biguns' was always the National press.

"To be fair Bryan, the biguns don't normally do write ups on the little league footie team or the village hall's craft fair."

"Steve, this one's a bit....." he pauses "controversial?" his face screws up in a baffled way, as a note of perplexity comes out in his tone.

"A nun got pregnant?" Steve laughs loudly.

"No, no, it's a Nazi. Well, Ex, well I'm not quite sure on the current political correctness to address this right." Steve glances at Bryan as he turns around from the windowsill. Just as Bryan says "Nazi" Steve thinks to himself how much he really does remind him of Danny DeVito.

"Did you say Nazi?"

"Look, it's all a bit hush-hush, you know how these things can escalate publicly. I've been informed today that Viktor Otto-Wolff has been taken to the Royal Brompton Hospital under armed guard."

"I don't understand, I thought his trial was in Rome?" "Well, he was taken ill, had a heart episode and the plane had to do an emergency landing into Heathrow."

"Go on" says Steve as he takes a seat the other side of Bryan's desk and drops his playful mischievous persona.

"The thing is I have a feeling we maybe being set up here. His PA, a Miss Addario contacted this office, it all seems very unusual and she has specifically asked for you to do the interview! The National press' hands are tied, as in politically. Those men in black at No.10 have come down hard, but I got a call from Larry, hot off the press, almost as if dropping a hint like a scud-missile."

Bryan twists his body uncomfortably back and forth on his swivel chair as he often did in moments of unrest or if he is particularly uneasy about a situation.

"We haven't just stumbled across it, this is no accident Steve. But could be a big seller with a large income if we were to pitch it right to the Biguns, when he's in Rome."

"Ok that is completely random Bryan, why ask for me?"

"Agree, the only thing I can think of is she's read something of yours, maybe she knows the Biguns will try to annihilate Otto-Wolff, but also knows that the media crazed society will not stop hounding him until they get their story."

"Do you honestly think the public actually care

what this man has to say for himself? After seventy five years, he's finally been caught and brought to face justice. The war may have been a long time ago but not many people are so forgiving for the war crimes these men committed." Steve replies with a significant perplexed expression.

"I know, but there is always a human need for curiosity. Wolff is 96 years old. One of the last left and he's never told his story, admitted or apologised for his part in the war. If he doesn't make it to trial or to Rome then the world will just never know, and he owes it to many thousands of people."

Bryan comes to a halt in swinging his chair, he looks completely straight on and holds Steve's stare.

"I want you to interview him."

Steve squirms uncomfortably the silence seems to last an abiding five minutes, only broken by the sound of high pitched beeps from the office's antiquated fax machine.

Bryan stands up promptly shuffles over to pick up the fax and idly pretends to read it.

"Are you sure Bryan?" Steve finally mutters, twisting anxiously at his onyx cufflinks.

"Honestly Steve, I think it would be great for this office. It does seem extremely unusual that you have been asked for by name that in itself is suspicious, maybe Miss Addario wants a lot less fuss. Journalists are in the most despised of genres akin to estate agents and politicians. We don't even know how frail or ill he is. I can make some calls, pass it by the Royal Brompton Hospital and take it from there. I just see the empathy in you. I see how patient you are with the elderly Steve. It's an honourable and admirable trait, when you did that piece on dementia there wasn't a dry eye in there" Bryan points out of his door towards the open plan office and Steve glances up from his stayed gaze at his cufflinks.

"In the meantime whilst I make some enquiries, I want you to gather as much information as you can on Otto-Wolff."

Steve shifts uneasily and does a single firm nod of his head and as Bryan lifts his mug of tea to his mouth, takes a very noisy slurp, he captures Steve's eye and can sense his apprehension and restlessness.

"I know your grandfather is Polish and his history, but I know you are the right one for this story. I wouldn't ask otherwise, let's flow with this, seriously what's the worst that could happen? Steve, ...Steve?"

Steve nods again, the anxiety in his face screams volumes. His mind jumbles altogether a hundred twisted thoughts all at once.

"This one could be the mother ship Mr Garrett. The 24 carat gold Ferrari."

Bryan sips again at his tea then holds up a photograph of a very young Viktor Otto-Wolff which he has printed off the internet. Steve reaches forward over the desk; hand out stretched takes the photograph and settles himself back into the chair to take a long look at it. At first glance Steve is taken aback by the normality of the young man. He wonders to himself what he had really expected, some kind of shifty looking psychopath. He just appears to be a handsome, well-groomed young officer in his uniform, probably in his late teens. It was the usual khaki/olive Nazi uniform with two pleated breast pockets on each side of the jacket. Two white stripes on the red Swastika armband ranking Otto-Wolff as an 'Oberfuhrer' a district senior leader. The jacket has an outer belt and a cross belt that goes diagonally from his right shoulder to his left hip. The collar of the jacket has patches on it which looks like a double leaf and Steve wonders if it could also signify some kind of ranking. The jacket also fashions the Totenkopf or 'dead head', a very renowned symbol during that time. The Totenkopf was the German equivalent of the skull and crossbones, a human skull and two crossed bones behind the head. It was the international symbol for – Death. The waistband hosts a holster and gun and Steve couldn't help notice that the hat he is wearing is too big for his head. The hat has a solid black peak on it and an eagle patch in the centre. The eagle is carrying a Swastika. The peak of the hat seems to come down way too far over his eyebrows. He has pale skin, very thin lips and a slightly pointed significant nose. The thing that captures Steve most of all is Otto-Wolff's kind, drawing, deep eyes. This is not what Steve had expected at all.

He felt it would've been better if the photograph told the story of a deranged lunatic, with two horns coming out of his head, but it didn't. Otto-Wolff looked a very normal well-groomed young handsome soldier. In fact, somebody you wouldn't think would stand out in a crowd, if dressed in normal civilian clothes.

Steve stares at him for a good couple of minutes, taking in every detail of the photo. 'What do you hide?' Steve thinks to himself, and directly at that exact moment he realises Bryan is right 'a human need for curiosity'. Steve looks at Bryan.

"Ok, I will do the interview if you can set it up."

Steve stands up and heads for the door, Bryan walks over to him, gives him an agreeing pat on his shoulder and says nothing. He knows that Steve's grandfather had been a prisoner of war for two years and spent a year in a mental institution, in a catatonic state, suffering post-traumatic stress disorder. Steve's family never knew the total extent of the torment his grandfather, Mikolai Borowski, had been through during his confinement, not even Steve's grandmother. She would always say 'Leave the past in silence, kill a root of a weed and the weed will not flourish and wreak disaster'.

On the very odd occasion when his grandfather would go quiet and into his own little world for a few days, his wife was the only person who ever managed to draw him out. She is English and had been working as an auxiliary nurse at the Bicêtre Hospital in Paris when she met Mikolai. She used to tell Steve, his brother Robert, his sister Michelle and his cousins wild stories of ghosts at the Bicêtre. About times when it had been a mental institution in the 18th century and how it was the birthplace of a curious machine, which had been designed at the hospital to decapitate a herd of sheep. The employees at the hospital were so delighted with their new machine it went on to become the infamous 'guillotine' in France. Steve and Robert used to take in all her stories with a strange delight and she used to refer to her grandsons as the 'gruesome children time forgot'. If the story had blood and guts or anything gory they loved it.

It was a typical Florence Nightingale story of nurse falls in love with the patient and patient falls in love with the nurse. Steve's, sister Michelle definitely preferred hearing the love stories and found them to be the most romantic stories ever. She would always say 'Oh Grandma this should be in a Hollywood movie' all starry eyed. Nobody could tell such amazing descriptive stories like his grandmother Molly Borowski.

Steve wonders what his grandparents would think of this assignment as he walks past three desks in the open plan office to his own. He notices nothing nor anybody else, just deep thoughts of Otto-Wolff, his childhood stories, guillotines, the holocaust and Bryan's rather out of control Boston fern on the windowsill. He sits in his chair and is instantly distracted by his computer screensaver, a rather amusing photograph of his earlier acrobatics which had been humorously photo-shopped to make him look like Batman.

Steve comes right back into the present reality and

he laughs very loudly, which is shadowed by sporadic bursts of sniggering from around the rest of the office.

Chapter 2

Steve sits on the underground train deep in thought and is completely preoccupied with his intriguing upcoming interview. The carriage is surprisingly unoccupied for 5:30pm on a Friday afternoon but he doesn't notice he's so distracted by all the thoughts jumbling in his head and his conversation with Bryan earlier that afternoon 'Why have they asked for me to interview him?' He reaches deep into his trouser pocket to retrieve his mobile phone and looks at all the playful photo uploads from the lunchtime antics – 12 Facebook notifications. Exiting the App, he searches the internet for Viktor Otto-Wolff. As he suspects, pages and pages of search results begin to appear. He decides he will start making notes, when he gets home, on all the information regarding his capture and the forthcoming trial in Rome. One thing that keeps jumping out at Steve the elusive Oberfuhrer was entwined with the word 'Ravensbrück'. Everywhere Steve looks, there is the word 'Ravensbrück', or 'The women and children of Ravensbrück'. He quickly learns that it had been a concentration camp in the northern area of Germany and was purpose built, mainly for women and children.

The loud rumbling, clattering and groaning sounds of the carriage as it rattles along its tracks and the eerily unusual quietness of its eight occupants gives Steve a very unwelcome shiver. He stares at each black and white photograph that comes up of the camp, its barracks, the kitchen, the disgustingly cramped sleeping arrangements and a small infirmary, although the hospital was not for the sick but for medical experimentation. There are some photographs of women and children working on site, a textile and leather processing company had built a factory. 5000 women had been used as tailors, shoemakers, furriers and producers of other profitable wears. On first appearance nothing particularly horrific or sinister shines through on the internet search.

He becomes intently enamoured by a little girl staring straight at the cameraman in a particular photograph and he is so deeply drawn into her eyes, it's as if they are whispering to him. The photo is tattered and stained to more of a sepia colouring and she was holding the hand of an adult, although she was the only person predominantly in the picture. The more Steve stares, the more he feels hypnotised by her gaze, as though she's staring right back at him. He's transfixed, this little girl has him in a trance; she had tangled ringlets in her hair and a dirty little face. The very kind of childish grubbiness you would imagine from a good day of outdoor play, rolling down hills, playing in mud, scuffed knees and other wholesome childish frivolity – but Steve knew that in this Fraulein's case that definitely wasn't why she was unwashed. Her eyes were sad, frightened, screaming. He tenderly put his finger on the screen and strokes her cheek, it was as if she was saying 'help me', Steve feels a lump appear in the base of his throat, and takes a sharp intake of breath. The train screeches with a high pitch, to Steve it sounds more like some kind of background music to a spooky movie with the high pitch screech the little girl's screams surround him. The encapsulating scream from this little girl's digitally captured memory; makes Steve quickly thrust his phone back into his pocket.

Steve sits on his balcony and stares out at the city lights. Closing his eyes every now and then, he listens to the sounds of the city, the music, the traffic and the people he takes in the smells of the various fast food restaurants below. He reaches for his glass of Sauvignon Blanc and looks up at the stars and as he takes a sip, a busy and bustling city of utter insomniacs, he thinks about the people during the war some eighty years earlier, staring up at exactly the same stars as he is at this precise moment. The feeling of surrealism and the overwhelming reality is sweeping, chilling and formidable. Half the men would have been away at war, the children would have been evacuated to countryside residences whilst the night guards, with their wind up sirens to sound an air raid would be on their watch.

He reminisces about the school trips he had taken and his childhood fascination with wartime museums and he smiles to himself as he remembers that they all had to dress up, as evacuees, as part of the school project. His mother had not really grasped the concept of early 1940 children's clothing and had been to the local charity shop to find a waistcoat and flat cap and came back with an ivory brocade satin waistcoat, quite obviously worn by a groom on his wedding day. She had endearingly said to Steve "Now maybe you were more of the wartime aristocracy Steve, there's always been Royals no matter what's going on in the world."

He never questioned her, but knowing full well that King George VI had the young princesses Elizabeth & Margaret, he never fully knew exactly which young Prince he was supposed to be though, he was certainly the best dressed evacuee at school that day. Taken in by an aroma of smoked bacon, blended with a strong scent of garlic, his apartment block is next to a trendy little Italian restaurant, quite a popular dining establishment. He takes another sip of his wine, acknowledging everything that his Grandad Borowski had suffered for the simple pleasures in life. 'All we take for granted' Steve nods to himself, recalling tales of long queues and ration books. He holds his glass up slightly, tilts it just a little to make a toast and says "Goodnight Grandad." -----

As the alarm clock sounds at 8am that Saturday morning, Steve launches one arm out from under the quilt and smacks the snooze button abruptly, buries his head under the pillow and finally emerges half an hour later and after hitting the alarm snooze a further six times. He stares at his stubble in the bathroom mirror above the sink, splashes his face with water to wake himself up a bit and decides the stubble could stay for the weekend. He continues to stare in the mirror, his mind flashing back to his home-bound train journey and the image of the little girl. He splashes his face again, decides to have a shower after his morning jog.

Throwing on his grey jogging trousers and white vest top, which fits tightly revealing his toned physique and broad shoulders, he picks up his iPod by the kettle in the kitchen, places the earphones into his ears, grabs his door key and sets off toward the stairwell. He moves swiftly down the stairs from Level 6 and halfway down stops to help Mrs Sanders with her four bags of shopping. She is a very flirty and spritely 79 year old who has a flat on Level 3. She always made no qualms in flirting with Steve.

"If only I was just a couple of years younger Mr Garrett I would eat you all up" she would say and he would always humour her and flatter her, which made them both chuckle.

She always applied way too much makeup and especially too much blusher to her cheeks, was always smiling and had a little pug dog called Berty. Struggling sometimes with walking him, Steve would always help whenever he could. On this occasion Berty is in the flat, Mrs Sanders couldn't cope with walking him and doing her shopping at the same time.

Steve takes the carrier bags out of her hands and carries them to her apartment, whilst she rummages through her large carpet bag looking for her door key.

"So what are your plans this weekend Mr Garrett? Taking a lovely lady courting?"

Steve places the carrier bags just inside her doorway and is about to answer when he notices the top of a headline on a tabloid, which is folded up in one of her carrier bags. He pulls it out slightly, the sub-heading reads:

'Nazi War Criminal in UK. At Undisclosed Destination' and pushes it back into the bag.

"Not this weekend Mrs Sanders, lots of work to do" and he heads back to the stairwell.

"Life is too short Mr Garrett..." she says jokingly "...you must learn to play once in a while."

He turns to face her and smiles "Well, I know where you are for that date if I get some spare time Mrs Sanders."

She giggles like a young lady and closes the door, Steve places his earphones back in his ears and sets off again but this time to the Newsagents. He picks up the appropriate newspapers and heads next door to the patisserie grabbing a Danish pastry and croissant...., not exactly what he had planned for a healthy detox and exercise weekend! He wanders around the corner to the park behind his block of flats. It was turning out to be a gloriously sunny day and he decides he'd read his newspapers and eat his Danish on the bench.

He settles himself back into the park bench, puts his arms outstretched on the back, closes his eyes and basks in the sunshine. He hears the laughter and noises of the children by the swings, the rattles of a skate board wheels behind him and the distant chimes of an approaching ice cream van, accompanied by the smells of cooking waffles.

"Hope you've put sunscreen on Mr Garrett," comes the familiar giggle from Louise as she completely blocks out his sunlight. He opens his eyes and without saying a word, looks down at the bench seat, telling her to sit next to him with his authoritative silence.

She sits down next to him smiling and tilts her chin up towards the sky, shutting her eyes as well.

"You were very quiet yesterday afternoon, everything ok with DeVito?" she says with a subtle tone of concern.

"Mmm, he wants me to interview that war criminal Viktor Otto-Wolff. He's here in London Lou."

"How on earth are you going to be able to pull that off? Are you going to do it?" she asks as they continue to sit there, eyes shut and heads facing the heavens.

"Yes I agreed to it, because apparently his PA asked for me specifically, it makes no sense? I've just been doing some research..." and at that he suddenly remembers his newspapers, sitting upright takes them out of the bag, hands Louise the Danish pastry which she bites into willingly, and he opens the paper.

Nothing particular was being reported except speculation he was somewhere in the United Kingdom and that a Rabbi from the Jewish community was expressing his concern.

"Fancy a coffee Lou?" He doesn't wait for an answer, he just takes her hand and pulls her up onto her feet, she smiles and as he gently brushes a tiny piece of pastry from her lip, he notices she's wearing a black Adidas crop top and jogging pants,

"Didn't know you jogged Lou?"

"Yes all the time," she replies knowing it is a blatant fib. She just wanted to 'bump into' Steve. They walk along the pathway through the park until they reach a little café two minutes away from Steve's flat, called The Fresh Bean, a very eclectic little coffee shop with very rustic solid oak tables and chairs, all hand made.

"What do you fancy Lou?" as they both stare up at the black slate menu board, above the large coffee making machines.

"Skinny latte please."

"Two skinny lattes please" Steve says to the young girl behind the counter.

They sit in the corner by the front window to do some people watching. "So what have you discovered so far Steve?"

"Sorry huh?" Steve replies.

"About Viktor Otto-Wolff?"

"Oh! Yes..." he chuckles "...he was an Oberfuhrer, which I'm assuming is a German version of a General or something. He was based at a concentration camp called Ravensbrück," Steve pauses for a moment, sips his latte looks up at Louise, and whispers "Did you know Lou the Nazi's did some horrific medical experiments on children? This particular camp was made up of mainly women and children. If children were disabled or poorly they were taken away from their parents and the parents were told that they were taking them to receive revolutionary new medical treatments with the possibility of cures. Instead they were just slaughtered in some twisted euthanasia programme."

Louise makes a little gasp sound and shakes her head.

"I can't even begin to imagine, I mean, I've seen documentaries and stuff, cried all the way through Schindler's List, but I don't even think I could begin to research or study it. For me, ignorance is bliss."

"Mmm, I know. My main concern is what do I say to him? I can't just blurt out 'did you slaughter babies and children?'."

"Huh, why not? They did terrible things Steve. If he's not guilty then why has he been in hiding for over 75 years?"

They both become instantly distracted by a very happy little pug walking solo past the window and as Louise laughs, Steve jumps to his feet "Berty!"

Quickly exiting the café he whistles "Berty here" and the little pug turns, goes straight toward Steve and wags his tail excitedly.

Steve picks him up, turns to the shop window, holds Berty's paw and makes a little waving gesture to

Louise and as she giggles and waves back, a very breathless Mrs Sanders appears around the corner,
"Oooo you naughty boy..." she wheezes. "...it seems as though you are my knight in shining armour Mr Garrett."
He bends forward and whispers in her ear "I think its fate Mrs S, we're destined you know."
Mrs Sanders raises her hand to her mouth and giggles again perfectly carefree and flirtatious.
"Indeed" she whispers back and takes Berty out of Steve's arms, cradling him in her arms like a baby.
"Do you need a hand Mrs Sanders?" Steve says as she turns and walks back around the corner. She stops, smiles, looks at Steve and without saying a word points reassuringly towards the coffee shop. Steve turns to see Louise staring with a huge smile across her face.
Steve nods back at Mrs Sanders and heads back into the coffee shop.
"My neighbour," he states, and catches a glimmer of adoration in Louise's eyes, as she tilts her head to the side and teases a few strands of hair away from her face. There are a few seconds of silence, which feels like minutes, neither knowing what to say. Steve's phone rings breaking the silence and he swiftly answers it.
"Ahh Bryan....yes thanks...right then, when?...no worries....I understand...ok speak later"
"The interview's this afternoon." Steve directs to Louise,
"On your day off?"

"Seems so, apparently we were the only ones to ask, but Bryan suspected that would be the case. I better go Lou I need to have a shower and a shave."

"Of course, no worries, hope it goes ok," she replies. Steve's already distracted by his thoughts at the unexpected suddenness of the interview happening so quickly.

Chapter 3

Steve works his way through the bustling crowds of people on Fulham Road and heads towards the Royal Brompton Hospital. He has compiled a few handwritten notes from his research and has also collected a few printouts of internet information which are all bundled together in his leather brief case. A beautifully embossed hand held case given to him by his grandfather on graduating university. He makes his way to the entrance of the hospital and notices two casually dressed men standing either side of the doorway, making a miserable attempt of being inconspicuous and thinks to himself, 'they just scream to the general public 'nothing much is happening here, but we are here so clearly something big is going down'. As he approaches the entrance the man on the right steps in front of him, pats him down, looks in the brief case and Steve shows him his identity badge from The Thames Charter.
"Miss Addario is expecting me." Steve shows him the ID badge again, the guard nods, steps to one side, allows Steve to pass and as he makes his way to the reception desk to enquire on Herr Otto-Wolff's whereabouts, a voice comes from behind him.
"Mr Garrett?"
A strong twang of an Italian accent, he turns and sees an elegant woman with perfect posture ad-

vance towards him with her hand outstretched. He takes her hand and shakes it "Yes".

"We've been expecting you," she says in her beautiful rolling European tone.

She is slim, about 5'7" in height but almost making 6' in her stylish black heels. She's wearing a fitted navy blue skirt suit with a white blouse and seamed back stockings. He notices the slight indentation of the clasp from her suspender belt through the very tight pencil skirt. She's very poised as she leads him through numerous corridors, like a catwalk model.

"My name is Ellia. I am Herr Otto-Wolff's Personal Assistant," she exclaims.

"Pleased to meet you..." Steve starts to reply but swiftly interrupted....,

"He has never agreed to anything like this before. Please keep in mind he is very ill Mr Garrett and he gets tired very quickly."

Steve gazes at her olive flawless skin and the subtle fragrance of a florally perfume. Her dark brown shiny hair tied tight into a flowing ponytail at the back adorned by a beautiful rhinestone and pearl barrette which almost matches the small pearl earrings and choker necklace.

"Ok I understand."

"Do not push him or agitate him, I warn you he is a highly stubborn man, if he refuses to talk then he won't talk."

"Ok..."

Ellia stops to a sudden halt and faces Steve.

"You are very lucky to be seeing him Mr Garrett,

please bear that in mind. Sit here, I will tell him you've arrived."

Steve takes a seat in the long corridor. He peers around the corner to see another two casually dressed guards standing either side of double doors leading onto a hospital ward and wonders to himself if he is actually 'lucky' to be seeing a remnant of a sadistic regime, at all. He opens the zip on his brief case and takes out the printout photo of Viktor, which Bryan had given him and looks at it again with intrigue. Steve closes his eyes for a few moments to take in what he is about to do. Not his normal dog show reporting. He begins to think about his grandparents Mikolai and Molly Borowski and realises he wishes that he'd spoken to them a bit more recently. He suddenly opens his eyes to the buzzing vibration of his mobile.

"Hi Bryan....yes I'm here just waiting...no, no problems getting in...will call you back."

Steve presses the 'End Call' button, he remembers the photo of the little girl he had found the day before and clicks on his history, bringing up the image again. She draws Steve in mystically with her eyes, that sadness, the fear, her unheard cries. Steve becomes deeply consumed by her trance once again, he finds himself telling her 'it will be ok.'

"Mr Garrett," he hears, and turns to see Ellia walking back towards him "Herr Otto-Wolff will see you now."

Steve places everything into his case and removes the digital Dictaphone and slips it in his jacket pocket. Ellia leads the way down the last corridor towards the guards and they stop Steve again proceeding to do the same pat down routine as their front door counterparts until they're satisfied he isn't about to do Otto-Wolff some damage. Steve feels his heart start to quicken and an unpleasant tightening of his stomach, he isn't normally a person afflicted with nerves but it dawns on him that his usual overwhelming confidence with his humour and flattery, will not aid him through this situation.

He's guided through the door that leads onto the ward, and he is surprised to notice another 8 to 9 men wandering around, quite clearly not doctors and watches as two nurses busy about. One doing paperwork and the other wearing gloves, carrying a small silver kidney dish with two vials of blood to be sent off for phlebotomy testing.

"In here." Ellia opens the door to a darkened side room.

"If you need anything I will be out here," she says and for the first time since meeting Steve she gives a slight smile.

"Mr Garrett is here Viktor" and she allows the door to close.

The curtains are closed as Steve stares at the man lying in the hospital bed. He has leads from his chest attached to a machine, which reads a heart rate of 155b.p.m, 'he is very tachycardic' Steve thinks to himself, wondering if Viktor is as nervous as he is. He has an oximeter attached to his left index finger and oxygen supplied via a nose tube.

Steve breaks his fixation on the medical exterior of the situation, to absorb the appearance of Otto-Wolff. Just like when he had been given the photograph of him the day before, Steve is astounded by the normality of this frail old man. He has white wispy hair and a grey moustache. A little stubble to his chin, but Steve realises that it is more likely to be due to his hospital confinement, rather than lax grooming. His moustache is incredibly neat and his pyjama top looks crisp with a starched collar and Steve notices the wrinkles and age spotted backs of his hands, his frail, bony hands. Otto-Wolff opens his eyes and reaches to his lap where his glasses are placed on top of a folded newspaper and slowly places them onto his face and looks up at Steve.

"Guten tag Mr Garrett." His voice is quiet and raspy, he takes a large intake of breath and winces in pain as he coughs. Steve promptly lifts up a glass of water from his bedside and Otto-Wolff shakes his head, making a 'no' gesture with his hand.

"Please sit," he says.

Steve pulls over a seat to the end of the bed and without even thinking it through or for any premeditated reason he turns and holds out his hand to shake. Otto-Wolff stares at the hand presenting itself to him, looks up at Steve's face and very gently and slowly takes his hand.

"Thank you for seeing me," Steve says and takes his seat.

"That never happens," Otto-Wolff declares softly.

Steve shakes his head with a puzzled expression across his face "sorry, I don't understand?"

"You shook my hand Mr Garrett, that doesn't usually happen."

"Please, call me Steve," he says glancing towards the blood pressure machine that was automatically inflating on Otto-Wolff's arm. Steve quietly presses the record button on the Dictaphone and Otto-Wolff watches Steve move the chair a little more towards the base of the bed. He notices Steve's smartly dressed attire, his brown hair and kindly blue eyes and he contemplates Steve's body language as he watches him rubbing the left side of his cheek and square jaw line with his hand, whilst rummaging through his papers in his briefcase.

"Angst haben?" Otto-Wolff says to Steve in his soft grainy tone.

"I, I'm sorry, I don't speak German," Steve replies anxiously.

"Are you nervous Steve? I am. I have been nervous my whole life. I am the connoisseur of nervousness," he smirks.

"Yes, yes I am sir. If I am totally honest, this is way out of my comfort zone." Steve shifts awkwardly and uneasily in the chair. He starts questioning if he should've just said that, or should he have admitted feeling nervous at all. Would Otto-Wolff see that as weakness?

"Ahh yes comfort zones, I like that expression..." His gravelly German accent becomes more clear "...my zone is not comfortable either, please call me

Viktor. Sir is not a respect I desire."

Steve is taken aback by the humility of the man. Maybe a lifetime of running or hiding had presented itself. Then Steve has a notion that he'd never considered before, his protectiveness towards his grandfather's past, his childhood fascinations with all that was WWII, the Nazi's were only humans too. He isn't sure if he can possibly allow or enable that concept, after all they were monsters. Steve scrutinizes the scenario briefly concluding that actually a lot of them just did what they were told, it was their job they may not have had a choice and they may have feared the results themselves that they inflicted on others. Steve's thoughts race.

"What do you want to know?" Viktor asks him.

Steve looks at Viktor, Viktor looks at Steve, and both men at a point in their lives knowing that this meeting of minds could change their ideas and realisations forever and neither one knowing where to start.

"Viktor..." Steve starts, looking for Otto-Wolff's acknowledgement that he'd used his forename as requested and Viktor gives a nod with a smile. Steve clears his throat anxiously.

"Viktor, I had a list of things to ask, a pile of information about... things...well, like the stuff I read on Ravensbrück but now I'm here I don't know what to ask you at all."

Viktor leans forward, picks up the glass of water and takes a few sips.

"Ugh it's warm..." he beckons Steve to lean in forward "...then let me make this easy for you Steve, don't ask me anything."

"But I...." Steve thinks he's completely blown his chances, with his lack of confidence and distant deficiency in forthrightness.

"I just want to tell you my story Steve. If you want detailed stories and tales of torture and murders, you will not get it. I have spent my life in an act of contrition. I have sought redemption, forgiveness. I have sacrificed the normal desires of a wife, a home, children, to give back to those who suffer. I never feared death, as I wanted to embrace a short life, as a justice for what happened during that period of time. But God's punishment to me was to inflict me with a long life, to suffer and to see their faces in my dreams every night. I'm not going to tell you what we were instructed to do."

Steve sits back in his chair stunned and wonders what he can ask him. What is he able to make out of an interview with a Nazi who is being brought for trial, if the man will not talk of his crimes?

"You do not need to hear about Nazi ideologies and policies. Who doesn't already know about humans suffering at the hands of our regime?"

Viktor pauses and takes some long breaths while Steve looks on, is it really worth taking this fragile old man to Rome to face a trial now?

"I will answer to all those questions and what I did, at my trial. I am not doing that today."

"Why did you agree to see me and be interviewed then?" Steve asks in a gentle but puzzled tone.

"Because, I want to tell my story. Me. I need to say I am sorry and I need to tell the world who Viktor Otto-Wolff is. I was never caught and taken with my colleagues to the Nuremburg trials. I spent my whole life running, hiding and avoiding capture...I kept secrets, many dark secrets and now I think it's time the rest of the world knows about them."

Steve begins to wonder if it is going to be an explanation of excuses, and actually begins to ponder if avoiding the subject made Viktor a selfish man, heartless and cold.

"How old are you Steve?"

"36," he replies and looks up at Viktor, trying to fathom his intentions.

"Do you have a wife? Family?" Steve is thinking who is actually interviewing who at this point, but shakes his head to signify that he hasn't.

"Do you want them someday?" Viktor seems very keen to know how Steve feels.

"One day yes, why do you ask?"

"I never had that, I wanted it so badly. I fell in love once..." Viktor pauses, twists his hands together and as he holds them, Steve observes a little tremor. He inhales three deep breaths and struggles with his words as each word is accompanied with a slight wheeze, "...a long time ago. She was beautiful and I broke her heart. I knew one day I would be found and I could not bear to bring that hurt and shame on her so she never knew who I was. I lived my life unable to forget and unforgiving. It is a weakness that thwarts the growth of any man, it poisons the very essence of a man, debilitates him. Not for one day did I ever forget who I was and would never forgive myself. I was the poison, and my sweet Heidi did not deserve to be poisoned, she held the key to my heart."

He catches his breath, closes his eyes and says "It is hard to understand how the best and correct decisions in your entire life are also the worst and most painful of ones."

"A bit like euthanasia?" Steve replies trying to trigger just a small reaction from Viktor and the notorious regime he was a part of.

But he just replies "...exactly."

"Without Heidi I wouldn't be the person I am today. That's what true love does to a person Steve, it changes your dreams, hopes, desires and views, but it sets your life on a different path. I still remember how exciting it all was from my every waking moment until I closed my eyes and I was filled with loving and sweet thoughts. I felt alive, the world was a gloriously colourful place, her smile and laughter carried oxygen through my veins. But I was inflicted with poison and I had to free her from the poison. Heartbreak itself doesn't live in a single moment, not even a month; hearts have the ability to crack and break apart for infinity. Oh, and I know what you tried to do there with that comment Steve. I am a cantankerous old fool with very selective hearing," he chuckles.

Steve finds himself smiling at the comment, no matter how inappropriate it was.

"So how did you end the relationship? What did you give as an explanation?" Steve questions.

"Ending something so precious was never going to be easy. I decided not to tell her I no longer loved her, I'm the poison and she didn't need the poison to obliterate all the self-esteem out of her. Oh, she knew I loved her very much so I told her that I had been relocated to another country through my job and had to leave for a while and that she would have to stay to nurse her sick elderly mother. Eventually after a few letters, it dwindled out gently for her sake. We didn't have all this fan-dangled technology like you have these days, no instant text messaging that would have made it much harder."

Steve shifts awkwardly in his chair, he considers the notion that humans can sometimes be nasty creatures and he looks at Viktor for a second and wonders if describing him from such a cynical vantage point may call him credulous or naïve. Steve isn't prepared to overlook Viktor's character flaws, nor his past in an idealistic or trusting view and he starts to question his own opinion 'can flawed humans have a fundamental goodness, benevolence nonetheless?'

Steve decides to go for it "Do you have a social conscience? Listening to your love of Heidi, it seems you acknowledge responsibility?"

"Define, 'social conscience' Mr Garrett?"

"Given the history of the war, do you have an inward sense of responsibility and concern for wrongdoings in society? Some things cannot be put right, but a conscience is the essence of humans to do what is right or wrong. Are you ever concerned by the injustices committed at that time?"

A dull heaviness falls into the room, an atmosphere that feels so unpleasant and cutting that a sombre dispirited Viktor looks vacantly downwards and replies "Jede sekunde jeden tag." (Every second, of every day).

"Excuse me?" Steve's tone is much softer than before, to get Viktor to indulge him.

"Always," Viktor responds in a deep thoughtful sadness.

Chapter 4

Viktor closes his eyes and all that can be heard are the occasional beeps of medical machinery in the room. Steve turns his Dictaphone off and stands up to stretch his legs, he watches Viktor doze for a while and peers round the corner of the curtain to look out onto the road and the people below. He looks downward at the hospital's main entrance and sees the two guards standing on the steps, the iron railings either side of the grand Victorian doorway hosts an ornamental Edwardian street lamp on each side, which frames the guards like the Beefeaters at Buckingham Palace. Steve begins to realise there is no press or paparazzi outside either and, as curious as that seems to him, he dismisses the thought.

He walks over to the door and pops his head out.
"All ok Mr Garrett?" questions Ellia who is seated outside the door working on an iPad.
"Yes fine, he's nodded off, is there anywhere I can get a drink?"
"Come with me," she says and places the iPad into her Michael Kors handbag.
She leads him down a corridor toward a vending machine.
"Have you known Viktor long?"
"Yes, about seven years and I've been his Personal Assistant, for five of those."

"How were you able to do that when he's been in hiding all his life?"

"He has his ways Mr Garrett. Most of our communication was electronic initially. I've become much closer to him, as a person, since his extradition was implemented."

"I must say, he is quite intriguing. I didn't expect to feel this way. My grandfather guards many secrets of his treatment during the war and all that I know is that it was pretty horrific."

"Tea or coffee, Mr Garrett?" Ellia says, turning to inspect the vending machine and places coins into the slot.

"Coffee please." Steve realises that Ellia, a total professional, is not prepared to divulge any information on her unique client.

"What made you take him or even consider working for someone like him?" Steve asks, changing his conversation down a less intrusive route.

"I studied law at university and was at a loss where I was going to progress forward in life. When his extradition came up I thought I would represent him but found myself in an entirely different role. Initially I believed that everyone constitutionally receives the right to counsel and defence, but becoming his PA was progressive," she replies placing more coins into the machine to purchase her own drink.

"What did he do for employment after the war?" Steve says sitting into a little alcove with tables and chairs overlooking the Royal Brompton grounds.

Ellia sits down at the table and looks at Steve.

"He was a farmer and made a good fortune which allowed him to keep busy and hidden away. He moved several times between the years of 1953-1995, then health issues started to slow him down. He sold his last farming land and went to Mexico and lived under the name of Viktor Schmidt until he was finally traced there by the Nazi bounty hunters."

Steve gazes out of the window, as he drinks his coffee

"Do you think he should face trial now?" He questions her without breaking his gaze. Ellia looks down at her skirt and pulls at it slightly as the hemline has risen,

"It's hard to say..." she starts "...I feel in my profession that it's never too late to face the consequences of ones crimes, especially if the crime or crimes are of a serious nature. It has also been a pleasure getting to know him as a person and everybody is now given the right to be rehabilitated."

"Rehabilitation can only be achieved if somebody has been convicted surely? Viktor has never been convicted," exclaims Steve looking back intently at Ellia.

"True Mr Garrett, but some people find it and face their demons along the way. We also have to consider that Otto-Wolff may have been acting under orders given to him."

They sit at the window for a while sipping their drinks.

"May I ask you a question?" She looks at Steve almost knowing exactly what is coming next, raises her eyebrow and nods in agreement.

"Why was I asked to come and interview him? Why me?"

"No particular reason Mr Garrett and I've been expecting the question. We both knew he was big news as it were. He despises the media on every level and basically said that if he had to do it, to find somebody in a lesser known capacity and give them a break in life. So I grabbed a handful of papers out of the waiting room and saw your article on Brexit and its local impact in your community. I thought it read very eloquently and here we are."

"Wow, you just never know who's going to pick up a local paper," he responds smiling to himself.

"Do you want to leave and come back?" she asks Steve.

"I think I will stay and wait until he wakes up if that's alright?" he replies starting to walk back towards Viktor's room.

Steve sits for a while outside his room and watches all the doctors and nursing staff come and go and a kitchen porter arrives with the dinner trolley. He takes a tray into Viktor's room a nurse leaves and tells Ellia that he is awake.

"You can go back in Mr Garrett," she exclaims as Steve opens the door slowly and stands in the door way. Viktor looks up at him,

"I've tasted worse I suppose" he says picking at the dry looking chicken fillet, pushing it around the plate like a fussy eating child.

"Doesn't look appetizing," Steve agrees.

"Please sit."

"I can come back after your dinner?" Steve replies, feeling that his presence is bad manners.

"Not at all, I think I will give it a miss anyway," Viktor pushes the hospital table away from his bed.

"I understand you're a farmer?" Steve says taking his seat again.

"I found great peace in it. I see you've been talking to the lovely Ellia? She's quite a young lady."

Steve quickly feels some kind of defence on Ellia's behalf is needed, so as to inform Viktor she has not betrayed any confidentiality about him at all.

"She didn't say much other than you were a farmer and lived in Mexico."

"It's alright Steve..." Viktor laughs "...she is a loyal associate."

Steve's agitation lifts and he settles back into a more relaxed seating position.

"I wanted to be alone. Farming is rewarding, but it gives a man many, many hours in his own company and time to think, reflect, ponder and learn who he really is. In that time I had to realise a multitude of regrets."

There is a knock on the door and a young nurse pops her head in,

"Sorry, please may I get an ECG printout for the Consultant?" Viktor nods and she bustles past the table with the dried chicken and shrivelled peas.

"Are you not hungry?" she smiles and Viktor lets

out a breathless chuckle. Checking the placement of the electrode pads across his chest, she applies the leads, turns on the ECG machine and takes a reading, tears off the printout and as she makes her way to the door, she turns and says,

"Thank you. Would you like me to see if I can get you a sandwich?"

"Danke" Viktor smiles and she leaves the room.

"There's definitely something about a nurses uniform, wouldn't you agree Steve?"

Steve smiles, but then thinks of his grandmother.

"My grandmother Molly was a nurse..." Steve announces quietly, "...she met my grandfather during the war, in a hospital."

"Where was that?" Viktor enquires his tone genuine, of real interest, other than just a bit of idle chit chat.

"Paris, The Bicêtre, he had been through some horrific times during a placement at a German camp. He never talks of it."

Steve is not mentally prepared to bring up his grandfather's experiences and he feels uneasy about mentioning it, but Viktor's sincerity has the overwhelming ability to draw him out.

"Was he a prisoner of war?" Viktor asks in a very soft tone, a real concerning sense of enquiry.

Steve shakes his head to say no and anxiously replies "Polish Jew."

A silence falls in the room once again and Viktor stares down at his hands and points to his beside cupboard. He says to Steve "Please get me my wallet."

Steve walks over to the cupboard, opens it, sees the wallet and hands it to Viktor. With his frail trembling hands he opens it and pulls out a small photograph from behind a credit card. He hands it to Steve and he studies the photo. It is very yellow in colour, but it's a colour photograph. There is a woman in a light blue floral dress sitting on a wall with a sea view behind her, she is smiling at the camera and has the face of a young girl in love, pleasant and happy. She has dark brown hair underneath a pale lemon coloured head scarf and is holding a rose in her right hand. It is a picture of happiness, fun summers by the beach. Steve looks up at Viktor. "Heidi," he says. Steve smiles and hands it back to Viktor. Viktor looks at her for a while, feels a burning lump in his throat and a tear slowly appears in his eye. He removes his glasses and tries to make nothing of rubbing his eyes.

"She was a Polish Jew too." Steve's mouth drops open just a little as he is taken aback by the revelation and sits himself back into the chair, beckoning Viktor to continue. Viktor places Heidi's photograph back into his wallet and puts it down on to his lap.

"Can I guess at what you are thinking?" Viktor asks.

"I am not really thinking anything, at this precise moment, just a little shocked," Steve replies to this astounding news.

"Don't start thinking that I sought her out to redeem myself. I did not know she was Jewish when we first met. I used to fill up my van once a fortnight with the produce I grew to sell at the farmers market and she would come to my stall and buy vegetables for her mother and neighbours. We would talk a lot and she was always laughing and I would live off her smile for the entire fortnight until I saw her again. But then this one time she arrived to do her shopping and handed me a lemon cake she had baked for me. She told me it was because I always gave her extra portions. I probably didn't even realise I had been, I was too busy admiring her and not concentrating on weighing out the measures properly."

Steve smiles and laughs a little, picturing the scene. "One day I plucked up the courage to ask her to accompany me to see Singing in the Rain at the movie theatre. I picked her up and took her flowers from my garden. I wasn't much at being a florist or arranging flowers, but she loved them all the same. It was at that moment, arriving at Heidi's house, that I observed various objects indicative of the Jewish faith, like the Shamash on the fireplace. It was not an issue to me, her faith, but my own demons battled in my head of my place in her life. Fate made sure that my heart would go to the very innocence I had once been a part of to destroy. I did not deserve to feel the love of one of God's creatures so pure, so giving and humble. We never spoke of the war, although I did have knowledge she had been in a camp, like your grandfather she did not feel the need to share her experiences. It would pain me alone at night wondering what she had seen or what had been inflicted on her. I deserved the nightmares Steve."

A knock on the door breaks the conversation and the nurse reappears with the sandwich.

"Hope it's not the chicken," Viktor sniggers and she giggles, collecting up his tray off the table. As she turns to exit the room the senior nursing sister enters, with a pot of medicine. Very stern, Steve mentally notes that she is a very 'old school' nursing matron type. She makes Viktor open his hand, to tip three tablets into it and forcefully hands him the glass of room temperature warm water he had drank from earlier.

"Refresh this jug of water nurse Jones," she bellows and the young nurse scoops up the jug and hurries out of the room, she writes down his clinical observations onto the charts and then leaves snatching the pot out of his hand in an abrupt manner.

"I can't work out if it's my presence or just her normal persona..." Viktor laughs "...maybe a bit of both."

Viktor feels a sharp pain shoot through his shoulder, down the side of his neck and permeate into his chest and he grabs his chest wincing. Steve quickly jumps to his feet to see if he is alright and reads on the oximeter that his pulse has peaked to 163.

"Do you want me to get help?" Steve says with a look of worry, though he doesn't wait for an answer and rushes to the door. Ellia jumps to her feet.

"What is it?" she says and also not waiting for a reply

shouts "NURSE!" Steve stands back as the nursing staff all run into Viktor's room. Sitting outside staring at the door he hears the clattering wheels of a trolley coming around the corner. Placed on it is a portable defibrillator and a male doctor pushes it through the door.
Ellia turns to the ward clerk at the desk and snaps "What is happening?"
Ellia doesn't wait for a response, she just turns and enters straight into Viktor's room with-out asking and despite what the medical professionals say to her. Steve wanders back to the vending machine, buys himself another coffee and takes his place in the seat he had sat earlier in the afternoon with Ellia. The daylight is starting to draw in a little and as he looks out of the window he watches a beautiful redness fill the horizon as the sun settles. He doesn't realise how long he's been there and still feels like he's not particularly made headway on his interview, he begins to think the inevitable and that he may not see Viktor again, when Ellia appears behind him.
"Mr Garrett."
He turns to see her and rises to his feet.
"He's ok..." she continues "...another episode, they are happening more frequently, but he is settled and going to sleep now."
"I understand..." Steve replies "...well, will you tell him that I appreciated his time and it was enlightening, if not eye opening to have met him."
Ellia interrupts "Mr Garrett, you may return to-

morrow. Herr Otto-Wolff has requested to see you again."

"He has?"

"He appears to like you, well for a reporter that is." She makes half a smile out of the corner of her mouth and holds out her hand to Steve. He shakes it and as she turns and walks back down the hallway, Steve watches her vanish back into Viktor's room. He picks up his brief case and makes his exit out of the main door. The guards have changed over shift as it is two different men on the steps as he leaves the building.

The sun has set even more and the street lights are starting to illuminate the paths and as Steve makes his way along the busy roads, walking through the bustling crowds he feels his phone vibrate. 'Louise Calling' the screen reads.

"Hey Lou......I'm ok just left.....Lou? Do you fancy dinner tonight I'm famished."

Steve needs some distraction this evening and Louise would definitely be that.

Chapter 5

Steve wanders up to Louise's door. She lives with two other girls, Rachel who is a hairdresser and a total wannabe WAG, and Melissa who works in a garage as a mechanic, complete polar opposites, but Louise always maintains it works quite well, all being different and uniquely quirky.
Rachel appears at the door and flirtatiously presses herself up against the open front door. She proceeds to twist her hair around her finger, as she gazes into Steve's eyes and calls out,
"Lou, Clark Kent is here!"
Steve smiles shaking his head. He pulls off his tie and undoes his top shirt button, places the tie into his bag and looks up to see Louise skip excitedly down the stairs, towards the front door. She grabs her handbag and stares at Rachel, grits her teeth and with a fake smile mutters "Ok thank you Rach". She may as well have just said "ok go!" but Louise is too nice for that.
Rachel turns back and looks at Steve.
"I think I may be trapped in a burning house later if you want to fly up and catch me."
Louise rolls her eyes, shuts the door and skips again down the steps towards Steve.
"She's interesting," Steve declares,
"That's one word I suppose..." Louise giggles "...you're still in your suit?"

"I didn't go home, came straight here."

Louise smiles thinking it is because he must have been so desperate to see her and Steve would allow her to believe this notion, as if he really knew what she is thinking.

"You look absolutely stunning," he notices looking her up and down.

"Oh....just something I threw on." Louise replies, knowing full well she's put on at least eight other outfits first. She is wearing a flowing red dress, tight fitted bodice with an A-line skirt, plenty of cleavage on show with matching red high heeled shoes. Louise grabs Steve's arm and says,

"Where are we going?"

"I'm not sure I haven't thought that far ahead. Let's go on the main high street and see what takes our fancy," he says assuredly.

They look at a couple of establishments and settle on a new Thai restaurant which is very beautiful inside, plush dark red furnishings and lots of gold ornamental Buddha's, stunningly authentic and the aromas from the Thai cuisine lavish the restaurant. A petite Asian lady leads them to their seats and hands them the menus.

"Would you like drinks?" she says in her Thai accent, smiling eagerly at them both.

"House white?" Steve asks Louise and she nods. The waitress acknowledges and goes off on her way to get their drinks.

"How did it go Steve?" Louise beckons Steve into a conversation he's hoping to avoid.

"Alright, I suppose. He wasn't at all what I'd expected and spoke of his regrets and the love of his life, a lady called Heidi, but he refused to speak of the war or his time at Ravensbrück."
"Oh, so he didn't say much about the trial then?"
"Nothing! Just that he would answer all the questions from that time in his life, at the trial."
The wine appears and the waitress asks if they were ready to give their food order. Neither one had even looked at the menu.
"Let's try the Thai Red Chicken Curry?" decides Steve, in his authoritative voice and Louise nods again in agreement.
"Have you spoken to Bryan?" Louise leans in to pick up her glass of wine and Steve quickly picks up his glass and they chink the tips smiling and collectively say "cheers".
"No, not as yet, I did tell him I would call later. He was more concerned that I had managed to get into the hospital to see him, but I had absolutely no problem at all. Bryan was right about the 'biguns' not touching the story. There was no press there at all."
"Really?" quizzes Louise with a look of perplexity.
"No one but me. Was very odd, don't you think?"
"So what did he look like?..." it's all Louise could think of to show some interest in the situation"... like Voldemort?..."
Steve looks at her quizzically.
"... A Psycho Nazi? No nose...Voldemort?..."
"Oh? You do say some random things! Err, old Lou,

like a very frail old man" and together they laugh loudly.

"Ok, so what are you going to do now, as you didn't get much for a story?" she questions again and this time a little happier with her statement.

"Well, apparently he wants me to go back and see him tomorrow."

Steve takes another sip of his wine "mmm".

"So, Clark Kent...?" Louise pauses and smiles over her glass of wine, opening her eyes wide catching Steve's glance "...have you been rescuing any more runaway dogs since this morning?"

They both laugh and Steve replies "All in a day's heroic work Lou, saving pugs, saving the world."

Their dinners arrive and they enjoy a relaxing evening of idle chit chat and socialising, Louise acts coy and flirtatious and Steve's more reserved, appreciates a gentle female presence. He thinks of Heidi sitting on that wall with the waves crashing behind her and wonders what became of her after Viktor had moved away,

"...so then Rachel said this lady had come into the salon and sai..."

Steve isn't really listening to anything Louise is saying and blurts out abruptly,

"LOU!"

"...yes?"

"Are you busy tomorrow? Would you come to see Viktor with me?"

Louise goes silent for the first time in half an hour and says "Of course, if you want me to?"

"I think YOU are just what I need."
Now Louise's heart jumps and flutters a beat, Steve telling her he needs her was more than she could ever hope to hear. Despite the details that it is for a Nazi criminal's interview was irrelevant. Steve 'needs' her.

He turns up at 10:30am sharp to collect her. Wearing a sharp Grey tailored single breasted suit, very pale blue shirt and no tie, he holds his little brief case under his arm and looks at his text messages when Louise appears at the door. As predictably assumed she wears a tight fitted black Body Con dress and black pointed kitten heels with plaited hair in a French braid style, teases down to one side and sits on her right shoulder. It's finished off with a black fabric rose securing the plait at the bottom. She has loose wisps of blonde hair that frames her face which blows gently in the soft breeze and she smiles at Steve as she skips towards him.
"You look gorgeous" he says.
"Thank you..." she smiles to herself "...so what's your plan today?" she asks thinking about the interview.
"Just getting him to talk would be a start. I think he'll like you Lou, we just need to draw him out."
They reach the outer corridor that leads to Viktor's room, all the security checks are maintained and Ellia appears at the door.
"Good morning Mr Garrett," she says holding out her hand to greet him again.

"Ellia, this is my assistant Louise Randall." Steve says shaking her hand.

She offers her hand to Louise.

"Pleased to meet you Miss Randall," she says and turns to lead them to Viktor's room.

Louise can't help noticing how beautiful Ellia is and how Steve watches her graceful postured walk and feels a small pang of jealous female rivalry gripe her stomach. This clearly reflects in the lemon sucking lip expression that overtakes her face. Ellia opens the door for them and they enter his room. The room is dimly lit and like the previous day the curtains are still firmly closed. He is clean shaven this morning, with fresh clean pyjamas on, he's reading his newspaper and looks at the three of them over the top of his glasses.

"Good morning Viktor, this is my assistant Louise Randall."

Viktor slowly slides his glasses off the end of his nose, gently folds in the arms and places them on top of the newspaper on his lap. In all that time he does not take his eyes off Louise. She holds out her hand to greet him and as he takes it turns it over with the back of her hand facing him, he leans forward, lifts her hand and with old fashioned gallantry kisses the back of it.

"Pleased to meet you Louise Randall."

She giggles at his old fashioned manners.

"Pleased to meet you too," she replies respectfully.

"Well, you'll need to collect another chair Steve," Viktor demands and unwavering his gaze from her.

Steve leaves the room, immediately returns with a chair from outside and as he places it behind Louise she gracefully sits down.

"Thank you for asking to see me again," Steve says taking his seat.

Viktor barely notices Steve's gratitude....

"So Miss Randall how do you know Mr Garrett?"

She coughs clearing her throat.

"We work together at The Thames Charter,"

"Do you enjoy being a reporter?"

"Well I don't normally do the reporting, I mainly work in admin, in the office really," she replies.

"So I really am honoured to have been graced by your presence then?" He retorts cheekily and a devilish smile creases the corners of his eyes.

"I suppose so..." Louise giggles "...Steve...Mr Garrett...asked if I would like to come with him today."

"Did he? And you were so overwhelmed about meeting an arrested criminal on a beautiful Sunday morning, you clearly couldn't resist."

Louise isn't sure how to reply and smiles awkwardly.

"...I believe you have a little more of an invested interest in our young Steve." Viktor went on.

By this time Louise is as red and blushed as a ripening rose and Steve interrupts jokingly to break the agitated atmosphere rapidly filling the room,

"Who couldn't resist all this charm hey Louise?"

Smiling warmly Steve beams back at her and Viktor just grins at the pair of them.

Louise looks up at Viktor "Does anybody fancy a

drink? I'm very thirsty."

Both of men nod and request coffee, Steve tells her where the vending machine is and hands her some loose change, Viktor watches her intently as she leaves the room.

"She likes you Mr Garrett, you would be a blind fool not to notice, I like her plaits there is always something cute and carefree about a young woman with plaits in her hair."

Steve smiles at Viktor's attention to detail, he thinks that he reminds him of himself.

"She's a lovely woman..." Steve agrees "...I find her refreshingly spirited; she makes me smile... A lot."

Viktor's facial expression glows with a contented smugness. Steve attempts to change the subject, "How did you sleep last night? You were quite unwell when I left yesterday."

Viktor is astounded by the genuine concern for his welfare and senses a real value of authentic heartfelt honesty in Steve's voice. Viktor knows he doesn't need the approval of anyone, he had spent a huge part of his life seeking approval, the reality is completely different, but knew that it was his fate.

"A little restless..." he responds "...hospitals are not designed for a pleasant night's sleep."

Louise reappears with the refreshments and hands Steve his coffee and places Viktor's on the table next to his bed; Viktor and Steve do not take their eyes off her as she moves around the room and takes her seat.

"So what has Steve told you about our meeting yesterday?" Viktor directs to Louise.

"Well, emm…" Louise pauses for thought momentarily "…He told me about Heidi?"

Viktor's face lights up, warm and illuminating as he hands Louise the same photograph he had shown to Steve, but this time it's meticulously placed underneath his pillow.

Louise looks at her, "She's beautiful. Did you marry her?"

"Sadly I could not do that to her, Heidi deserved better than the likes of me."

"Where was this taken?" Louise continues, not allowing a silence to fall or the conversation to dry up. Steve leans back into his chair, he knew the freshness of Louise's innocent inquisitive personality would capture Viktor's assiduity and he turns on his Dictaphone, securely resting it in his pocket.

"Cavalaire-Sur-Mer in Provence…" Viktor's expression is so sincere "…I took her there for a week it was the singular most magical week of my entire life. She holds the key to my heart."

"That is so romantic…" whispers Louise, "…did you give her that rose she's holding?"

"Yes and if you look closely I gave her that heart shaped locket she is wearing as well. It was beautifully hand crafted with mother of pearl cherubs on the front, although you won't be able to see it in too much detail, in the picture."

From what Louise could see, the locket was quite slim in width, she couldn't quite make out if it was an antique gold but had a very unusual old brassy look about it. It was a good 3" length and two little cherubs sat comfortably in the centre.

The room falls quiet as Viktor tries to catch his breath. Coarse wheezing sounds with each exhalation were becoming more regular and decadent from the decline of his heart. Louise leans forward and slips Heidi's photo into Viktor's frail hand, and he nods in acknowledgement.

"Are you religious Steve?"

Viktor's question takes Steve a little by surprise, considering the past and the regime's view on certain religions it certainly isn't a question Steve is expecting to be asked. He thinks for a moment about Viktor's statements of living his life in contrition and always seeking forgiveness, of him being a self-loathing man, unforgiving and not forgetting.

"Not particularly." Steve replies.

"I never believed in the concept of going to a heaven or a hell, even though many would say that Hell is where I am heading, if that is the case then so be it. But I always believed that there might be something more than this life we live and how about you Miss Randall?" Viktor says turning his attention to Louise.

"Oh yes, I believe in God!" Louise beams at him, which also takes Steve by surprise. He's never taken Louise to be a spiritual person, but much more carefree and ditsy about life. "I believe that God loves everyone who seeks forgiveness."

Viktor smiles at Louise's innocent and honest remark and takes another sip of his coffee. He starts to choke a little on the fluid and struggles to catch his breath. They both jump to their feet Louise gently pats and rubs Viktor's back as Steve runs out into the hallway. A nurse rushes in just as Viktor manages to clear his throat. She reads his pulse on the oximeter and notes down his general obs onto his hospital chart.

He snaps a little "don't fuss please I am fine."

Ellia appears and is standing staring at Viktor at the foot of his bed.

"I have quite an audience," Viktor responds.

"Yes you have..." Ellia says sternly, fussing over straightening his blankets, "...I am beginning to think you like the attention."

"If you smiled once in a while you would be a beautiful woman," Viktor replies.

"It's very overrated. Now do you wish to rest?" By this point Ellia is disposing of his coffee, tidying the bedside table and putting his glasses back into their case. Viktor shakes his head in the negative.

"You might be right Ellia, I think I like the attention," he says smiling at Louise.

The nurse and Ellia leave the room and once again it is just the three of them together. Viktor beckons Steve and Louise to come closer, they drag their chairs so each of them are either side of his bed and he holds out his hand to Louise. She takes it willingly. Viktor stares at Louise's perfectly manicured red nails and closes his eyes. He drifts off in his mind and flashes back to the moment he gave Heidi her locket. She was wearing red nail polish too. A young Viktor had stood behind her as he took the locket from her and Heidi held her hair up, whilst Viktor fastened its clasp and he lent down to kiss her gently on the nape of her neck.

"I can still smell her perfume," he says slowly opening his eyes. "I have to tell you my burden. I have to confess my secret."

Chapter 6

Steve looks at Louise, who is already looking back at him, and they both collectively look towards Viktor.

"Do you want us to get a priest?" Steve's perplexed face screws up above his left eyebrow and Viktor makes a very breathless attempt of laughter.

"If it was or had been that easy I would have done it during the last 75 years Steve...a priest?" He chuckles and coughs uncontrollably.

"I'm not qualified to impose an act of penance Viktor, I'm just a journalist."

"You are so much more than 'just' a journalist Steve. That is just a job title. Many people have that title, but when you take that title away, you have the person. You are sitting in a hospital room, with a Nazi criminal, on a Sunday and sipping tepid vending machine coffee. Now, how many other people on this planet can say that right now?"

Steve laughs, through his nose in agreement and nods his head. Viktor gently squeezes Louise's hand and smiles at her, she looks back at him with an overwhelming feeling of adoration, like the way she did when her grandfather used to 'steal' her nose.

"No, I just want to share my burden, I haven't got very long now and I must put it right before I die."

"What?" Steve questions. He realises at this point that there is no way Viktor will make it to Rome to face trial, but will he find out the mysteries that surround this charming old man, even though Steve fought not to find him charming at all.

"What do you need to put right Viktor?" Louise asks, whilst using her free hand to gently stroke the back of his hand, which is firmly holding her other one.

"We committed some terrible crimes. I don't want to go into all that, I mentioned this yesterday."

Steve nods his head again in agreement and acknowledges Viktor's request.

"I want to tell you about a secret mission assigned to an elite group of scientists and some of the guards at Ravensbrück. We were assigned to carry out medical experiments and treatments on the children, the healthier children of the camp."

Steve abruptly interrupts "That's not secret Viktor. That is very common knowledge. It was one of the first things that came up on an internet search when I was researching information for my interview with you."

Viktor lifts his finger, with the oximeter attached, to his lip and kindly hushes Steve. Steve settles back into his chair feeling a little reprimanded.

"Yes, yes I know, many rumours were made from the speculations that were sparked back then. But what the gossips didn't know was the real reason for the experiments. We weren't just assigned to test medicines or revolutionary new treatments, we were assigned to test a substance called DNA1333, specifically just that. There had been other variations of the substance that we were to discover had failed. It wasn't intended to kill. We were to watch it, study its form and its capabilities, progress and growth."

"What was its purpose? Was it a preliminary cure for something or some disease?" Steve asks as he checks to confirm his Dictaphone is definitely switched on.

"It was a genetic growth hormone. Artificially designed to stimulate the pituitary gland and release these hormones into the bloodstream. Hitler wanted to create the Aryan Race. A race of perfect physically fit human beings. History tells us that the holocaust was to eliminate humans that didn't fall into his ideals and that he would create his idea of perfection."

"But weren't these the blonde hair, blue eyes? Hitler's idea of the perfect race?"

"That was his idea initially yes, but he knew that dominant genes can reappear in ancestors in many generations down the line. He knew hair colouring and eye colouring were both superficial. So the regime decided to rethink their ideas of 'perfection' and what a super race should be. DNA1333 was initially tested on 16 imprisoned children aged between 5 & 10 years old, it didn't matter if they were of Jewish descent as Hitler's aspirations were to 'Germanize' them. It was 8 boys and 8 girls that eventually progressed from this formula. There had been the ones before them, where the previous growth hormone serum had failed and produced mutations."

"So what happened? Did the artificial hormones actually work?" Steve questions eager for an answer.

"We were ordered to build an encampment, a secure secret enclosure, to study the children. Watch them develop and grow, all of them. The 16 with DNA1333 were mixed with the ones who did not die from the previous growth serums. They had a freedom to play and learn, isolated from all other human contact except for the scientists and guards studying them. The hormone was tested in a few animals and plants also, it proved to be successful. These children were strong and had the abilities of iron-men. The children with mutations also grew strong but suffered severe mental problems, outbursts and uncontrollable anger. A guard had been felling a tree in the encampment and I witnessed one child lift the entire trunk above his head and throw it at the guard. He missed him, but we were more astounded that a 7 year old boy was able to lift a tree trunk some 8 feet long and 30" in diameter above his head."

"Was the boy punished?" Louise gasps.

"No Louise, this was all part of the study, to watch their capabilities and development. The enclosure covered a vast amount of land to the north of Ravensbrück and covered a secure area of approximately five square miles, with woodland and lakes. Plentiful in food and fresh water streams, everything the children needed to develop."

A very loud knock on the hospital room door stops Viktor in his track,

"He's very weak, who has ordered this?" Ellia is heard talking in a sharp tone of anxiety and hysteria, much higher pitched than her normal flat monotone Italian accent.

"Herr Otto-Wolff, I am so sorry, these men have come to see you, I had not passed authority on it but they have papers…"

"Ellia, please calm yourself, if they have 'papers' it must be important" Viktor smirks at Louise however she is more distracted by the appearance of two very intimidating looking gentlemen in black suits at the door. One of the men is about 6'1" and the other is a couple of inches shorter. Straight faced, making no expression at all, they hand Ellia the paperwork and she fumbles looking through it frantically.

"These gentlemen are from the Simon Wiesenthal Centre," she continues.

Louise notices the taller gentleman's ID badge attached to the waistband of his trousers. It has his photograph and name, which she can't read from this distance as she's sitting too far away to focus, but can see the emblem on it. It is three quarters of a blue star and the quarter that is missing, on the left side, shows, what appears to be blue flames rising from it.

"I think you must leave Herr Otto-Wolff for a while Mr Garrett. I shall join you shortly." Ellia holds the door open for Steve and Louise to leave and closes the door behind them, leaving Viktor, Ellia and the two gentlemen in the room by themselves.

Steve and Louise stare at each other in silence, he grabs her hand and leads her to the double doors which head to the hallway and takes her outside.

"Let's go get a bite to eat," he says quietly, Louise agrees and they head towards the main entrance. They pass the security guards protecting the front door Louise asks,

"Who were those men Steve?"

"Nazi hunters Lou. The organisation investigates and searches for Nazi criminals they have probably come to discuss his trial."

"He can barely drink his coffee without choking I don't know how they will get him to Rome."

Steve agrees.

"Are we going home now?" Louise continues and takes out her mobile phone from her handbag to check the time.

"No, we'll come back. That can't be it, that's not all of it," Steve says, he lifts Louise's chin up from looking at her phone and looks deeply at her. Louise looks at him with a confused appearance,

"But he told us Steve he confessed to the experiments, it's what he wanted to unload."

Steve cups his hand around her chin affectionately, "I'm not so sure Lou. We already know the Nazi's performed human medical experiments. I don't think Viktor's big confession was to name the substance they were using for clinical trials. If that is all it was Lou, then why would that have been so difficult for him to confess these past 75 years? If he is being genuine and honest that he had spent his life hating himself, then why not come clean with this information, years ago? We don't know it all, I just have a gut feeling on this and it was when he said about needing to put it right. How can he put the war right Lou? I doubt he has built a time machine out of a DeLorean or borrow one from Christopher Lloyd and going back in time."

"You're right, he did say about needing to put it right. That's an odd statement to make, I'd never thought of that."

Steve strokes the side of her plait, slides strands of her fringe away from her eyes, he is very distracted in his thoughts, as he is unconscious of his romantic grooming actions.

"What are you thinking Steve?" she says in a soft adoring voice, revelling in Steve's sudden attention.

Steve looks back at the hospital door, 'we need to get back in there' he thinks to himself.

"...no, he still wants to tell us something Lou, we'll go get that lunch but we are definitely coming back."

Heading down the driveway past the car park, suddenly from behind they hear calling. Turning in unison, they see Ellia waving her arms to them and rushing through the hospital entrance.

"Mr Garrett please wait!." she says as she catches up with them, catching her breath "...please don't leave."

"We're going to get some lunch, would you care to join us?" responds Steve.

"Mr Garrett...."

"Steve, please call me Steve," he replies.

"Steve," Ellia normally being so composed, so efficient, diligent and painstakingly correct is now finding herself lacking in accuracy and in a place she's not mentally comfortable. Ellia was not used to letting down her guard or composure.

"Steve, I know you do not know myself or Viktor and you are here to write just an article for a newspaper, but I do not want you to leave," she hesitates and looks earnestly at Louise and Steve's faces, who look back at her just as meaningfully - "Please stay?"

Ellia stares out of the corridor window just along from Viktor's room and turns slowly to place coins into the vending machine. She stops still and turns to face Steve,

"He likes you Steve, he has done nothing but talk of you since you came and I don't often see him open up like this. I have been his PA for so long now I have forgotten how to be anything other than that. I feel like my life is about to change so dramatically. I have been so preoccupied and busy I haven't prepared myself for any eventuality or for what is about to happen."

Steve likes seeing the vulnerability in Ellia, seeing her acting human and not like a staunch militarian. He watches her more relaxed body language as she circles her finger over the rim of her cup, her posture more rounded and forward at the shoulders. Steve decides to bite the bullet and in a gentle tone tries to divert Ellia from her current thoughts.

"What do you know of Viktor's time at Ravensbrück? Has he discussed much with you?"

Ellia looks up and sighs, "A little. Viktor is very guarded about that time. Every now and then he would just mention a snippet, but that would be it, literally a snippet and nothing I could string or piece together like a jigsaw, all random moments. You have been the first person I am aware of that he has talked to."

They are suddenly interrupted by the emergency light above Viktor's hospital door flashing, sudden moments of shouting and nursing staff rushing with a trolley into his room, both the men from the Simon Wiesenthal Centre are ushered out of the room. Ellia gasps as if in complete slow motion, gulping for oxygen, she drops the coffee cup. She looks up and sees three doctors run into the room, past the men in black suits and as they stare up the hallway towards Ellia, she turns away from them. Louise leans down to pick up her coffee cup and goes off to fetch some paper towels, to clean the spill.

"I need to be down there!" Ellia's voice is panicky as she moves to head down the hall, Steve gently grabs her arm,

"Not yet Ellia."

She stops and looks down to the ground and as Steve notices her glazed eyes filling with tears, he can tell that Ellia is really not comfortable with this emotion. He comes to the assumption that crying is something Ellia would consider as highly inappropriate and a sign of weakness.

After a few moments they watch two doctors and 3 nursing staff leave Viktor's room, accompanied with the cardiac crash trolley. Ellia makes her way along the corridor and see's one of the doctors shake his head negatively to the two investigators. She stops in her tracks, still gasping for breath. The doctor turns to her "He is weak and he had a very strong cardiac arrest"

"You mean he's not...." Ellia lets out a huge sigh between her hyperventilating and adjusts to regulate her breathing, "but I thought you said to the investigators...."

"That Mr Otto-Wolff is far too weak for any further questions at this time," and the doctor turns towards the desk to write up his notes.

Steve appears at Ellia's shoulder and she turns to grab his hand "He's still alive."

Going into the bedroom tentatively, Ellia sees one last nurse and doctor, still doing observations at Viktor's side. His eyes are closed and his face seems to look very small, smothered by the oxygen mask which covers his nose and mouth. Ellia sits beside him and takes his hand, (sentimentality she is not accustomed to), and all these overwhelming emotions consume her normal persona and the symbolic mask she wears. Viktor's breathing slows, every inhalation is visibly a struggle and Ellia sees his face has changed, changed in less than an hour.

The doctor exits the room and Louise appears in his

place. She gently puts her hand onto Ellia's shoulder.
"We really should leave you Ellia."
Ellia puts her hand up towards her shoulder and holds onto the back of Louise's hand.
"Please stay," she whispers and looks up at Louise, she turns to see Steve slowly enter the room. The three of them stare at Viktor in silence, the spacing between each of his breaths seems to last longer than the previous one. Very slowly Viktor opens his eyes just slightly to see Steve, Ellia and Louise all looking at him, they all notice a very slight movement in the left corner of his mouth and a smile from underneath the oxygen mask. They decide to stay with him and all take up seats around his bedside, just staring, no one speaks and they're all deep in thought.

As the day starts to draw in, a dusky light takes over the room, but none of them seem to notice. They become aware of a very slight movement from beneath the sheet and as Viktor's hand appears, he pulls down the oxygen mask.
"Viktor please leave it on it's to help your breathing," says Louise rising to her feet to assist it back on his mouth. Viktor grabs her hand and she sits on his bed next to him, not for a single second taking her eyes off him.
"Listen..." he says, almost unrecognisably as he struggles to speak and inhale at the same time, "...

you need to know....."

Steve sits upright, torn between his conscience of whether turning his Dictaphone on, whilst a man is clearly dying is highly inappropriate or not, but he sets it to record nonetheless.

"I need to say about the DNA1333..." he stops again and puts the oxygen mask back on his mouth for a few intakes of breath, he pulls it down again "...we were to watch their development, the children I need to save the children."

"What do you mean Viktor? How are you able to save them, it happened years ago, the war is over?" questions Steve in a confused, desperate for answers, kind of way.

"Exactly! The war ended Steve. The war ended."

Viktor squeezes at Louise's hand and she cups his hand tightly with both her hands. Thoughts race quickly through Steve's mind, 'the war ended?' he thinks 'but of course it did, what is he trying to say? How can he save the children? What is it he needs to put right?' Steve suddenly feels a sweat break out on his forehead,

"Viktor, what happened to those children? When the war ended?"

Viktor beckons Steve to lean in closer and he gets down onto the floor, kneeling and resting his elbows on the bed next to Viktor, the opposite side from Louise.

Ellia turns to Steve and says with a sense of confusion.

"What do you mean Viktor? What is this about?"

"Steve..." Viktor replies "...that is my point and that is my confession. The war ended, that was it and it was over. Many people came looking to arrest those involved in Hitler's regime. We had to leave."

"Did you kill them?" Steve asks.

"No. We just shut the door to the encampment where they lived and we left them behind."

Louise takes an extremely shocked intake of air and her mouth opens in total surprise, in absolute horror. Steve rubs his hands over his head trying to take in the information. As Viktor puts his mask back over his mouth, Louise sees the glimmering of a small tear roll off the side of his face.

"Did anyone ever go back to save them?" Steve bellows sternly.

Viktor shakes his head "No, they were the children the world forgot. People carried on, made and rebuilt new lives after the war and I never found the courage in me to go back."

Standing up and walking extremely quickly out of the room, Steve stands in the hallway beside the door, leaning his back against the wall and bending forward holding onto his knees. He needs air and he is so angry he needs time to absorb the information and gather his thoughts.

Ellia stands in front of Steve "Does anyone want to explain what is going on?"

"I'm so angry Ellia, I just need space from him right now. He is a spineless, heartless coward. These men were all just narcissistic, sadistic, cowards." Steve's tone is loud, sharp and almost aggressive which leaves Ellia taken by surprise at Steve's anger. She had not seen that side of him, Steve was always content at the empathy he had shown Viktor, despite the dark history and who he is.

"Yes they were. Terrible things happened, unmentionable crimes, but you must not let it upset you now, our grandparents would not want us to feel sad now. They gave their children and grandchildren freedom from these monsters."

"Those children were victims of an experiment, would not have had their freedom. They were incarcerated and left behind..." snaps Steve with a sour bitterness in his tone "...they never knew that the war was over!"

Louise, looks toward the door and wonders if Steve and Ellia are alright. She knows Steve would be very angry and tangled up in a web of emotions, torn between beginning to feel a slight fondness to a man which he had previously loathed, for all the demons his grandfather Borowski had spent a lifetime battling. She knew that his grandfather was still fighting WWII from time to time.

Looking down at Viktor, she finds it difficult herself to see beyond the frailty and feels him gently squeeze her hand and lets out a discontented sigh.

"Louise..." he whispers gently "...pass me Heidi please."

Slipping her hand under his pillow, she brings out the photograph. She holds it up for him to see and they both sit and admire his love, his Heidi.

"She has the key to my heart," the exasperation and

sweetness in his face and tone Louise acknowledges that he really did truly love her.

"Louise," his words are barely recognisable and obscure.

"Yes Viktor?"

He looks admiringly into her eyes for a few brief seconds.

"You are so lovely and vibrant, just like my Heidi. Your abundant heart wills equal happiness."

He becomes very quiet and she kneels down beside him, takes a cloth and wipes his brow. His breathing is so sporadic and waning she begins to wonder how she has found herself in this ambiguous situation to start with.

"It's in the numbers," he just about gets his words out.

"What numbers Viktor?" she replies confused, unable to fathom or decipher his statement.

"DNA1333" he whispers. He slowly closes his eyes utters a faint "Gott verzeih mir" and as his hand goes limp in Louise's, he finally lets go. Very gently his head falls slightly to its left and the machines go from a considerably inconsistent bradycardia beeping to a definite flat line. Louise pauses for a split second and calls "NURSE!"

Chapter 7

Steve and Louise sit quietly sipping a well needed glass of Prosecco, in the Regency Rose wine bar. This particular Sunday evening is a little more unusual than their normal social meet ups. Steve's features are troubled and sombre, as if he knows this is going to haunt him somehow. Can he carry this secret or burden himself now, wondering 'what if' for his whole life, like Viktor had? Steve's normally calm and pleasant demeanour is being rattled with the anger, consuming his mind and gut. He feels unintelligible words, spewing through his brain, like a volcano releasing pent up emotions. His hands close into fists and every so often he has to consciously relax his face when he feels it contort into fury. Louise says nothing, more because she does not know what to say. She feels changing the subject; however that may usually seem to be a good thing, this is not one of those moments. She listens to people chat in the wine bar, like a humming background music. She shifts uncomfortably, thinking of ways to break the silence and every moment presents itself inopportune and untimely. The tension becomes so intense Louise thinks she can hear the blood pumping in her ears.

Without asking Steve if he wants another drink she leaves the table and goes to get in another round. She gazes across the bar to see a young couple laughing and in love, Louise watches the way the females body language is open and comfortable, touching the man's knee without realising her flirtation.

Picking up the two glasses she turns back to Steve, she can see that his mind is consumed with Viktor's horrific revelation. He hasn't even noticed she has moved and Louise places the glasses onto the table. She takes a penny out of her purse and pushes it across the table, until it bumps Steve's hand. He looks down at the penny and looks up at Louise, "a penny for them" she says in a sincere subdued compromise.

"I'm so sorry Lou," Steve realises his detachment from his surroundings.

"I understand," she replies and takes his hand across the table. He smiles, just for a split second, but that is enough for Louise.

"What will you write in your article?" she continues.

"I don't know?" Steve looks down at the table to consider all the ramifications and consequences of making such a huge declaration. That a group of forgotten children may have possibly lived and grown up in an isolated world, alien to the rest of the world in which it is embedded.

"I have no idea what to tell Bryan either," he adds and feels a burning acidic agitation in the back of his throat and upper chest. He often has some form of gastric discomfort during moments of complete distress.

"Steve, Viktor said something to me before…" she

pauses at her statement "...well, he whispered 'it's in the numbers' and when I asked him 'what' his last words were 'DNA1333'. I wasn't sure what he meant?"

"He was a psychotic old fool it meant nothing, other than what they did to those poor kids!" Steve's voice raises, Louise can tell he is clearly afflicted with anxiety and mental torture.

"Sorry Louise..." he realises that his anger should not be directed or channelled at the wrong people, "...the numbers were the titled formula they used honey, that's all." "That's ok Steve but he also said some German which sounded like 'gott verzy mer'?"

Steve can't sleep. He feels a great loathed hatred for Viktor and is antagonised that someone can make him harbour such emotions. He despises the prejudice against millions of innocent people, for discriminating them for race or religion.

He opens his laptop abruptly to start his article

- I am extremely disgusted with immoral, insanely selfish, spineless people. Why do these people exist? As far as I am concerned, people without compassion may as well just die! -

Staring at the words on the screen, he deletes it all. Thinking back to his conversation with Louise, he opens an internet window, searches for German translate, and then voice activates 'Gott verzy mer'

GOTT VERZEIH MIR – GOD FORGIVE ME.

He shuts the laptop down, sighs deeply and he flops his head back onto the pillow and stares at the ceiling. Steve begins to realise he must have exhaled a hundred sighs at this point. He glances over to the alarm clock by his bedside, 3:23am….another sigh. By the time his 6:50am alarm sounds he realises he probably finally drifted off some 45 minutes earlier. Feeling mentally and physically drained, he showers, deep in thought, shaves deep in thought, dresses, eats and goes to work deep in thought.

He sits idly at his computer screen, not even knowing where to start or what to type.

"Steve," Bryan's voice bellows from across the room, he walks into his office and expects Steve to follow.

Steve walks across the open plan area Louise looks up at him and squeezes his arm, knowing his mind is in overdrive.

"Good morning Steve, well how did it go?" He asks and beckons him to take a seat.

"He passed away Bryan. Yesterday afternoon." Steve takes a seat and looks up at his boss.

Bryan sits down the other side of his desk, pulling a facial expression of surprise,

"You were with him?"

"I'd taken Lou with me the second day. I wouldn't even know where to begin or where to start any form of article Bryan. He refused to talk about the trial or any of the accusations against him. It was as though he just needed company."

"Do you think he knew he was going to die?" asks Bryan gently.

"Almost certainly he did. He wanted to talk about a girlfriend he let go because he never wanted her to know his past." Steve halts and wonders to himself whether he should tell Bryan of the experiments and abandoned children. What if they had died? What if they had survived? What if they still existed in this artificially created Nazi world? How would he ever know? How would the modern developed world ever know? Maybe they had been found? Surely Viktor would have been aware if they had been? Was Viktor's only reason for seeing Steve to burden him with all this knowledge? Dozens of ifs and maybes had kept Steve up most of the night. He feels a burning reflux of acid filling his chest and throat and promptly pops an antacid into his mouth.

"I'm sorry I put you through that Steve..." Bryan continues, "...would you like a couple of days off?"

"No I think I would like to work Bryan, it'll keep my mind occupied."

"Well, a treasure has been discovered, washed up on the banks of the Thames by Town Hall near London Bridge, some jewellery and medals. Maybe you can go along to see what that's about. I have the info here.....erm, found by 2 young lads named Martin Chalmers and Toby Wright. I have their contact details, quite a haul apparently...."

Steve gazes at the wild Boston Fern on Bryan's window sill, not really taking in the information.

"Steve, are you sure you are ok?" Bryan sees the strain across Steve's face and noticeable tired bags under his eyes.

"Yes, yes sorry Bryan" Steve reaches across to look at the information.

"I will make some phone calls and see if I can interview the boys."

Getting up he leaves Bryans office, Bryan watches him exit and suspects that Herr Otto-Wolff's death is agitating him a lot more than he is letting on.

Louise looks up at Steve as he passes her desk,

"Did you tell....." she starts but Steve hushes her and whispers,

"No."

Steve sits at his desk and makes some phone calls on his new assignment. The treasure find is being held at the Southwark Police Station along Borough High Street and as Steve leaves to make his way there, he contacts the boy's parents to arrange interviews with them for when they finish school.

He finds it refreshing for a while to distract his busy brain from the weekend's distasteful revelations. He takes photographs of the find and the war medals that are suspected to have been from the Boer War around 1899-1902. The jewellery pieces are a very beautifully handcrafted gold bangle bracelet and a necklace. The gold bangle has roses entwined around it and between each rose there are rubies. The necklace is gold with perfectly spaced diamond and ruby stones that go the entire length of the necklace, with a larger ruby droplet at the centre, encrusted with diamonds. Steve takes photographs of all the pieces and speaks in detail with an antique specialist, who is also at the police station, intrigued with the discovery.

He interviews Martin and Toby who are both very excited about their find, as any young lad would be about finding missing treasure. Steve is very refreshed and focused as he makes his way back to The Thames Charter. He walks into the kitchenette and flips on the kettle Louise makes a little cough behind him to get his attention.

"Louise," Steve smiles.

"Someone's here to see you Steve..." she says in a low tone. "...she's in Bryan's office waiting for you."

"Who Lou?" Steve says trying hard not to peer around the corner and be obvious to stare across the office.

"Ellia," she whispers.

Steve plonks his mug harder than anticipated onto the work surface.

"What does she want?" He doesn't make eye contact with Louise, just glares at his mug.

"I don't know, but she's been in with Bryan for about 20 minutes. I tried to text you but I had no signal."

Louise moves forward to stand next to him and pulls herself a mug out of the cupboard "are you ok?"

"I was just picking myself up this morning," he replies. It dawns on him that this situation is not going to leave him anytime soon.

He stands at Bryan's door,
"Ahh Steve, you have a visitor."
"Hello Mr Garrett," Ellia says in a much gentler Italian tone than her normal direct forthrightness.
"Ellia" he acknowledges.
"I was hoping it wouldn't be too inconvenient to talk to you for a while please?"
Steve realises that he couldn't recall Ellia once saying 'please' or any gratitude during the weekend he spent in her company.
Bryan gets up, "Please use my office, I have things I need to be getting on with elsewhere," and he shuts the door behind him.
Steve and Ellia look at each other. He notices that Ellia is still meticulously dressed in a little black number. No make-up on and her hair is loose around her shoulders. Not quite the sophisticated secretarial look he was accustomed to.
"What have you told people?" she asks.
Steve is taken aback by the sudden abrupt statement. 'What have I told people?' The irony that Ellia could possibly consider that the weekend's events were of fun idle gossip is incredulous.
"Ellia, I know I am a reporter but this is not something I pick up the phone and start bragging about. To be completely honest with you I wish I had never come to meet Viktor at all. I feel like he has placed a curse on me. So in answer to your question I have not said anything to anyone. What did you tell Bryan, as to why you wanted to see me?"
For the first time the roles shift. Ellia becomes

demure, almost submissive and Steve is the outspoken and ultimately frank.

"I am sorry..." she lowers her tone again "...I just told your boss that I wanted to share the funeral information with you and would like to invite you to attend."

"Attend his funeral?" Steve's voice is still slightly raised and still finding her temerity unbelievable.

"I need to talk to you," she replies softly realising Steve is not happy by her presence.

"Well you are here talking to me."

"No, I would like to meet up with you, please. More private than all those eyes out there looking in at us," she acknowledges.

Looking out of Bryan's door, he sees Bryan, Louise and three other staff members trying to make it look blatantly obvious they are not nosing in at them.

"Why?" he asks her.

"I think we both need to get our heads around all of this. If you have been thinking anything like I have, a hundred questions bouncing about in my head and I have no one else I can talk about this to. Please, meet up with me?"

Steve notices the uneasiness and anxiety in her face. He realises that she is battling with Viktor's untimely proclamations as much as he is. Did he want to go over the same thing again and again or just let it all go and move on? Sighing, he reaches inside his jacket pocket, pulls out his business card and hands it to her.

"It has my mobile number on it. Call me this evening we'll arrange to meet."

Ellia holds on to the business card and looks up at Steve, her big brown eyes glaze with impending emotion.

"Thank you," she mutters softly. She teases her hair to one side and hooks it behind her ear. Steve observes she has no jewellery or make-up on, that she looks pained and actually a little frightened.

She slips his business card into her handbag and stands up, "I will call you," she says holding her hand outstretched to shake Steve's.

He doesn't respond verbally but shakes her hand and walks to the door to hold it open for her to leave. She vacates the office space frantically escaping the numerous eyes transfixed on her. Ellia's ability to captivate attention is almost enchanting.

Chapter 8

Throwing his suit on his bed, Steve climbs into his jeans, puts on a tight fitting grey t-shirt and decides he needs to go for a walk to clear his mind. He picks up his mobile phone and wireless earphones to put them all in his pocket, he hesitates momentarily and puts them back down onto the table. He doesn't want to deal with Ellia's call just yet. He switches the mobile off and leaves the apartment. He stands outside Mrs Sander's door and knocks firmly.

"Berty get back, BERTY BACK!" He hears coming from the other side of the door. It opens just about three inches as a chain secures it.

"Oooh Mr Garrett..." she squeals in a delighted tone "...and to what do I owe this pleasure?"

Unhooking the security chain, Steve looks at her and tries very hard not to laugh out loud. She's standing in front of him wearing a dark purple dressing gown, wellington boots and a very extravagant large teal green coloured hat, with a black feather; the kind of outfit you would expect to see on Lady's Day at Ascot, back in the 1970's.

"Nice hat," he says and she could see the cheekiness in the corner of his eyes.

"Thank you for noticing. I wore this for the Silver Jubilee," she sniggers.

"I was wondering if I could walk Berty?"

She laughs and links her arm into Steve's and leads him into her lounge.

It is very eccentric in taste. To the right of the room is a green velvet chaise longue with gold wood trim. It sits against the rear wall, with African tribal wooden faces along the wall immediately above it. The wooden faces are not situated very high up as Mrs Sanders is only 5' tall and is too fragile to stand on a step ladder. There is a large painting of her husband in the centre of the wall, a very well-groomed looking man, greying hair, wearing a housecoat and a cravat, holding a smoking pipe. Little cuckoo clocks, placed in very odd places around the room, make loud ticking noises as the pendulums swing from side to side.

Steve stares inquisitively at a stunning pottery vessel, it stands at about 2 feet in height.

"You are always mesmerised in that piece, whenever you are here." She's says smiling at him intently.

"There's something quite fascinating about it, where's it from?"

"Qumran in Israel…" she responds enthusiastically "…my husband and I met there you know, he was a university assistant to the professor of Archaeology back in those days. They were doing a dig there. We met one evening in the hotel restaurant. Oh he was so romantic," she grins to herself and drifts off momentarily into her own memories. "This piece is a cylindrical scroll jar. It is believed that these are the same jars found in the Qumran caves where they found the Dead Sea Scrolls."

Steve acknowledges warmly not too sure if he believes her eccentricities. Berty jumps up out of his basket and runs to greet Steve, wagging his tail & he crouches down to make a fuss of him intently.

"Hello Berty" he says scooping him up into his arms, "want to go for a walk?"

Mrs Sanders pulls his lead off a hook in the corner of the hallway and hands it to Steve heading back into the kitchen,

"I've been baking today Mr Garrett. I have some biscuits for you."

She hands Steve a bag of biscuits and he gracefully accepts them and kisses her on the cheek. She shrieks, "Oh Mr Garrett, people will talk!" she laughs as Steve heads for the door.

"Say, 'see you soon'" and he takes Berty's front paw to wave at Mrs Sanders.

"Behave boys," she replies still touching her cheek where Steve had kissed her.

Steve and Berty walk towards the park and he lets the little pug have a run and sniff about. Steve sits on the bench and keeps one eye on Berty while happily people watching. He gives Berty one of the biscuits Mrs Sanders has baked, the little pug gives it a sniff and walks away from it, which makes Steve roar with laughter. He sits there for quite some time deep in thought and Berty lays beside his feet all puffed out and panting.

"We have to stop meeting at this bench," says a familiar voice. Louise sits down next to Steve and makes a fuss of Berty.

"I've been calling you for ages..." she continues "...I was just on my way over to see you."

"I left my phone at home Lou. What's wrong?"

"Steve, I have something to tell you," she says very quickly hoping not to give him the opportunity to interrupt.

"Listen, I know you said that Viktor's words about the formula were just its name, or code, but it was the way that he said it Steve. It was kind of cryptic, I just couldn't get it out of my head. To be honest it's been driving me crazy, he really emphasised it, like it had a bigger meaning and I've been trying to figure out what he was saying, So I've spent hours doing research and came up with something. I'm not sure if it does actually mean anything but I need to tell you." Louise barely comes up for air, trying to get it all out at once.

"Go on?" Steve is intrigued by Louise's proclamation and sudden passion in the situation.

"He said it was 'in the numbers'. I did a lot of internet searching for 1333 but, nothing came up, and then I realised he was saying it as thirteen and thirty three, not as individual figures, but two sets of numbers."

"Yes he did, I didn't think anything of it?" Steve sits himself upright and turns to face Louise. She has aroused his curiosity and has completely captivated his full attention.

"Do you remember he asked us if we were religious, right before he choked on his coffee and the nurse came in?"

"Yes I was rattled that he was searching for some kind of divine forgiveness for the things they had committed, you were a lot more compassionate than I was about that."

"Well..." she pauses for a second or two "...Steve the fourth book of the Bible is called Numbers, he said it was 'in the numbers' and chapter 13 verse 33 might interest you. Look I printed some things off."

She pulls some papers out of her handbag and hands them to Steve.

Numbers 13:33 "And there we saw the Nephilim, the sons of A'Nak, who are from the Nephilim, and in comparison we seemed like grasshoppers, both to us and to them"

"What does this mean Lou? What are the Nephilim?" Steve says intently curious.

"I printed this from Wikipedia..." she pulls a page out from underneath the previous printout "...basically the Nephilim were from the sons of God or fallen angels who had sex with earthly women and gave birth to these hybrid humans, they were giants. Many archaeologists have claimed to find huge skeletons many feet high. Some interpretations referred to them as the super human race, Demigods or Titans. History tells of giants in stories right through ancient folklore. But look at this, I put in a search for Nephilim and Hitler, read this Steve, it comes across as a conspiracy theory but I think....." she stops, Steve stares at the pages, the photos of huge skeletons, he tries to absorb the information all at once,

"Lou, I think you might have something here,"

- Hitler believed the Atlanteans were a superior race. He was obsessed with their culture. The Nazi symbol was a sun disc in the talons of an eagle – a symbol representing the parents of the Nephilim. He blamed the Jewish people for the destruction of the Aryan culture. –

"Why did he blame the Jews for the destruction of this people?" Steve says and looks up at Louise attentively.

"Because according to Bible legend the Nephilim were wiped out during the story of the great flood, you know Noah's ark and all the animals. Noah was a direct descendant of the Jews. Later the Jews made sure of the Nephilim's destruction whenever they reappeared to the Earth. According to this conspiracy Hitler believed that the parents of the Nephilim, the fallen angels or demons, used or manipulated various world empires to destroy the Jews like the Egyptians, Romans, Arabs etcetera. These demons made an agreement with the German government to exchange knowledge of powerful technology for the systematic execution of the ones that wiped out the Aryan Race – The Jewish people."

"Why have I never heard of any of this before?" Steve is astounded. He sits back into the bench, still shuffling the pages.

"So Viktor was right, the German government were

recreating these Nephilim or the perfect Aryan race. I always thought Hitler's hatred for the Jews, was that he blamed them for Germany's economic crisis and he convinced his government of this. You're a genius Louise Randall!"

She smiles, a warm feeling waves through her body as he calls her a genius.

"Do you think the DNA part of the formula just stands for its genetic code? Was DNA that advanced or had even been discovered back then?" she asks him.

Steve laughs heartily at Louise's question.

"You come here to find me with all this information about giants, biblical scriptures, Viktor's hidden messages and you ask me what the DNA stands for? You are too cute Lou..." and kisses her on the forehead, "...well done, you are very clever Miss Randall."

She blushes and smiles at him, proud of herself that Steve is extremely impressed with her. She just needs to please him. She has a sense of spirited gratification.

"Ellia wants to meet up with me, she needs to talk apparently. She mentioned about going to Viktor's funeral." Steve has a look of distaste appear across his expression and his lip curls up in disgust.

"Do you think you will go to the funeral?"

"I haven't decided; I'm still shocked by the invitation to be honest. I meet this old man at the weekend and now I'm being asked to attend his funeral." Steve sarcastically grunts "Well, it's not like there will be hundreds giving him a grand tearful farewell is it?"

"Steve….." Louise pauses momentarily "…if you decide to go, I can accompany you?"

Steve turns on his phone and pours himself a glass of wine, slumps down onto his sofa and watches messages and missed call alerts appear on the mobile screen. Some calls from Louise, some from Ellia and one voicemail from his mum. A text message beeps through.

'Hello Mr Garrett. I have tried to call. I know you must feel I have acted inappropriately today. I would really like to talk to you. Please. Ellia.'

Steve fires up his laptop to do some research on the Nephilim and becomes astounded on all the information available about them and the direct links available between these hybrid humans and Hitler's vision. There are pages and pages of images of their skeletons discovered around the world.

If Steve's head wasn't already full to bursting it certainly is now, taking in an overload of material. His mind wonders back to the children at Ravensbrück, that the Nazi regime had experimented on. Had they succeeded in recreating these 'giants'? The super race? Had they survived?

He grabs his phone to call Ellia but hesitates once again as he is brought to a halt by his mobile Search History. His little Jewish girl stares back at him again. Something about the photo begins to take

Steve away for a moment as she looks at him with that dirty little face. 'Those eyes...' he thinks to himself '...what are you trying to tell me?'

He screen shots the page to save her image into his photo gallery. Something about her drives Steve with motivation. He immediately dials Ellia's number and as it starts to ring he hangs up, let's out a big sigh and takes a sip of wine for courage.

He pauses for a few minutes staring at the phone and mutters "Sod it!" and in a moment of slightly aggressed confidence hits redial.

"Hello Steve," he hears Ellia's voice, soft melodic tones of her beautiful Italian accent.

"Ellia?" he replies.

"I wasn't sure you would call..." she says "I..." she halts.

"Yes?" Steve realises that she is entirely uncomfortable with the situation she is finding herself in and so is he.

"Ellia, what do you know about the Nephilim?" He asks very quickly, not giving her much time to continue with whatever she is about to say.

"Nephilim?" Ellia is totally thrown by the question. "Well, as I understand it they were the offspring of angels, this is a strange question Steve."

"Not really. Miss Randall did some research regarding the DNA1333 serum they tested on those children at Ravensbrück."

"And?"

"When you and I were talking outside his bedroom, he told Louise it was in the numbers. She found this

Bible verse in Numbers 13:33 about these people, the Nephilim, a hybrid of super humans. Ellia did you know any of this before yesterday?"

"Not that no, I was hearing it for the first time when I was with you. I know of other things but definitely not this." She pauses for a second "I cannot sleep Steve I cannot function coherently right now. I know it is a huge plea for such a brief encounter, for me to request that you might accompany me to his funeral, but I don't know anyone in England. I hurt that he has cursed us with this knowledge Steve, but I cannot do this alone."

"Where will the funeral be?" Steve didn't really want to ask or to know, but felt compelled to ask. He hears the quivering tremble in Ellia's voice, not wanting nor intending to give her false hope. Steve displays sensitive empathy, it's who he is - it's what he does best.

"Just a small cremation and then he has requested I scatter his ashes in Provence on my way back to Italy."

"Provence?" enquires Steve, trying to remember where he'd heard this already, sometime recently.

"Yes, Cavalaire-Sur-Mer, the place he took Heidi. It's his most treasured memory." Ellia waits deliberately causing a gap in the conversation, in the hope that Steve will fill the silence with his reply, whether to attend the cremation or not and Steve, revelling in the silence, uses the moment to gather his thoughts. Why is Ellia so quick to dismiss the information he has just shared about Louise's dis-

coveries? She had changed the subject very quickly. Is she telling the truth about Viktor's confession or did she actually know? Why is she so desperate to get a reporter that she has only just met to accompany her to his funeral? Is it because she is all alone in England or is she covering up more mystery to all of this?
"Yes I will go to the funeral, text me the date and time Ellia."
"Thank you Steve..."
He gives her no option to reply or continue her sentence and hangs up the call.

Chapter 9

The morning of the funeral is a dreary cold one. It has been a continual heat wave for over a fortnight and Steve stares out over his balcony thinking how ironically appropriate a dismal grey sky is, completely fitting for the send-off of a dismal grey character like Viktor. Steve had cleared it with Bryan to attend the funeral and asked that Louise come along. He doesn't wish to spend the time alone with Ellia and feels that as Louise is the one Viktor opened up to at the very end, it's fitting.

Steve stands in front of his full length mirror wearing his sleek Hugo Boss black suit, white shirt and a black tie he twists on the onyx cufflinks and straightens his jacket sleeves from the cuff. He looks down, towards the marble kitchen work surface, at a collection of newspapers that have been there a few days.

Head Line: 'Nazi War Criminal Viktor Otto-Wolff dies at 96'.

He screws up his face in bitterness and looks back into the mirror 'right, get today over with and get back to normality' he says to his reflection. He rubs a little hair wax through his hair before he heads towards the door and hears a little scratching noise from the other side. He opens the door Berty rushes in and runs around his living room.

"You are such a naughty boy," comes the voice of a very breathless Mrs Sanders climbing the stairs.

"I am very sorry Mr Garrett…" she wheezes "…Ooo look at you all fine and dapper today" she says patting his jacket lapel.

"Berty come here you bad doggie."

Steve smiles and crouches down, "come here boy" he pat's his knee and Berty runs up to him.

"I'll carry him down for you" Steve scoops up Berty and locks his door.

"Where are you off to today looking so dressed up and handsome? Somewhere nice?" asks Mrs Sanders and takes the lead slowly down the stairs. She wears a pink fuchsia beret on her head and a jade knee length 50's swing dress with layers of netting petticoats puffing it out at the sides. Steve chuckles to himself; he has definitely fallen in love with the quirkiness and eccentricities of Mrs Sanders and is becoming quite protective of her.

"Do you have children Mrs S? I don't think I have ever asked you before?"

Steve can't remember a time when Mrs Sanders had ever had a visitor or seen any family members.

"Sadly Mr Sanders and I were never blessed. We always wanted them, but it wasn't to be. We didn't have the options of a little bit of medical assistance, like they have these days. I have my Berty. But we had a good life, we travelled the world. Oh the things I have seen Mr Garrett."

She smiles and turns to him and as she reaches her doorway he passes Berty into her arms.

"Oh no, he has got fur all over your nice suit. Wait here."

She places Berty into the living room and closes the door so that he doesn't escape again. Rummaging through a drawer in the large mahogany dresser situated in the hallway, she pulls out a lint roller and hands it to Steve and he slides it over his suit picking up the dog hairs.

"You seem so sombre these past few days?" She questions him.

"I'm going to a funeral Mrs S. but it's not a person I wish well of or have any regard for. I feel I'm doing it out of duty, but I feel so torn up inside."

He goes quiet, he's usually so positive around Mrs Sanders, always kept their relationship very light hearted, she looks up at him and fluffs off a couple of dog hairs from his arm.

"A dragonfly starts his day not knowing he only has that one day. Whether it's a good time spent or a bad time…., that is the dragonflies' choice. Life happens regardless of the path we travel along. And whether that path was good or bad, unlike the dragonfly we have the opportunity to try and make some good out of it." She looks up at Steve, can see that something deep is vexing his soul. She doesn't pry.

"You know Steve…" she starts, she seldom ever calls him by his first name but feels his torn anguish needs a little gentleness "…a famous literate once said 'we've got this gift of love, but love is like a precious plant. You can't just accept it and leave it in the cupboard or just think it's going to get on by itself. You've got to keep watering it. You've got to really look after it and nurture it', whatever it is that is bothering you, to resolve the situation you need to take care of it, it won't go away or be resolved unless you deal with it."

"That is a beautiful quote, was it Shakespeare or some famous scholar?"

"John Lennon," she giggles and Steve laughs. He takes Mrs Sanders hand and kisses the back of it and looks at her, smiling cheekily.

"Mr Garrett!.." she shrieks "...I keep telling you to not feed the gossipers!"

He bows at her and she curtseys back holding out the sides of her swing skirt, shuts the door giggling to herself most charmingly.

Louise and Steve stand to the side of the parking area outside the crematorium at the Kensal Green Cemetery. It is a perfect rectangular building with a flat roof something like a child would draw. A cream coloured building with a grand entrance way, there are Roman styled pillars with two small black doors either side. There are glazed windows behind the pillars that span the entire length of the pillars from top to bottom and a glass door leading into a grand foyer. Flowers lay as tributes to passed loved ones in the magnificent glazed atrium, between the chapels.

They stand together quietly observing people come

and go in and out of the building as a hearse pulls in and a few members of the press arrive. Viktor's death has been of much more interest than his hospital confinement. Steve finds this all very strange and is perplexed how he had landed that privilege, or not so privileged meeting. Either way, he couldn't help shift the suspicion that Viktor's capture and trial created a lot of disturbed enthusiasm. His death seems absorbed in even more scrutiny and curiosity. Bryan had said it was all hush, but Steve knew the press, he knew if they wanted to find him they would have done just that.

The paparazzi start snapping photographs of the hearse and the coffin, a news reporter stands over on the grassed area, across the road and they use the crematoriums main entrance as a backdrop. A camera crew stand around him and then others start to appear doing the same from various locations. Louise notices a black BMW pull up outside the building which stops directly behind the hearse. The driver steps out and opens the car door behind the driver's side. An elegant lady steps out, she looks to be in her late 40's or early 50's smartly dressed in a couture fitted black dress. The driver pulls a wheelchair out of the boot and assembles it, places it by the car door and as the elegant woman leans into the car; she assists an elderly lady out of the car and into the wheelchair.

Louise taps Steve's arm and gestures by nodding her head over to the left as they see Ellia walk towards them. Louise admires the sophistication that surrounds Ellia, like an aura of magical colour. She is dressed in a tight fitting peplum black skirt suit, her hair piled high on her head into a neatly placed bun. She steps over towards Steve and holds out her hand for them both to shake, Louise greets Ellia and smiles sympathetically as Steve reluctantly shakes her hand. Ellia picks up on his reluctance and says in a quiet tone "Thank you both for coming. Please do not be alarmed but you will be sitting family side. I have not had you placed with the rest of those vultures over there," she points to the press.

Steve is still suspicious of the VIP treatment they are receiving for somebody they feel no loyalty toward, let alone a misplaced connection for. They had met Viktor briefly over one weekend. Just one weekend that would give them the burdens of nightmares for a very long time, and now they are 'fake family' at his funeral.

The clouds begin to cast a spooky shade over the crematorium and surrounding area, creating eerie shadows on the ground.

"Looks like rain." Louise says and breaks the awkward atmosphere.

"Well God won't be weeping down teardrops of rain amongst this bunch of mournful souls."

"Steve!" Louise nudges him embarrassed and a little shocked, but Ellia looks away accepting how Steve must feel about it all.

For as long as Steve could remember, the idea of death had never really affected him. He had always felt it was a life process that it was just the end stage of a persons' life and that is all. But Viktor's death has shifted something within him and he knew that Viktor had changed his scope of life completely and nothing was ever going to be quite the same again. He has an overwhelming feeling of doom, depression, toward Viktor. An entire melancholic depressive atmosphere surrounds him in a way he can't describe and that he's not comfortable with.

A tall gentleman gestures at Ellia from the large glass doorway and slowly everybody makes their way inside the crematorium.

Louise notices how extremely quiet it is and they both sit in the row behind Ellia. She glances around to see how many people are in fact sitting on the family and friends side and shifts uncomfortably for there is literally a dozen people and all seated estranged from each other. It is very clear nobody knows each other, brief encounters of people that have known Viktor over his 96 years. The woman Louise had noticed helping assemble a wheelchair outside walks up beside her. Louise looks on intently. A frail elderly lady sits in the wheelchair's large padded seat. She is dressed totally in black from head to toe and is wearing a black felt hat with fine netting that comes down over her face. Ellia stands up and gently kisses the woman on both her cheeks, very continental style and does the same with the younger lady pushing her. The wheelchair is placed in the front row beside Ellia and the younger woman sits down next to Ellia. On the other side of the room towards the back the press assemble quietly. Louise feels sad how a life has passed, that hardly anybody is there to show their respects. Steve, however, is much bitterer about it all and isn't surprised by the lack of respect being shown at all. He thinks how surprising it is that there isn't an entire Jewish community outside the crematorium protesting. He never takes life for granted, but Viktor had taken the lives of innocent ones for granted. Those lives were important to other people and he begins to realise from that moment that death is not just an end stage of a persons' life. It is more than that, deeper, meaningful, going beyond and further than the written boundaries of a person's life. It intimately torments, affects and haunts all the people that are directly and in a lesser way, indirectly connected or associated with the person who they are mourning. This is the significance of Viktor, he has affected Steve, he's haunting his every thought and as a result it torments him. Chopin's Piano Sonata No.2 plays quietly in the background and everybody is asked to stand as the pallbearers carry the casket along the aisle and place the casket on the stand at the front between two large wooden pillars with candles placed on top of each.

A beautiful flower arrangement is placed on top of the coffin, lush in colours of reds and pinks, with occasional sprays of greenery.

Steve feels a shiver in his body as a hymn begins, a droning mumble of voices sing softly from around the room. A tall elegant gentleman begins the funeral. He says a few opening words and a prayer in German. Steve begins to find the whole thing creepy and disturbing. He feels dizzy and his breathing becomes erratic. He isn't a person who has ever experienced a panic attack before, but it seems he may be about to. He thinks to himself 'deep slow breaths' and is quite relieved when everyone is asked to sit.

For such a small turnout, he feels very stuffy and claustrophobic and pulls a tissue from out of his trouser pocket to wipe the buds of sweat from his forehead.

"You ok?" whispers Louise noticing Steve pasty colouring and hearing his breathless panting.

"I feel nauseous."

Steve balances his elbows on his knees and buries his face into his hands. He only hears his heartbeat in his ears and nothing being said in the funeral service. The pounding becomes unbearable and he quickly stands up to make his way out of the exit towards the back. He can feel everybody's eyes turn their glance toward him, and as he finds himself being suffocated, the walk to the door seems to go on forever. Ellia turns around and glances at Louise and without saying a word, Louise shakes her head negatively that he's not ok.

He bursts open the front doors lunging his body into the fresh air, stretches out his arm to grab one of the pillars and slumps his way down onto the floor to a seated position. He leans back against the pillar, tries hard to regulate his breathing and feels tingling sensations in his fingers and, without notice, leans forwards and vomits onto the gravel in front of him.

Chapter 10

The people attending the funeral start to slowly make their way out of the doors, Louise hurries over toward Steve who now sits down at the bottom of the driveway.
"Steve," she says in a really mellow concerning tone. He looks away, not wanting to make eye contact with her, a sense of embarrassment, demasculinized and a self-conscious uneasiness overwhelms him.
Louise remains quiet as she knows he doesn't want to speak. She feels confusion, worry and generally edgy. This Viktor situation brings out such intense emotions within them both, more so with Steve. She glances over, a car pulls up beside Ellia at the main doors and the elderly lady hands something to Ellia who kneels down to take it.
Steve and Louise are too far away for Louise to focus clearly on what is going on and she watches intently as Ellia leans in, kisses the lady on both cheeks, acknowledges the woman escorting her and then heads down towards Louise and Steve. Louise looks away quickly, she doesn't want it to appear that she's witnessed anything and as Steve notices her heading towards them, he groans rolling his eyes. He stands himself up, brushes some dust off his trousers,
"Are you ok Mr Garrett?" Ellia asks and tries to make

eye contact with him.

"I'm fine I must have eaten something, had a bit of an unsettled stomach," he says incredibly defensively.

"Thank you for coming," Ellia continues, Louise nods at her, but she and Steve both remain silent.

"Are you coming back to the..."

Steve interrupts her knowing she is going to enquire about the wake. He wants no more of it, keeping up a fake persona, living and acting a charade is not his style.

"I won't be coming to the Wake thank you, I have things I must do today."

Louise again shakes her head, saying no, but remaining silent. She wants to go to the wake and meet the old lady. She has intrigued Louise, but out of respect for Steve she declines as she knows this subject has to, very quickly, be forgotten and she needs to get Steve out of here.

Steve lies on his sofa and stares at his television screen, but not really watching it, re-runs of Friends on the Comedy Channel. Once again his thoughts start to race about in his mind, like a twisting kaleidoscope of Viktor, the forgotten children, the funeral it just went on and on. He can feel himself falling into a rut, drowning in his own head and can't think of a way out. His thoughts are sharply interrupted by the ring of his landline telephone. He sits himself up and reaches for the handset on the coffee table in front of him,

"Hello?"

"Mamies petit soldat" comes the familiar voice.

"Grandma!" Steve's face lights up contented and a net of safety envelopes him and he smiles.

"Are you ok Stephen? Your mother says that nobody has heard from you for a couple of weeks."

"Grandma may I come over and see you and Pops?"

Steve grabs his house keys and jacket and slams the door behind him. He needs to be grounded and family time is just what the doctor would prescribe.

He stands outside his grandparents' house and has, for now, forgotten Viktor and all his curses. He stares for a while, this is home. The little front gate is shut, there are bushes either side of it, making a perfect square around the front garden. It looks exactly the way a little child would draw a house with its little square hedged surround. He opens the gate and steps onto the little path looking adoringly at the variety of gnomes sporadically placed on the grass, amongst the tubs of flowers. Baskets hang from the porch way of the front door but since his grandparents barely use the front door, he walks the path that runs down the side of the house to the open backdoor, also adorned with hanging baskets and shrubs. As he looks over the back garden he smiles to see more gnomes and an ornamental wooden windmill, about three feet tall with sails that turn in the wind. Most of the garden decorations have been gifts, to his grandparents, by their children and grandchildren over the years. Each little gnome has their own story to tell.

At the bottom of the garden is a large wooden outbuilding, where each of them would spend a few hours every day in recliner chairs, reading their newspapers and magazines. He sees a movement from the outhouse and wanders down to the bottom of the garden where he finds Grandad Borowski resting, with his feet up on the recliner, bifocal spectacles halfway down his nose and the newspaper flopped on top of his chest. He's snoring and Steve smiles to himself staring at his grandfather with great love and adoration.

He is a tall man, around 6'1"; everybody says that's where Steve gets his height from. He looks at the ageing lines under his eyes and across his forehead. Large tufts of hair sprout across his eyebrows, out of his ears and hairy nostrils. He looks eccentric, but Mikolai Borowski is far from eccentric. He is a quiet man, always deep in his thoughts. Sometimes he's so far away in his mind, he becomes lost. He has always been this way, Molly his wife is the 'hub' of the family. Very talkative and flamboyant, she watches over them all, with great love and pride like a mother hen. She is definitely the dominant one in the family. Steve kneels down by his grandfather's legs and rests his head onto his lap, like he had done as a child, safe, secure, Pops was his hero. Mikolai makes a sleepy snuffly sound and rubs his nose, feeling a little disturbed and as he opens his eyes to see Steve looking up at him, Mikolai chuckles, snorts out of his nose and pats him on the head.

He takes his glasses off his nose, folds in the arms,

puts them onto the little mahogany table beside him and folds his newspaper, turning his attention to his grandson. Neither of them saying a word, Mikolai knows Steve is troubled. He's not seen Steve regress into the familiarity of his lap for a very long time. The last time this happened Steve was stressing over his dissertation many years earlier. Whilst Steve wonders about the pains his grandfather kept secret, Mikolai wonders what is troubling Steve. He strokes Steve's hair and Steve is happy to be caressingly groomed by his grandfather. He gazes from Mikolai's lap out onto the freshly cut lawn and watches a squirrel run its way along the length of the fence, he can see just behind the hedging. The squirrel is so carefree, scurrying along, such a simple life.

"Talk to me son," comes the familiar raspy deep husky voice of Mikolai, beautiful notes interlinked with a Polish accent.

"I wouldn't know where to start Pops," Steve's voice is soft, with an edge of melancholy, desperate and trembling. He sits himself up to look up at his grandfather and Mikolai smiles lovingly with his eyes, he doesn't like seeing his Grandson so vexed and troubled.

Mikolai and Molly have two daughters, Steve's mother Annetta and her sister Adalene. Steve's brother Robert is 3 years younger and his sister Michelle is the baby, 10 years Steve's junior. He begins to wonder when he last caught up with any of them. He has spoken to them and all text each other regularly, but he realises how his job has consumed his life. He has not had any one to one time with any of them for longer than he cares to remember.

Adalene and Uncle Gerald have one son and one daughter. Steve's cousin Rene is a year younger in age. He is Steve's best friend, not just family, but his lifelong comrade and partner in crime. Steve always loves Rene's attentiveness to their relationship and begins to feel guilt for his lack of availability recently. Rene and Steve look very similar and quite often passed as brothers when they were children. Steve looks at the family photograph in a plain chrome frame besides Mikolai which had been taken some 10 years earlier at his grandparent's golden wedding anniversary and he chuckles at his geeky looking floppy haircut and Rene and Robert trying to look cool in their beany hats and shades. Michelle was only twelve in the photograph and was pulling off very fetching braces on her teeth, frizzy hair and wearing a Busted boy band t-shirt. Rene's younger sister Rosa was 18 in the photograph and had the moodiest sulky face. She had wanted to go on a girl's holiday to Ibiza, but had to attend the family event instead.

Steve chuckles "Do you remember how stroppy Rosa was that day?"

"I told Adalene to let her go on the holiday. Rosa apologises every time she sees that photograph now. Wisdom comes with age - age also makes people take time to down tools and listen. As you can see I'm rushed off my feet today Steve." Steve laughs aloud again, Mikolai just smiles and watches his grandson intently.

He pulls himself into Molly's chair opposite his grandfather and slowly rubs his hand over his face anxiously and takes in a large slow intake of breath. "Pops, I met a…..how can I phrase this?... a unique gentleman, through work recently and his presence in my head is driving me insane."

"Sounds like my head with your grandmother" Mikolai replies in a cheeky mischievous way. Steve smirks and unconsciously starts rubbing his palms against each other and stares idly at the rug on the floor.

"This man has made me think about a lot of things I've never considered before. I've just taken for granted that some things should never be spoken about, but they should be talked about. Or at least I need them to be spoken of Pops."

"I'm not following you son. Who is this man, what did he say?"

At that Steve shifts his stare from the ground to quickly making eye contact with his grandfather.

"Pops, I need to know, I know that this is hard for you. Grandma and mum will go mad for me asking, but I just have to know now…" he pauses for a few seconds and softens his voice "…what happened to you in the war?"

He had said it, if there was ever a scenario of a cat actually sitting in a bag, then that cat just leapt right on out of it.

Mikolai sits slowly back into his recliner and turns

his head to glance out over the garden. Steve looks on intently at his grandfathers' expression, just to check if he has angered him.

"It was a long time ago Steve," Mikolai responds but continues to gaze over his garden. Steve sits silently, he's blurted out the family's forbidden question and now isn't sure how to back track it. His last intention is to upset his grandfather. There has already been enough upset recently.

"I was extremely messed up for a very long time. If it wasn't for my Molly healing me mentally the best she could, I don't know what would have happened to me."

"Were you harmed in any way? Tortured?"

Mikolai shakes his head "Not all suffering and pain that hurts the most, are physical Stephen. No, my pain was mental. I would have rather been beaten, those bruises heal. The bruises in my mind are permanent."

Mikolai sighs deeply and lifts his glasses off the table and puts them on his nose.

"Come with me Stephen."

He stands up and they both make their way down the path heading for the house and as they reach the backdoor, Steve ducks to avoid collision with the array of hanging baskets. They are beautiful; lush in pink, yellow and purple pansies, some with sweetpeas' Molly's pride and joy and she often makes baskets by request for neighbours and friends.

Mikolai enters the backdoor and Molly is busy French polishing the large dining table just inside the entrance. It is a small reception room, with the kitchen to its right and a white wood painted door to the left, which leads onto two lounges. One is a small lounge where Mikolai and Molly spend their evenings together, and the grand lounge at the front of the house which is for entertaining and if, on the off chance, the Queen came to visit for afternoon tea! Molly would often tell her grandchildren the Queen is coming one day and to their knowledge the Queen has never come over on the invite of afternoon tea. The rooms are adorned with an array of family photos, ornaments and large vases with artificial flowers in them. Molly turns and does a little clap when she sees Steve come through the backdoor and she puts down her cloth, grabs his cheeks with two flat hands and pulls him down to kiss him. She always wears a very sticky, thick, pink lipstick which lingers on Steve's face for some time after. He used to hate that as a child.

She grabs the cloth and polish and puts them into the large pockets of her frilly gingham waist tied apron and she places a large vase display of fresh flowers onto a lace doily in the centre of the table.

"Drink?" she asks Steve.

"Coffee please, Grandma," he smiles as she continues to fuss over miniscule cleaning details and the re-arrangement of photographs, as she heads into the kitchen.

The kitchen is tiny. There is a sink underneath the window which isn't well lit due to the hanging baskets blocking the daylight the other side! To the right of the sink there is a deep cupboard and the oven and to the left of the sink is a pine French dresser displaying Royal Dalton crockery, floral teacups and saucers. Further to the left of the dresser is the entrance to Aladdin's Cave, or the larder. Steve and his cousins were always enamoured by this cupboard, it is deep enough to walk into and it hosts floor to ceiling shelves, with enough food to feed an entire street for a month following an earthquake or zombie apocalypse. It houses so many tins of Spam and tuna, his grandmother could open a shop. He knows her food obsession is due to lack of food and rationing during the war, Molly became obsessed with making sure that in the unlikely event of any major catastrophe happening, her family would be well nourished. She flips on the kettle and signals to Steve to take a seat.

"Molly we will be back shortly my dear. Stephen and I are going to talk man stuff," says Mikolai patting Steve on his back.

"Is that right? Well whatever that 'man stuff' is, make sure you don't make a mess, I've just hoovered," Molly mutters to herself.

Chapter 11

Steve follows Mikolai down to the front lounge, passing walls of family photographs that date back to the turn of the 20th century, beautifully posed starchy looking pictures of Mikolai's parents with his Grandparents. Large Victorian style dresses and Stephen's great, great grandfather in a very fetching top hat. Steve's sister Michelle would stare at these photos for hours as a child. Behind them comes the recognisable coo of the cuckoo clock as its little bird pokes out proudly to announce the hour.

They enter into the lounge and Steve instantly remembers that he wasn't allowed to play in there as a child and is still terrified to touch anything, even though he's an adult now. Under the huge bay window is a crushed red velvet two seater sofa with two matching chairs either side of it. The arms of the sofa and chairs have beautiful embroidery anglaise protectors on them with matching ones that sit over the backs. The curtains behind are also a lush red velvet drape with cute Austrian ruched nets in the window and the main wall hosts a stunning ornate fireplace with an open fire which is only lit during winter months, when the family gather together. There stands an extremely archaic and enormously outdated television set to the left of the fireplace. Along the nearest left hand wall is a walnut and brass side board that stores photo albums spanning decades of the Borowski's lives with each other and their children and grandchildren.

"Have a seat Stephen," Mikolai gestures towards the sofa.

As he sits down slowly he watches intently as his Grandfather opens the furthest right hand section of the sideboard and never takes his eyes off him for a single second. Mikolai reaches towards the back of the shelf and pulls out a small wooden box he caresses the top of it, shuts the side board door and sits himself down in the chair next to Steve.

Mikolai concentrates at the closed dark wooden box for a while. Steve can tell his grandfather is anxious to open it and he can't help but wonder if asking about Mikolai's time during the war, is about to open more than the Pandora's box, that his grandfathers wrinkled hands clench onto so tightly.

"I'm sorry Pops, I shouldn't have said anything. I...."

"Shh..." his granddad hushes Steve and says softly "...I just need a moment son."

Steve looks at the little wooden box it is about 6 inches in length, 4 inches wide and only about three inches in depth. On the lid it has exquisitely carved wooden daisies intertwined with ivy, four carved daisies to be exact and the ivy vine engraving going down the side of the box, which means you can only fit the lid to the bottom in one certain direction.

"Stephen, I have never found this easy to talk about. For many years I punished myself for not doing more at the time...." Mikolai pauses and looks up from the box at Steve. Steve is already puzzled. He leans forward slightly and grabs his grandfather's arm empathically and Mikolai sighs moving his arm away from his grandsons hand, he interlinks his fingers into Steve's and grips his hand tight. Steve is incredibly touched by this gesture. He struggles to remember the last time he had held his granddads hand. Even then, it was probably when Mikolai held Steve's hand to protect him as a child, but this time, this actual moment, it is Steve protecting his grandfather, the ultimate role reversal.

They sit like this in silence, both completely transfixed on the box. Steve is curious as to its contents and Mikolai terrified to let its contents out. Neither speak, especially not Steve. He realises that he may have to sit there some considerable time until his Grandad feels comfortable enough to let the demons fly out.

Suddenly their silence breaks by the lounge door flying open and Molly standing in its doorway with a tray holding two cups and saucers, a small plate of biscuits and a sugar bowl,

"That wretched squirrel has just jumped at me whilst I was pegging out the laundry and...." Molly stops dead mid-sentence and lets out a small gasp, as she sees her husband holding the box "...Mikolai!..."

He holds up his hand and shakes his head quickly. She turns to look at Steve, but he doesn't know what to say. She places the tray down on the coffee table in front of them nervously her hands trembling slightly.

"It's ok my darling, it's time that they knew," Mikolai's voice is firm but gentle. She didn't question it nor argue or disagree. She had learnt over the years that this particular subject was only her husbands' burden to bear or share. Without a word she turns towards the lounge door to leave, she hovers for a second and looks at him, he looks up at her and winks knowingly and she exits the room.

"You have to understand Stephen, Grandma is very protective. This box holds the reason I met her in the first place."

Steve begins to feel very unsettled by his questioning and is uncertain of the serious impact this may have on his grandparents. Could his grandfather's confronting his fear become a challenging test for Mikolai and Molly or is his fear unrealistic or out of proportion with what may be expected in their situation? Steve has no idea what to expect, maybe he is being irrational, but thinks he mustn't over think this or judge, as he has no idea of the enormity of his Grandfather's experiences.

Mikolai lets Steve's hand go, and slowly opens the box. He picks up a square piece of fabric like an appliqué or a sew-on motif. To the left of the fabric is a yellow star and on the right were a set of numbers. He places the appliqué out onto his knee and looks back at the box. Lying face down inside, is a small photograph and very slowly he turns it over. He takes a long time studying it. He caresses his finger over it and then in silence he hands it to Steve. Steve looks up at his granddad, who beckons him to take it. Steve holds the photo and recognises the lady in it as the lady is in a photograph on the wall in the hallway. Steve had seen her all his life. It is Mikolai's mother but in this photograph she is holding the hand of a little girl. 7 or 8 years old, the young girl has long blonde hair, and her smile shows her two top front teeth are missing. She has a little pinafore dress on with a pale blouse underneath it, scruffy droopy socks at different lengths on her calves and scuffed black ankle boots. Next to her stands a young man of about 13 or 14 years old wearing a flat cap, white shirt and high waist trousers supported by braces over his shoulders. The little girl is smiling up at him, a toothless smile and he is reciprocating, grinning back at her.

"Is this your mum, Pops?"

He nods and Steve continues "I recognise her from the photos in the hall."

"That is me Stephen," Mikolai points to the young man in the photograph.

"Wow Pops, I don't think I've seen any photos of you at that age. I've seen you as a small boy and in yours and grandmas wedding day photos. You look so much like Robert here."

Mikolai laughs "Well, Robert looks like me."

Steve smiles at his chronological error.

Steve has recognised his Great Grandmother and Pops, the mystery can only be concluded in the young girl. He looks up at his grandfather, but holds onto the photograph. This is the one thing that defined all that Mikolai was. What led to the Bicêtre hospital and to his Molly.

"Her name is Hannetta, she was..... my sister." The words seem to fall out of Mikolai's mouth with extreme difficulty his lips are tense as he says it. He feels a tightening in his throat and a dense heaviness on his ribs. A very small tear eases its way over the small age lines that frame his eyes and glides down his cheek bone, glimmering in the daylight that shines through the lounge window. Steve has never seen his grandfather cry, he has seen him consumed in his own world, far away in his thoughts, sad, distant and lonely, but never cry.

"I didn't know you had a sister, Mum never mentioned it."

"Well, Annetta wouldn't mention it son. Your mother is named after her in a roundabout way, but you know I always call her Annie. Sometimes calling her by her full name was hard for me, even without the H"

"How old is Hannetta here?"

"She was 7. It was taken in January 1940. It's the last photograph taken of the three of us. My father died a year earlier of Tuberculosis, so I was providing for the family. My Uncles would always be there to help us whenever we struggled but it was never a burden for me and I took the responsibility of providing for them very seriously and enjoyed doing so. Hannetta would come and sit on my lap every evening and read to me, kiss me on the cheek before going to bed and say 'I love you Miki' and that made the long working hours for a couple of coins all worth it. I never felt that pleasure in me again until your mother came along, and slowly as Adalene arrived and then my Grandchildren I began to feel the joy I had once felt with Hannetta and to protect you all, where I had failed her."

Mikolai stops and sighs again and he leans forward to pick up the saucer holding the cup of coffee, places a digestive on the edge of the saucer and he looks out of the window sipping at his drink.

"Maybe I became overly protective of Annie and Adalene, but they never complained."

"Why do you feel you failed her Pops? What happened to her?"

Mikolai looks down at the yellow star fabric patch on his knee he picks it up and almost feels its curse.

"We had these sewn on our clothing."

"I know," Steve whispers in an almost inaudible tone, he can't imagine the scenes.

"I will never forget that day, it haunts me every night. My mother had just come through the backdoor with a basket of freshly laid eggs, I was polishing my boots and Hannetta was sitting at the dining table eating an apple. It was the 18th January. A very cold day and I'd been out earlier cutting logs for the fire as our cooker was an old wood burning stove and provided heat for the house."

Mikolai sips at his coffee for a second to gather his thoughts. The smallest of tremors in his fingers makes the cup clank against its saucer in a repetitive clinking sound. Steve grabs the cup and places it onto the tray.

"You're going to burn yourself Pops."

"We hadn't even heard them coming, there was no noise in the street to alert us to anything out of the ordinary, but then again we were the first house to be targeted. I just remember the knock. Well it wasn't so much a knock, more like 5 hobnail boots hammering at the door. I hadn't even reached it when it swung open and smashed against the coat rack hanging in the hallway. One of the pegs hit the small window of glass at the top of the door and it smashed it into tiny shards of glass. The next ten minutes or so happened so quickly and are just a haze of memory in my head. I have tried to piece it all together, but it's all jumbled like a puzzle. I remember being told to put a coat and shoes on. One of the soldiers picked up Hannetta, she screamed and bit into his hand. This wasn't a good move, he took one swipe at her and she flew across the kitchen hitting her forehead and splitting it against the work top. I tried to run towards her but two soldiers grabbed me and dragged me backwards up the hallway to the front door. I could hear my mother calling out reassuringly to Hannetta 'it will be ok, it will be ok' but Hannetta was frightened. Her screams alerted the rest of the street of the sudden invasion."

A silence falls in the room as Mikolai reaches into his trouser pocket to pull out a handkerchief and rubs it against his nose and wipes his eyes. The two men sit together in silence for a couple of minutes and Steve continues to stare at his Great Aunt, one he had never known anything about. Mikolai twists the yellow star in an anticlockwise motion through his hands.

"We were all bundled into a convoy of trucks along the street and all that we could do was to sit there, with armed soldiers surrounding each truck, waiting for our neighbours to arrive. The scenes of distress from each family, as they were evicted from their houses, have their own stories to tell. Hannetta sat on my lap with her arms tightly around my neck, as my mother used her apron to stop the bleeding from Hannetta's split head. We were transported on a four hour journey until we reached a sorting point. This was where I saw my mother and sister for the last time. A selection process commenced, we all had to give our names and skills. I was placed into a long line of males set for labour work. The females and children were put into different lines. I looked up and down the line from a distance frantically trying to find my mother and Hannetta but I couldn't see them. The fear in all the men's eyes, as they tried hard to look over and find their wives and children was something I will never forget. As men we need to protect and cherish our women, provide for our children. God just made us that way. All the men were put onto a train and that was that."

"What happened to you after that Pops? You were still just a child yourself, where did you go?"

"Ahh well that all seems irrelevant now. From that moment on, all I could think of was to survive. I needed to live and one day to find them again. But that wasn't to be. When the war was over and your grandmother's time at the Bicêtre had come to an end, we went back to Poland to my home. If ever I prayed hard in my life, that was it, I prayed that they would be there waiting for me when I returned, but that wasn't to be. The house had been ransacked and stripped of anything of value. It was desolate and dusty. I salvaged a few items that would have been of no value to anybody else and found a few photographs, the ones hanging in the hall and this one. I wrote a letter to any of my family albeit Hannetta, my mother or my uncles, just in case they came to the house searching for us and pinned it to the kitchen door. I left the home address of Molly's family in England, if anyone needed to find me, but no one ever came. Everything I suffered and endured through the rest of the war was of no significance. Eventually after a few years I sold the house and the new owners promised to pass on the address in the off chance somebody would turn up. All I wanted was to hear Hannetta say 'I love you Miki' just one more time. What really tortured me was the not knowing what she had to endure, if she lived or died. As news spread, rumours and gossip of the mass genocides occurring. The mental cruelty was too much to handle, that is how I ended up at the Bicêtre, but my escape from the camp is a whole different story."

Steve shakes his head as he strives hard to comprehend his grandfather's words and grapples to deal with such intense tragedy, Mikolai's struggle to protect his family, his struggle for freedom, for existence.

"Excuse me a moment Stephen."

Mikolai stands up and leaves the room and Steve sits himself back into the sofa. He ponders over the photograph and then quickly grabs his mobile phone and takes a picture of Hannetta, his great Grandmother and Mikolai. He then hurriedly puts his phone back into his pocket and places the photograph and yellow star back into the box. Molly quietly enters the lounge and Steve jumps up and wraps his arms around her.

"I'm sorry Grandma," he starts.

She pats him knowingly on his back, kisses him on his cheek and replies,

"I know you must have had your reasons my darling."

He does have his reasons and his hatred for Viktor and the Nazi regime has just escalated through the roof.

Chapter 12

Steve sleeps surprisingly well that night. He is shocked when he's awoken by the sound of his alarm in the morning. Despite having to attend the funeral of Viktor and the revelations from his grandfather all in one day, he has the best night's sleep in several days. He arrives at The Thames Charter and decides that today will be a fresh start to move on, to forget Viktor and to leave behind the past couple of weeks. He feels happy and he positively struts, head up, into the open plan office, looking extra dashing.

"Good morning beautiful." He says to Louise as he kisses her on the cheek. Taken completely by surprise at this gesture, Louise blushes with a cheeky smirk on her face, as two other female office associates giggle and exchange gossipy glances at each other.

The morning goes smoothly and Steve begins to feel exactly like Steve again, mischievous, happy and chilled out. Bryan sends him out in the field to report a star studded movie premier. This is more like it. Louise is asked to write the article regarding Viktor's funeral. She has written most of her article and decides to scour the collection of photographs that she has downloaded off the internet, taken by various members of the world's press who had also attended the funeral.

She idly scans through various pictures for a few minutes, ones of the hearse arriving, the coffin and the people attending and then freezes at a set of photos that were taken after the funeral. She sits bolt upright in her chair, flicks through the photos again and again. She throws the printed downloads onto her desk and grabs her mouse to bring up the images she's printed off. As she speedily whizzes through the photos, she finds the one's she's searching for. The angle of imagery is from the front of the elderly ladies transport. She scrutinizes a set of still shots which shows the lady passing Ellia something from around her neck. Louise enhances each photograph and zooms in on the item sitting beautifully around her neck. As the enhancement is distorted and fuzzy from her computer, she highlights the photographs and sends them via email to young Ben downstairs in I.T. She can't get out of her chair fast enough and hurries along the corridor towards the stairs, knocks paperwork out of Bryan's hands and scattering the pages everywhere.

"Sorry Bryan!" she gasps, bending down to gather up the pages.

"In a hurry Miss Randall?" Bryan chuckles as he watches her in a tight fitted skirt and high heels, rummaging all over the floor.

"Here..." she says handing the papers in disarray to Bryan "...sorry I don't think they're in order!" she shouts as she runs through a door leading to the stairs.

She hurries down the stairwell and notices Ben on

his way up.

"Ben!" she gasps catching her breath. He has a look of surprise as he sees Louise very excitable to see him, "Err yeah?"

"I need your genius computer brain NOW!"

Grabs his oversized grey jumper and drags him back down to the I.T. room.

"Glad to know I'm needed for something," Ben states sarcastically as Louise pushes him to his chair. A young I.T apprentice, 22 years old and fresh out of university, Ben looks completely stereotypically like a computer geek. Steve always tells Ben that he will be the next Bill Gates. He has red auburn hair, has been growing a beard for the past 4 months, wears silver rimmed glasses and is extremely freckly. He is not extremely fashion conscious, but his intelligence is exceptional, and to be fair The Thames Charter bosses know he is way too good to be their I.T. guy.

"I sent you an email; I need you to enhance some photographs please."

He brings up the images onto his screen and Louise moves in much closer to him, to watch him doing what he does best.

"There..." Louise says and points at the elderly ladies neck.

Ben starts to zoom in and uses digitally enhancing programmes to crisp up the image, Louise grabs a chair and sits next to him not taking her eyes off the screen for a single second. All in all it takes about five minutes for Ben to bring it up and just as he is about to speak Louise lets out in high pitched hysterical "HEIDI!"

Her mouth drops open in disbelief. She shakes her head puzzled, rubs her hands together anxiously, "No it can't be?"

He hands her the print and she stares at it still dazed and confused, but there it was the heart shaped locket with the mother of pearl cherubs, embossed onto its front, the same locket Louise had seen in the photograph Viktor had shown her at the hospital.

"I take it by your reaction you are surprised to see this?"

"Yes..." Louise's tone is a lot more subdued now "...yes I am."

"Can you see in any of the other photos, if she passes it to this woman next to her?" she says and points to Ellia on the screen.

Ben enhances each photograph one by one in series, as Louise continues to stare at the necklace, beginning to mull it over in her mind, 'How does Ellia know Heidi? Does Ellia know a lot more than she was letting on? Does Heidi know more about Viktor than he had realised?'

"It looks like a key Louise," Ben says as the most recent image Ellia is taking a small key from Heidi.

Each still shot shows, the elderly Heidi opening the locket, taking out a small 2" key from the inside and handing it to Ellia. Louise whispers under her breath 'she holds the key to my heart' repeating back Viktor's words. Ben prints off the other images and again Louise just sits there staring, mesmerised at the key in Ellia's hand. It is a golden or brass in colour.

"Can I help with anything else?" questions Ben, Louise is lost in her thoughts she doesn't hear him at all.

"Pardon?" she looks up at him with an expression like she has just seen a ghost.

"Anything else?" he repeats himself.

"Oh, no thank you... Ben thank you, you are truly a star."

Very dazed and troubled she slowly exits the I.T department. She continues to ponder each photograph as she goes back up the stairs to her desk she flops herself onto the chair. Bryan avidly watches her very stunned body language, completely opposite to the highly rushed hysterical one some twenty minutes earlier.

"Louise, can I speak to you for a moment please?" Bryan bellows from his office doorway. "...hello! Louise?"

She looks up at Bryan confused and flustered, hides the photographs under some other papers on her desk and goes to his office.

"Please, Miss Randall, take a seat." He says gesturing at the chair. She sits and pulls the bottom of her skirt down and looks back towards her desk very distracted.

"Miss Randall.... Louise, I'm not going to beat around the bush here, but the fact of the matter is, you and Mr Garrett have been acting extremely odd ever since the Otto-Wolff assignment. Steve hasn't said much at all about it and I may be getting old Miss Randall, but I am not a total idiot."

"Yes Bryan." Louise shifts herself uncomfortably in the chair.

She knows Steve has not given Bryan all the facts of Viktor's interview and she certainly doesn't want to betray Steve's trust but she also knows she is not about to pull the wool over Bryans eyes either.

"I'm going to get us a coffee, and when I come back I think you and I are going to have a little chat."

Bryan leaves his office and gives Louise time to gather her thoughts. She isn't sure what to say and what not to say. Is she about to expose the centuries' darkest post war secret? A can of worms that Viktor himself had hidden, that he had never had the courage to expose or resolve himself? Starting to feel the intensity and full realisation of how Steve had been feeling, suffering and struggling regarding this matter, she wonders if Viktor knew that Ellia had more knowledge about Heidi than he had realised. Louise feels nauseous. Will Bryan just think it is an amazing story of Nazi corruption and expose it, or will he use discretion? She isn't able to gauge how he will react. He is, after all a journalist, sensationalism at its worst. He re-enters the room and sits down at his desk, pushes Louise's coffee across the surface towards her and she feels like a child sent to the head masters office for misbehaving.

"Whatever is troubling the pair of you, I'll do my best to help Louise."

She looks up at him, she sees genuine concern in his eyes. Maybe he wouldn't want it ousted?

"Bryan, I don't know how to start?"

"Well, we have all day Louise, you can do this now or I can bring you back in tomorrow, or the next day, it's up to you. I'm just concerned about you both, Steve especially, he's always been somebody I've admired for not being phased by most things. However, I have heard about what happened at the Kensal Green Cemetery..."

"You have?" quizzes Louise, looking extremely perplexed.

"Yes, I had a phone call from Ellia, enquiring if Steve is 'OK'. She gave me a detailed description of what happened during the service, she is very keen to speak with him."

"Oh right..." Louise begins to realise that this is not going to go away anytime soon, Bryan wants facts and what exactly is Ellia's game?

"OK, but this is not going to be easy," and Louise begins to fill him in on all that she knew to date.

Steve returns to the office buzzing with footage of the movie premier highlights and starts uploading it all onto his computer.

"Where's Lou?" he asks a colleague employee, wanting to share his days outing with her.

"She's been in with Bryan for nearly two hours."

Steve looks up and sees Louise with her head looking downwards and Bryans face contorted, frowning with his elbows on his desk and rubbing his closed eyelids with his fingers, which he often did under times of pressure and tension.

Louise comes out to get the images Ben had enhanced for her and notices Steve is back in the office.....

"You better come with me," she says.

"Oh Louise you haven't?...." Steve's 'good day' just came crashing down around his ears as he follows Louise back into Bryan's room.

She drops the pages onto the desk and as Bryan slides them about the desk to view them, no one in the room says a word. Louise looks to Steve and points at the photos on Bryan's desk and he tilts his head to view the photos, puzzled he looks back at Louise as the recognition starts to sink in. Steve suddenly leans over and grabs the photos to study the scene and holds them tightly in his hand, his skin pales and he feels his heart beating in his chest. Taking a few seconds to absorb the information in front of him, he freezes, wide eyed, lets out a sudden sigh and opens his mouth to speak, but no words come out.

He feels light headed wipes his brow, overwhelmed until a barely audible raspy tone trembles out of his mouth "Is this?... Is this Heidi?"

"I think it might be?" says Louise.

Bryan says nothing. Still trying to absorb all the facts, to him this is all brand new information and his mind is coming to terms with the experimental child subjects that the Nazi's had walked callously away from.

"Does Ellia know Heidi?" questions Steve.

"No idea, I've only just uncovered this info myself," Louise replies. Bryan interrupts, booming in disbelief, "Shouldn't we be calling somebody?"

"Like who?" Steve responds taken by surprise at Bryan's frustration.

"Well, like the United Nations, Downing Street, I don't bloody know?" says Bryan, as his phone rings and grabs the handset with real aggression.

"What?" he answers it rudely and then slams it back onto its base, places both hands on top of his head, Bryan swings his chair around to stare out of his window with his back to Steve and Louise. Waiting for him to speak, they exchange looks at each other. Bryan remains silent for several seconds, the vein in his neck is pulsating and he grinds his teeth angrily.

"Ellia is in Reception!"

Chapter 13

Ellia appears at the door accompanied by the receptionist and enters the room very slowly. She can sense the tension in the room, nobody speaks, Bryan faces away from them and continues to stare out of the window. Steve gives Ellia the filthiest look of disgust. He begins to wonder the nerve of her Ellia who just keeps reappearing like a bad smell. Louise keeps her eyes transfixed onto the desk and glares at the photographs Ben had enhanced for her she is consciously not making eye contact with any of them. She feels overwhelmingly nervous and starts to tap her beautifully manicured gel nails on the wooden arm rests.
It takes a moment for Ellia to realise what Louise is transfixed on, she leans forward and picks up the photos off Bryans desk and lets out a large sigh.
"I think I owe you all an explanation."
Steve lets out a very sarcastic snort from his nostril and shakes his head. Bryan finally swings his chair around to face the other three.
"An explanation?.." he starts "...huh! An explanation she says! There's more to this? And there I was thinking this couldn't get any better!"
"I understand this might all seem very strange." Ellia responds.
"Strange?" Bryan's cynical disbelief is highly judicial, and Steve reflects Bryans unfavourable searing

and contemptuous tone. Louise is much more indulging to hear what Ellia is about to share, if a little pessimistic that it will have any effect on her work colleagues, least of all Steve. Ellia contemplates her hard to please audience and knows that she is not going to pass off any trivialities. This is serious and she has some sincere, totally bona fide explaining to do. Steve collects a couple of chairs and shuts Bryan's door. Ellia sits down almost in slow motion, quite solemn in fact and for that moment Louise moves her transfixed stare, to give Ellia her full attention.

"So I'm correct in thinking that you all realise this lady is Heidi?"

Nobody acknowledges the question they all collectively look at her, no expression on any of their faces. "Heidi is my Grandmother."

That one sentence breaks the silent glances. Louise gasps and her hand slaps firmly against her open mouth, wide eyed. Bryan throws his arms up into the air and Steve jumps to his feet "WHAT?"

Ellia looks away from them all and studies the photographs, quietly and genuinely replies "Yes."

"Did Viktor know?" Louise asks her voice heartfelt and cordial.

Ellia shakes her head signalling that he didn't know "No."

She is frank and forthright with her reply. Louise feels compelled to believe she is telling the truth and having met Viktor she thinks this to be right and true, but also wonders what vested interest

Ellia has to work on such a personal level with him in the first place.

Ellia takes a long drawn intake of breath "My grandmother is the lady of mystery in this game, I'm....We're...just pawns of the mystery."

"Oh I didn't realise experimenting on little children was just a 'mysterious game'?" comes Bryan's still sharp cynicism bellowing through.

"No! I must start by telling you all, that the revelation of those children was as fresh and new to me exactly at the same time he told Mr Garrett and Miss Randall. The encampment they lived in, I did have some minimal idea about, but the children, I had no idea about and neither did my grandmother. Please- .....let me tell you my grandmothers Heidi's story."

No one moves, no one says a word, the plot thickens and history is getting darker.

"My grandmother, then Heidi Babik, was taken to Ravensbrück during the war, she is Jewish. She was one of the lucky ones, as an established seamstress, her skills were valuable. She could cook well, sew and was a very fast typist. She had been an accountant before the war, and a very good bookkeeper. They used women with skills as free labour. She would have to take meals each day to a small group of doctors or scientists, well, that is what they called themselves, down a network of tunnels underneath the Ravensbrück camp. Nobody else knew these tunnels existed. Grandma even believes that most of the other Nazi staff and soldiers didn't even know. She never told anybody because it would have cost her, her life. She would only be able to push a food trolley along the tunnels until she reached a soldier. The soldier guarded a caged gate that blocked the width of the tunnel. She never saw beyond that. The entrance to the tunnel led from behind a large fake fire place in the Oberfurhers office. Her discretion was paramount she would have been shot for sure, if she had told anyone. In the evenings she would leave to go back to her sleeping facility but would hide and watch the soldiers and scientists leaving at night. They never saw her, nor met her during the day. She studied them all the time. She would watch as suspicious boxes, packages and deliveries would be taken down the tunnels. She never saw the contents of the deliveries, but knew something unusual was happening down there and the only evidence she ever had of this was when one night, as they were all leaving to go to their quarters they were all laughing loudly, lighting cigars, shaking hands and drinking wine. It was a definite celebration, but what made it even more unusual was one of them was carrying, what grandma thought, was a large toy rabbit. It took her several minutes to realise, it was actually a real rabbit, dead, but real. The soldier carrying it was a good six feet tall and held it up by its hind legs. It was over a meter in length and he struggled to lift it. The next day in the kitchen the women found a massive supply of freshly cut meat pieces and they were told to make a stew for camp. Out the back of the kitchens was a fire pit that had been burning throughout the night. She saw a small tuft of animal hair and concluded it must have been from the rabbit. Over a couple of weeks she watched intently and for a brief time they ate well for a concentration camp. Limitless supply of vegetables and meat and the strange packages kept on disappearing down the tunnels. She saw a huge hoard of Hazard warning signs delivered one day, she questioned what the dangerous hazard was once and was hit for being indignant."

Ellia pauses for a moment her audience was captive, waiting for her to continue.

"Many years later after the war, back in her home town she would often frequent the markets. She was nursing her very sick mother at the time. One day she noticed one of the soldiers from the tunnels that she had watched every night. He was selling farm produce in the market. At first she was frightened he might recognise her, so she avoided any contact. She realised over time that he was one of the soldiers who would already be hidden away in the depth of the tunnels, when she started work. When she finished her day she would watch them leave each night. She came to the conclusion that she looked entirely different, nourished, healthier skin, wearing normal clothes, not the striped garments they were provided with in camp and her head had been shaved bald in the camp, to prevent the spread of head lice. Her hair was beautiful and long by now, so she braved it, eventually curiosity had got the better of her, the war was over, she had nothing to fear anymore and she walked up to his stall. He did not know who she was at all and was quite enamoured by her grace and beauty. She eventually found herself in a situation she could never have imagined nor dreamt of, she fell in love with the enemy, but she fell in love with the man. If Stockholm syndrome ever needed clarifying or a case study then Heidi Babik was the ultimate subject. She adored him and he worshipped her."

Louise has tears stinging her eyes, she doesn't say anything, she doesn't need to, but her eyes say everything. Steve can see her thoughts and emotions aloud, that they have just discovered a world of darkness and beauty all at once. As Ellia tells Heidi's story, a story she had heard a dozen times before herself, actually repeating it for herself she begins to feel the hurt and pain that her grandmother's life had been subjected to. She knew that Heidi had always told her children and grandchildren that a life is so precious.

"The necklace was Grandma's mystery. Unsolved, she never got to know the secrets it told, but she knew it meant something. She wasn't sure if it was to do with his childhood past, a family heirloom, the war or their future. He would tell her it was the key to his heart. He had taken her to France, to Provence...."

"That's the picture he showed us, that holiday," Louise is now being swept away by the romance of the story.

"Yes, he never knew that I had seen many more photos of that vacation, but then he never knew Heidi was my Grandma. They had gone to Provence, my grandmother told me it was the most magical love stricken holiday of her life, but obviously my grandfather was never privileged to this kind of intimate information. None of us knew anything of Viktor Otto-Wolff until after my grandfather's death, grandma never spoke of him. We never knew the secrets of the necklace she wore her entire life. Oh, we had seen it, always, she had just told us that she had bought it as a treat for herself many years ago and was just 'fond of it'. It holds a key inside, well I gather you have seen that?" she points at the enhanced images.

Ellia pauses momentarily, she looks into the faces of the other three "May I have a drink?"

The silence breaks "Yes of course," Louise jumps to her feet "Usual Steve? Bryan?"

Ellia has started to soften Bryan and Steve's cynical judgements and their general facial expressions are relaxing. Louise is dizzy and whimsical with romance, Steve still has his reservations and Bryan is astounded by the past few hours of explosive realisations.

He turns to Steve, "You know mate, in all my years of journalism I've seen many things, been shocked by many things too. But in all those years I have never been on such a roller-coaster of shock and emotions in a tiny space of time."

"Yeah, you know!" expresses Steve, knowing full

well everything Bryan is going through.

Louise bustles excitedly back into Bryan's office with a tray of beverages and a small plate of biscuits. She shuffles snuggly back into her chair, takes her mug and holds it intently in front of her, grinning like a Cheshire cat at Ellia to continue.

"Where was I?"

"The necklace and your Grandfather's passing" exclaims Louise, by this point bursting with rosy red flushed cheeks, which seemed to enhance her 'fire engine red' lipstick grin.

"Grandma used to tell us that she believed the secret key was hidden in the necklace by Long John Silver himself. He gave it to his young love, so no pirates would ever find the key that opened the chest to their hidden treasure."

Like a child taken to another world Louise almost scolds herself with her coffee, wanting to do a hyper excited little clap, and manages to splash her white fitted blouse. She signals to ignore her and that she doesn't care. Steve smiles to himself, he is becoming very fond of Louise's fresh love of life, childish endearing innocence, but highly intellectual and bright. She sees life as so magical she is never judgemental and always sees the good in everyone. Then he recalls that it is exactly why she is sitting there at this precise moment in time and the whole reason he took her to meet Viktor in the first place, her love of people, and a romantic story.

"When Viktor went away my Grandma knew he held many dark secrets. She had seen him at Ravensbrück in the mysterious tunnels. She said he would often wake at night screaming from his dreams. She told us he was the love of her life but knew his demons consumed him. She never hated him for going away, despite the heartbreak she went through. So my grandma eventually met my Italian grandfather. They married, had three sons, a daughter, seven grandsons and four granddaughters, even some great grandchildren now too. She has led a fulfilling and happy life. She loved my grandfather. As he was getting frail, I can remember my sister Maria going through her first heartbreak, over a boy called Marcus. Grandma was watching granddad pottering about in the garden and my sister was sobbing into her lap. She patted Maria's head and stroked her hair and said 'you know dear, there are two types of men, broccoli and chocolate. The chocolate ones are exciting, naughty and you know they are very bad for you, that my dear was Marcus. The broccoli men are much more boring and predictable, yet you know they will look after you, they are healthy and good for you' Maria looked up at grandma and laughed wiping her tears away 'so what type is granddad?' she replied 'broccoli dear, he is broccoli.' I never really grasped what grandma was referring to at the time, but now I get it. Well I did when she told us about Viktor he was obviously her 'chocolate man'. It all started about 8 years ago I will never forget that day. We were all gathered at grandmas for a family Sunday meal. Everyone brought a dish Italian family gatherings are always very special. The television news was on in the background, and everyone was bustling about, chatting over each other. In a large family that size, you have to be very loud to be heard. Grandma was carrying in a large pitcher of wine to place on the table, when she stopped suddenly she was staring at the television set. Her hands started shaking and the wine was spilling over the edges. Uncle Angelo stood up to take the pitcher and silence fell in the room. We all looked at grandma and then at the television, to see what she was staring at. The newsreader said 'Viktor Otto-Wolff', Uncle Angelo had not quite taken the pitcher, when grandma let go of it. She gasped both her hands over her mouth and the pitcher smashed onto the terracotta floor tiles. She then ran out of the room. My mother and aunties ran after her, whilst my uncles hushed all the children and turned up the television volume. My grandmother took till the early hours of the morning to tell us her story. The older grandchildren were allowed to stay up and listen. She started her story at about 6pm and finished at 2am. Not even her own children had known she was in Ravensbrück. Many, many tears were shed that night, even from my uncles. She had not seen Viktor for over 50 years and there he was, in her dining room on the small television set. They had displayed a photograph of him as a young Nazi soldier and as an old man. The item said that he had been found in Mexico and they were going to attempt to extradite him for war crimes. This is where I came into the story. I was a young, fresh out of law school solicitor, I had worked on a few law suits and had a fantastic placement within a good law firm. The family all got together and asked grandma if I should try to represent Viktor. It took grandma several weeks to decide but she wanted to meet him again and of course ask him about the key. She also wanted to tell him all about what she had hidden from him and her time at Ravensbrück. I flew to Mexico and befriended Viktor, eventually my role within his personnel changed and I became his Personal Assistant. I was to bring him back and liaise with the Italian officials to get him to Rome for his trial. I was by his side for a total of 7 years and he never knew Heidi was my grandmother. We had all decided that we would wait until he was in Rome before bringing Heidi back to him. As you know over the past few weeks, that was never to be. My Auntie Leticia, who is also grandma's care nurse, flew grandma over to England when Viktor was taken ill..." Ellia sighs deeply "...they landed half hour after he passed away."

Louise wipes a tear from her chin with the ball of her hand and places both index fingers under her eyes to stop more tears. She pulls a tissue from a box on the side of Bryan's desk. Ellia's presence in Viktor's life wasn't so sinister. They had all jumped to conclusions.

"This is why I am here today, my grandmother, Heidi would really like to meet you both. You were by his side when he went and she wants to see you

and thank you. She was hoping to meet you both at the Wake yesterday, but you were quite unwell Steve. Would this be ok with you....?"
Louise sharply ends Ellia's sentence with a resounding and confirming "YES!"

Chapter 14

Ellia goes off to make a telephone call to her Aunt Leticia, to see if her grandmother Heidi is up to receiving a visit from some very keen guests. Louise skips about the office, she drops into her chair and swivels it around 360 degrees a couple of times, like a child. Steve is a lot more relaxed about Ellia's presence. He squats down next to Louise, still stares at the funeral photo of Heidi and her necklace, "So Lou, What am I?"
"Sorry?" she laughs wandering exactly how to answer such an elusive question.
"Am I Broccoli or Chocolate?" smiles Steve.
Louise sees a glimmer of the cheeky Mr Garrett she knows and loves.
"Well..." she starts "...a lady never reveals such matters!" As she taps him on the head like she's patting a dog. She grabs the matching jacket to her skirt suit, puts it on to hide the recent coffee stain and wiggles off down the office, feeling very amused with herself.

The black London taxi pulls up outside the Savoy Hotel with the four of them on board. Louise looks up at the flags that fly above its beautifully green lit sign and the glorious golden Peter of Savoy statue, guarding the entrance, between the flags.
She whispers to Steve, "Henry III gave this site to

Peter of Savoy in 1346 and he built a palace here originally."

"Very impressed Lou, did you just Google that?"

"No..." she giggles "...it was my year 7 history project."

As they step out of the cab and walk up to the grand entrance way, Ellia takes the lead a few meters ahead.

Bryan turns to acknowledge his two work colleagues "This Heidi lady must have some money eh?"

As they enter its stunning reception area, Louise spins full circle to take it all in, admiring every detail. They follow Ellia intently as they proceed to walk down a beautifully decorated corridor, pale blue carpet, and long Asian style rugs that stretch through the centre of the floor. The walls have deep width terracotta, vertically striped wallpaper, and hosts delightful double lamp displays along the walls. The trimming at the top of each wall lead spectacularly detailed architrave, framing the corridors like giant sized pictures.

Ellia comes to a halt and knocks on one of the bedroom doors. Her Aunt opens the door Steve and Louise now recognise her as the woman pushing Heidi in her wheelchair, at the funeral. Ellia greats her Aunt, kisses both cheeks and Leticia then proceeds to do the same with each guest. Heidi is sitting in a green recliner chair by a grand ornate window. The window is full length and is open just an inch or so, letting a gentle breeze slowly float the

nets and drapes, which tickles the base of Heidi's chair. She uses the electronic mechanism controller to bring the chair into an upright position.
Ellia reaches down and gives her grandmother a big affectionate hug. Heidi holds her granddaughter's face with both her hands and kisses her on the forehead, she admires Ellias beauty,
"Bella piccola rosa" (beautiful little rose)
Ellia turns to the side and holds out her hand to introduce Steve, Louise and Bryan to Heidi. Bryan reaches forward and holds out his hand Heidi gracefully nods and shakes his hand. Louise does the same, she is completely spinning out mentally, that she is meeting 'The' Heidi. Heidi senses Louise's excitement and love. She places her other hand on top, making Louise's right palm the filling of a Heidi hand sandwich. Heidi then turns her head to look at Steve he steps forward and also offers his hand to her. She takes it gently and in a balletic movement pulls him closer to look at him. He kneels beside the recliner chair, a little confused by this gesture and she kisses him on both cheeks.
"Molto bello," (Very handsome)
She smiles warmly at him "Se solo ero 50 anni piu giovane." (If only I was 50 years younger)
Her daughter- in- law Leticia roars loudly with laughter and Ellia rolls her eyes at Heidi. Steve thinks the laughter is all very well, but he has no idea what is going on, so he politely smiles.
Leticia brings them all some seats and they sit in a semi-circle facing Heidi. She takes a moment to

look at each of the keen beaming faces looking back at her. Louise can't help but notice how elegantly dressed she is in her lilac woollen twin set top and cardigan. With a grey pleated skirt that has a subtle purple thread through its weave. The necklace sits gracefully around her neck, lying snugly on her chest. Louise breaks the silence,

"May I look at the locket please Ms Babik?"

Heidi's face lights up and she laughs "Nobody has called me Miss Babik for a very long time. That was my maiden name dear, it is Addario now."

She holds up the locket and Louise moves in closer to examine its mystery, its beauty. She certainly can't believe she is seeing it in reality. She takes a while to study the little cherub guarding the front.

"Are you feeling any better now Mr Garrett?" Heidi asks earnestly.

"Oh yes thank you, very much, I am fine now. Please call me Steve."

"And you must call me Heidi..." she replies enthusiastically. "...you had us all very concerned Steve."

Steve starts to feel his bitterness towards Ellia and Heidi was a definite over reaction, on his part. He begins to feel extremely sorry for her, having been involved with Viktor in the first place, even if she had loved him dearly.

"Well, I understand my lovely granddaughter has told all of you my story. I wanted to be here to see Viktor one last time and tell him the truth about me."

"I don't think you owed him the truth at all, I think

he owed you an explanation Heidi," said Bryan still coming to terms with everything.

"That maybe, we both kept a lot of secrets from each other wouldn't you agree? I have to be completely honest I was very shocked at the things Ellia told me, about what was really happening at Ravensbrück, the giant rabbit does not seem so peculiar a story after all these years."

Heidi offers them all some refreshments but they decline with gratitude.

"So I suppose you are all wondering why I wanted to meet you?" she continues taking in the expressions on their faces. Actually not Bryan, Steve nor Louise had thought about why Heidi might want to meet them at all, the thought hadn't even crossed their minds. They were all just ecstatic and keen to be meeting the lady behind the photograph kept securely in Viktor's wallet for several decades. They look at each other a little puzzled by Heidi's comment and turn their attention immediately back to her to carry on.

"The thing is..." she starts "...it wasn't until Ellia explained that Viktor closed the doors to their secret experiment at the end of the war leaving everything hidden behind, that I began to wonder if it was still all locked up? For all I knew of my own time at Ravensbrück everything had been cleared away at some point. This news has come at something of grave despair to me; I have not slept at all."

"I can certainly relate to that" Steve announces in complete agreement.

"So this is why you are all here. I have a proposition to put to you, I will understand if you were to decline...."

"Go on..." Louise's words eager and firm if a little confused and excited all at once.

"I am too old for new adventures, but I need to go back to Ravensbrück, I need closure. I feel my life has an unfinished chapter that needs to be put to rest. I want you to be my eyes." Heidi's tone is a little tense and reserved, not knowing for sure how to ask them. The silence in the room is numbing, the only sound from a car engine starting up from the road below and it is almost a suffocating silence which engulfs the three of them.

"You want us to go to Ravensbrück?" murmurs Louise, so softly and indistinctly she isn't sure if the words had come out of her mouth at all.

"I have money for the mission. My husband Giovanni was extremely wealthy, we had many vineyards, I will fund everything entirely and whatever you need, you will have."

Nobody could move; nobody knew how to react. This is definitely not what any of them had expected at all.

Ellia stands up and walks around behind Heidi's chair, she places her hands on her grandmothers shoulders and Heidi lifts her right arm across her chest to hold on to Ellias left hand.

"I have put a very small skilled team together, six in total. They are used to exploring abandoned man made tunnels, four are ex-military and two are professors who specialise in war and archaeology. At this stage they know none of the real story behind this expedition, just that we are to excavate hidden tunnels that my grandmother remembers from her time at Ravensbrück. One of the professors has visited the place many times and has profound historical knowledge of Ravensbrück he was extremely excited to hear about these secret tunnels. I leave in two days and fly to Berlin where I am to meet them at Fürstenburg which is a small town nearby to the camp. We have all the essential safety equipment, food, medical supplies and protective clothing...."

Heidi interrupts Ellia "and the key my dear, you have the key?"

"Yes grandma it is very safe."

Ellia looks up at Steve and Louise "Grandma just wonders if the key has anything to do with the site."

"Viktor told me it held many secrets and I was to hold the key to his heart. I never knew what that may have meant until now, maybe the key has something to do with the secrets at Ravensbrück? I do not know? Ellia dear, I think we should keep it safe in its proper home."

Heidi holds her hair to one side and Ellia undoes the clasp at the back of her neck and then hands Heidi the brassy coloured locket. Heidi holds it in her hand, caressingly strokes the pearl cherubs, holds it up to her lips and kisses it. Ellia kneels down next to Heidi and she places the locket around her granddaughter's neck. Heidi strokes it one more time and quietly says,

"Oh Viktor, what did you do?"

Ellia places the key back inside the locket and flings her arms around her grandmother tightly. For a few moments the small group just sit motionless at Heidi's unexpected proposal.

"You do realise we will need to discuss this Mrs Addario?" Bryan says sympathetically to Heidi.

"Are you forgetting you are reporters Bryan?.." Ellia looks at him "…why don't you think of this mysterious quest as possibly unravelling one of history's biggest stories ever to be told?"

She had a point, this really was the story Bryan had set Steve on in the first place. Bryan's own words were 'a human need of curiosity.' He had wanted a story on Viktor and it certainly looked as though he would get one – a massive explosion of a story.

"It's totally funded Bryan, it will not cost The Thames Charter a penny," reiterated Heidi again.

Bryan turns his attention to Steve and Louise, "I will have to stay to manage the office this is entirely your decision guys. Ellia is right though, it will certainly make a headline or two?"

Steve turns to look out of the window he pulls the net around him so he can stare over the grounds of the Savoy Hotel. A few days ago he was flitting off to do a report at a local Bake-off charity fundraiser event and now he's being offered to fly to Berlin and unravel the world's best kept secret. 'How did I get here?' he thinks to himself. For a minute he

takes his mind to his grandfather Mikolai Borowski. He reaches into his pocket and looks on his phone, at his little great auntie Hannetta, he had only just learnt about. He flicks through the photo and stops at the image of the small girl, he had found when on the tube researching information on Viktor. She had the ability to hypnotise Steve, there was just something about the image, her ringlets, the grubby unwashed face staring back at him, but it was her eyes, it was always those terrified, innocent eyes. They screamed at Steve every time 'help me'. He tightly grips his hand around his mobile handset, clutching it with his fingers 'maybe I can help you sweetheart' he thinks to himself. He knew logically that it was impossible to save her now, but maybe this is his destiny for her, for Hannetta, for Mikolai and now Heidi. All their existences had been drawn together to create this moment in time, as if the powers of the universe had pulled them all in alliance with each other to bring justice back, for the ones that were forgotten. He comes out from behind the net curtains and says firmly, "Let's do it!"
Louise instantly jumps up and lets out a squeal, claps her hands together excitedly and flings her arms around Steve's neck for a happy hug, and for a split second he tightens his arms around his dramatic, excitable, frenzied friends waist, pulls her tightly towards him and presses his lips against hers. Rather quickly Louise's excitable body movements become limp and calm as she melts intoxicated by Steve's sudden amorous passion towards

her.

Bryan lets out a very awkward cough from the back of his throat and turns to Heidi "Can we book separate hotels for these two?"

Collective laughter bursts out around the room, except for Louise who has gone so fuzzy headed and wobbly legged that she has to sit down, feeling a bit dazed. Leticia leans in towards Steve and thanks him gratefully for his decision to help her mother-in-law.

"You have no idea what this means to her Mr Garrett."

"To be honest I am doing this for myself too. I couldn't go on having the knowledge, that I do, about the situation, this is right, I have to do this," he sincerely replies.

He had woken up that morning with the firm decision to put Viktor Otto-Wolff behind him and by this same evening is going on a quest to find out what Viktor had done. He chuckles to himself in disbelief 'unbelievable Steve'.

Bryan shakes Steve's hand "You're doing the right thing mate."

"I hope so Bryan, I really do..." his voice contemplative, very serious and deeply thoughtful, "...are you sure you are ok with all of this Louise?"

She is still contemplating Steve's lustful impromptu kiss, blushing and trying to compose herself.

"Am I ok with this? Oh my goodness, like, is this really happening? Seriously?"

Her happiness just envelops the room, her love of the romance behind it all, she hadn't even contemplated rummaging through dirty old tunnels and what hideous delights might await them, she grabs hold of Heidi's hand.
"Yes, yes I am ok with all of this. I am going on a real ADVENTURE!" She screams the word so loudly and roars loudly with laughter, everybody reciprocates her. A refreshing moment of howling breathless kind of laughter fills the room.

Chapter 15

Steve and Louise have just two days to get everything sorted, packed and ready to go. He nips downstairs to see Mrs Sanders but she is not at home, so decides to go for a run over the park and a visit to The Fresh Bean to read the newspaper. His mind buzzes and he finds it very difficult to concentrate on anything.
"Well, if it isn't Clark Kent," comes the familiar chortle of Rachel, Louise's hairdresser housemate.
"Good morning Rachel."
"I see you've got Lois Lane all in a tizzy I hear superman here is flying her off on a holiday?" Rachel's forthrightness is never forgiving in her blazė attitude. Without being asked she invites herself to sit with him. She did love a gossip and given Louise's recent behaviour this is too good an opportunity to miss.
"Have a seat..." Steve rolls his eyes sarcastically "...it's not exactly a holiday, its newspaper work, business."
"So she tells us, all expenses paid to some cute little European destination. Won't even tell us where in Europe, just that she'll need to pack for all eventualities and doesn't even know how long she'll be gone, very romantic..." the whole time she looks into her compact mirror applying lipstick "...I'll have a regular mocha please."

Steve is mesmerised by her oversized fake nails covered in sparkling rhinestones. Steve does his second eye roll in less than a minute of Rachel's company and goes to the counter to buy her a drink. He listens to the mumbling inaudible chatter from around the coffee shop and ponders on Rachel's words, about the length of their time away. He hasn't given it too much contemplation, but she is right though it could take days or months. He turns to face his table and his thoughts are utterly broken by Rachel beaming at him. This makes him more nervous than the journey to Ravensbrück.

"Yum thank you. I'm 'well-jel' of Lou going away, so are you going to tell me where you're both going? Or are you using work as a cover-up to Louise and whisking her away to Paris or something?"

"Rachel, it's of the highest National Security, if I tell you they might have to find you and kill you, for knowing about it or the CIA......if the CIA find out that you know, who knows what will happen?"

"A 'no' would've sufficed thank you." She retorts being rather unimpressed.

"So, how are things going with Anthony?" Steve changes the subject knowing full well the 'Anthony' subject was currently a very sore distasteful issue with Rachel. Louise and Melissa were strictly forbidden to even mention his name.

"He was a complete waste of spa.. (Rachel's phone rings 'Barbie Girl' ringtone.) 'yep......ok....thanks I will be there in ten.' Well it seems you have been saved Steve, my car is fixed and Mel has it in her garage. You make sure you look after her ok? She likes you Steve, a lot, don't play her along if you don't feel the same way. She has a very warm and loving heart and is too sweet for her own good."

He knows Louise is just too 'nice' and knowingly nods at Rachel in agreement. She grabs a very multi-coloured Louis Vuitton handbag off the table and totters out wearing extremely high heeled wedges that she can barely walk in.

Louise calls Steve's mobile "Hey, you just missed your house mate.....Rachel....the usual...the world revolves and exists purely for her kind of stuff. Yeah, I'm packed are you? I'm going to pop into the office to sort that out......our train to Heathrow is at midday. Ok. Laterz."

He just finishes his latte when Mrs Sanders suddenly appears at his side.

"I came knocking for you earlier." He greets her with warm fondness. She pats the back of his hand "Mr Garrett! I do hope your intentions were completely dishonourable!"

He struggles very hard not to break into raucous laughter, at her attire today. She had wrapped a floral bed sheet around her and tied it, with a cushion attached at the back.

"Nice cushion Mrs S."

"Thank you it's my kimono attempt for celebrating the Chinese New Year."

"It's August Mrs S?"

"Yes they are very peculiar with their celebratory dates, all backwards that side of the planet."

Steve's body convulses in spasms, as he tries hard to stifle his laughter, but looks more like he is having a seizure or suppressing a coughing fit.

"So what did I owe the pleasure of such a dashing visitor?"

"I'm going away for a while Mrs S and was wondering if you could check in on my flat every now and then, make sure it's not flooded or burnt down."

"Where are you going?" She interrupts excitedly.

"I'm going......."

"Are you taking a lady friend?"

"Well actua….."

"Oooo what's her name?"

"The thing is….."

"Oh how exciting Mr Garrett, you are being very secretive aren't you? I will ask no more questions!"

Steve sniggers to himself and thinks that maybe asking Mrs Sanders isn't the best of people to ask. She would more likely be the reason his flat might get flooded or burnt. She wanders off up the street, not realising the cushion tied to her back, balancing on her buttocks, has now fallen off and is sitting on the side of the curb.

Louise and Steve sit waiting for Ellia in the departure lounge. British Airways Flight BA981 to Berlin Schőnefeld Airport read the boarding passes.

"I think I might go and have a nose at the duty free," Louise says and makes a beeline for the perfume counter. Steve makes a few phone calls to home and his grandparents. He has really enjoyed the relaxed atmosphere and the way he feels about the situation, the last couple of days. He has discovered that Fürstenburg has a rather wonderful local beer brewed in the Black Forest region that has been established since 1283. It is now owned by Heineken and he thinks that a brewery tour and a few pints sound like a wonderful start to the trip. He even decides to do some interviews and an article on the brewery, given its spectacular history. He thinks to himself, 730 years of brewing beer has got to be pretty good stuff. He is quickly interrupted, from his thoughts of a nice ice cold pint, by 3 rather smelly sticks, being shoved under his nose.

"Which one do you like best?" Louise beams, holding the paper strips, all with a perfumed scent on.

"Hard to tell with them all under my nose at once Lou," he laughs.

He smells them all individually to humour her.

"Which one of them did you like best?"

She holds up the first one and exclaims "I do quite like this one actually," and smells it again.

Without a seconds thought "I'm glad you like that one Lou, because that's my favourite too. You should definitely get that one."

Louise smiles happily and moves swiftly back to the perfume section. Steve just grins to himself knowing he has been extremely clever. A little tip he'd learnt from his father, so he didn't have to spend the next hour deciding on perfume scents, handbags, dresses, or anything else a woman is trying to decide on.

Ellia arrives and greets them both with continental kisses.

"I'm so excited Ellia!" Louise hugs Ellia very tightly, rather taking Ellia by complete surprise, but daily she is becoming very attached to Louise's zest for life.

The flight is delightful the three chat, laugh, and start to get to know each other really well. They speak of their childhoods, their families, their education and places they have travelled to. Ellia has the most to tell about her family, as it is so large. She buys them champagne for the flight it is all very charming and quite sophisticated. Louise sprays Ellia with her new perfume and manages to get most of it directly into Steve's face, and he spends the next half an hour complaining his champagne tastes more like Dior than Brut.

At Berlin's Schönefeld Airport they catch a train to Fürstenburg, it is about an hour's journey, with all their talking and becoming acquainted the entire flight and train journey pass extremely quickly.

They grab their luggage as the train pulls into the station. Ellia lets go of her suitcase handle and runs towards a very slim built man, with wild unkempt greying hair and large spectacles, which seem to ultra-magnify his brown eyes. She greets him in her usual manner and turns to Steve and Louise,

"I would like you to meet Professor Hans Tassin these are my friends Stephen Garrett and Louise Randall."

All the common greeting pleasantries are exchanged.

Hans grabs Ellia's and Louise's suitcases and leads them out of the station.

"The Professor has a rather invested interest in the war and the Nazi ideologies, he has written many papers on these subjects."

"He looks like Doctor Emmett Brown from Back to the Future" Louise whispers, all giggly, into Steve's ear.

"Well, I won't be getting into his Delorean if he's fascinated with the war Lou." They both stifle their chuckles.

Hans smiles at them, a lot. It is almost as if he is forcing the smile, not knowing how to act in a social setting, so to keep a smile fixed permanently to his face is the best way to resolve his inability to cope in surroundings with other humans. He wears a tan tweed jacket with leather patches on each of the elbows, it is single breasted and the buttons are undone. Under the jacket is a pale green checked shirt, he wears worn down khaki-green corduroy trousers with dark brown brogue shoes, but the shoes are highly polished and shining.

They follow him to his car, and smile as he tries very hard, to fit the luggage into the boot of his old style Beetle.

"Don't be fooled Lou, it has a flux capacitor inside," Steve says quietly, but Louise's response is less than quiet as she squeals the loudest snigger.

"Sorry, sorry..." she tries to justify her random out-

burst "...I'm just excited."
Hans stands perched in the door of the driver's side, whilst he piles bags on the roof and secures with elastic bungee straps.

They pull up at a stunning little hotel built on the edge of a lake. Fürstenburg is situated amongst the Lake District of Mecklenburg, with breath taking miles of forest land that hosts around a 1000 large and small lakes. The hotel looks like an oversized wood cabin and has wood decking that extends out towards the lake, with a small jetty attached. The views are quite phenomenal Louise stands there speechless, takes in her initial surroundings, not quite believing this is where she would be living for the foreseeable future.
"Beautiful isn't it?" Ellia says to her.
"Incredible Ellia, just utterly fairy tale and romantic" Louise replies and feels full of love and giddy headed.
To the side of the hotel is a large oak pagoda with tables and chairs for its guests, outdoor heaters sit on the patio, which looks over the lake and the hotel boasts it's very own private beach area.
"One of the lakes is so massive it is named 'Muritz" which means small sea. Most of the lakes have areas of sand, like mini beaches." Ellia continues to watch the excited happiness in Louise's face. Steve and Hans collect the suitcases from their precarious positions in and on top of the car.
"I think I would like to see Muritz, ahhh that fresh

air, I can even taste salt in the air Steve! So much nicer than the bustle of London..." Louise states whilst skipping up to Steve and then kisses him on the cheek "...I'm going to love it here, you may not get me back to the city."
She grabs the handle of her suitcase and gracefully makes dancing footsteps towards the hotels reception.
The hotel is called Kleine Stranhütte (Little Beach Hut).
Hans goes to the receptionist who greets them with a big smile and checks them into their rooms. They all agree to meet each other at the bar for a drink, before going to the restaurant for dinner in an hour's time.

Steve throws himself onto his bed and places both hands behind his head, as he takes in his surroundings he lets out a long, very happy and contented sigh. His double bed is dressed with a crisp white quilt cover adorned with intricate embroidery around its edging. Large built in chrome wardrobes with full length mirrored doors are to his left and in front, at the foot of the bed, is a long side board with the normal kettle and refreshment facilities. Next to the television is a selection of sight-seeing leaflets, displayed out on the surface like a fan. The room has its own balcony over-looking the lake and the bathroom has a huge Jacuzzi bath.

Steve and Louise stand on the patio area, outside by the pagoda and watch the sun in the horizon disappear into the lake, bursting sensational colours of crimson yellows and oranges across the base of the sky. Louise is a 'dream to look at' thinks Steve as he is distracted by her beauty. He watches her hair blow majestically in the gentle breeze coming off from the lake and it makes the hem of her chiffon lemon coloured maxi dress float around her ankles caressing the tops of her feet. He stands back a couple of meters and without Louise's knowledge takes a photograph of her staring out over the water. A graceful radiant Louise silhouetted against a painted array of yellow, pink and orange. The clouds glimmer as the slow darkness sets in and the first glimpse of the night's moon peeks above the trees in the distance. Stars begin to appear above them, like little sequins illuminating the lake and makes it glisten.

"You look amazing Louise."

Steve is swept away by the beauty and romance of the setting and this precise moment in time. He slips his hand softly into hers and squeezes his fingers around her small delicate hand and feels the softness of her skin.

Chapter 16

"Everybody I would like to introduce you to Dr Caleb Beldman" Ellia says to the ever growing group at dinner.

He is 6' tall, African American, 37 years old, extremely well spoken and articulate. Caleb has a stunning Adonis look, dark eyes, slim, muscular and lustrous hair. His face is so strong and defined it could stop a person in their tracks and a prominent jaw that curved sharply to his neck. His presence within the growing group definitely makes an impact with Ellia and Louise who are quite stricken with his beauty.

"Where are you based in the USA?" Hans asks keenly, more interested in Caleb's profession than his awkwardness toward idle chit chat.

"I studied at Boston University and lecture there now. I'm with the Conservation Department and I specialise in Geology." His voice deep, crisp and commands the attention of the rest of the room.

"Please tell me more about these tunnels Ellia".

"I only have my Grandmothers description to go on. We know that the door led from the Oberfurhers Office," she replies watching Steve chasing peas around his plate.

"Is this a GPR Dr Beldman?" remarks Hans and he looks in awe at a tall piece of equipment that stands grand next to Caleb's suitcase.

"What is it? It looks like lawn mower with laptop strapped to the handle bars" Louise giggles.

"Yes it is Hans and please, call me Caleb." Caleb smiles at Louise "Its full name is Ground Penetrating Radar......It's like an x-ray machine that lets me see underground, it uses electromagnetic radiation to detect objects or subsurface structures."

"Like a big metal detector?" she questions with a massive smile. "Yes sort of. It picks up various metals, but also tells me what rocks, soil, water or structures maybe beneath the ground by sending up radio wave frequencies."

"That's so clever..." Steve says, "...what are the plans for tomorrow?" he says and looks at Ellia, as he tucks into his rare sirloin steak, having given up on the pea chase.

"I was thinking we should head over to Ravensnbrück, go to its museum and have a look around. We need to wait for the rest of our team to arrive, so I'm open to offers Steve."

"I quite fancy a nose around the brewery if anyone cares to join me?"

"I think you could twist my arm on that one Steve..." Caleb agrees "...I think it's got to be done before we delve into the serious stuff."

"Are you joining us Lou?" Steve says and turns his attention to her.

"I would like to take a trip over to the Palace, I read the information leaflet and it looks absolutely breath-taking."

"Well then, I shall accompany you Miss Randall, I

would prefer a coffee on the grand lawns of the Duke and Duchess than a visit to the brewery," Hans acknowledges.

"And what about you, Ellia do you fancy tagging along with Hans and I?"

"Thanks for the offer Lou, but I do have a few things to do and prepare for our new arrivals." Ellia gets up from the table "Good night everybody I am ready to turn in, shall we all agree to meet, at say, 10:30am to visit the site and museum?"

Louise wakes up by a piercing ray of light through the crack in the curtains, a beam glows and reflects off the wall behind her bed. She stretches her arms up above her and smiles taking in her surroundings. She notices her phone flashes on the bedside table. She grabs it and sees a voice message from Rachel, puts it on loud speaker as she makes her way to the bathroom. Voices boom from the handset, intermingled with screeches of laughter and high pitched voices "Hey girl has Clark Kent proposed yet? We've not heard from you? Take it you got there safe?" Rachel squeals.

"Hi Lou, MISS YOU" shouts Melissa.

Louise is giggles as she looks into her bathroom mirror. She makes her way downstairs and meets Hans in the restaurant at the breakfast bar.

"Good morning Miss Randall, did you sleep well?" He says, picks up a croissant and a small tub of jam.

"Like a log thank you."

Sitting by the window in the restaurant, Louise looks at the suns glorious presence overlooking the lake it filters through the leaves of the trees that curtain the hotel. "Tell me more about yourself Hans, what is it about the War that fires such an interest in you? I personally find it all extremely hard to digest." Louise says and sips on her coffee.

"When I was a young lad my Grandfather gave me his war medals from the first world war. I think my passion started from then. I learnt and read about the world wars, but to be honest I study all aspects of peace and war, the human greed, power, the cost of war, its backgrounds and the aftermath....." Hans looks up and sees Caleb walk towards them both "...take Caleb for example and the civil war in America...."

Caleb takes his seat and winks at Louise "Hate to disappoint you Professor Tassin but I'm a little too young to remember it."

"Yes, yes of course, I do apologise, I was explaining to Louise that I study aspects in the science of all wars not specifically just World War 2. I was about to discuss the complexities of the American Civil war, how it all started but how it ended up implementing the freedom of black Americans from slavery."

"My ancestors were slaves at a cotton plantation in South Carolina," Caleb says subtly interrupting Hans' train of thought.

"Were they really?" Hans replies with a genuine sincerity in his face.

"Mmm" Caleb mumbles and bites into slightly burnt toast "I think this is a discussion for this evening with a large port Hans, I don't think I can cope with a deep debate over the Southern politics regarding secession and the dissolution of the Union over breakfast." Caleb laughs loudly.

Ellia and Steve appear at the restaurant window. They'd been for a jog. Ellia catches her breath "Good morning. I hope you all slept well? I'm just going to grab a quick shower and will meet you all in bit."

"Are you not eating?" Louise says and exchanges admiring glances at Steve.

"I woke early Lou, I've already eaten and went for a jog along the lake it's so beautiful. The sunrise off the lake was amazing; it looked like a floor made of solid gold."

The five of them cheerily walk through the quaint streets of Fürstenberg. It's approximately 90 kilometres north of Berlin. The town's surroundings are exquisitely stereotypical in European detail, like Scandinavian postcards. The residents of Fürstenberg sell high-quality food and drinks, the streets buzz with eclectic restaurants and boutiques. The high street hosts a butcher, a bakery, a chocolate shop and the infamous brewery.

"They are all extremely happy people" Louise says.

"Why wouldn't they be? Look at their surroundings," Steve replies and takes in the lush green views and the magical lake the town sits on.

"Every bit of Fürstenberg is designed for a thriving community" Professor Tassin says as he moves in on the conversation, "Resourceful infrastructure, the charming buildings and striking architecture. A tiny society focused on a productive balance between work, family and recreation."

"It's a pocket sized fairy-tale," responds Louise and looks over to see the top of the Palace poking its way above the line of trees.

"Do you think that the people knew?.." Steve hesitates... "About what was happening over the other side of their lake?"

Hans pauses for a short time and replies "It's very difficult to answer. The whole entire planet was in disarray. Every street throughout Europe was buzzing with either Nazi or Allied soldiers. However the people here would have definitely seen a lot of traffic passing through the streets, even if they did have some idea, really, what could they have done?"

"Very true," Caleb replies.

They arrive at a bridge that overlooks the lake. It's quite wide and camouflages itself majestically amongst the trees. The bridge is wooden and arches itself elegantly over the peaceful river. In the centre of the bridge are two lengths of metal tracks that start at the top and finish at the bottom where the stairs align.

"What are they?" Louise whispers to Ellia and just as she is about to answer a young man on the top of the bridge arch slots his bicycle wheels into the metal runner and glides the bike smoothly down the stairs. Ellia and Louise smile to each other and she responds "Well that answers my question." They

stand on the bridge and look out over the still lake.
"It's so peaceful you can't imagine something so sinister happened near here." Caleb says and watches the gentle ripples in the water.

"Look..." Hans says and points over to the other side of the lake "...you can just see the top of the Ravensbrück memorial, it was put there in 1959."

They arrive at the Ravensbrück site, Steve notices how quiet and surreal the place is and feels a shiver radiate in his body as he thinks about its dark history. No one says anything and standing together they stare at an army tank just outside of the camp.

Hans breaks the silence and speaks in a quiet tone "It was put there by the Soviet army which liberated the camp in 1945."

It stands on a red brick plinth and beside the tank is a fantastic sculptured statue of 3 women that were prisoners in the camp.

"The statue is named 'Mutter-gruppe' or Mother's Group..." he continues, "...the large bronze monument over at the entrance is one of the female prisoners carrying another lady, its title is Mahnmal Tragende which translates as 'Woman with burden' it was designed by Will Lammert and was positioned here with the other statues and memorials in 1959."

Louise looks up at them, the two statuesque ladies look gaunt, skeletal and severely undernourished. The group collectively stare at her and the person she struggles to carry. Steve feels empowered by her inner strength and what she signified to thousands of women and children who had been incarcerated. It is almost spooky the way she dulls and blankets their senses, a feeling that something is about to happen or could happen is being kept hidden away behind her.

They find it difficult to talk with the atmosphere that surrounds them is like an emptiness or a dream that still doesn't make sense.

"It's very surreal" Louise whispers.

"Dali once said his definition of surrealism was to make the normal look abnormal and abnormal look normal," Hans says to Louise.

"It's the pained expression of desperation in their faces Professor Tassin; she looks so lonely and scared." Louise feels a tension tighten in her body and a flutter of nervousness in her face. Her cheeks heat with a burning pinch and a little sweat moistens her palms. The dim reality begins to dawn on her; she is sensitive and compassionate about humans. She tries to calm her breathing and mentally tells herself that she has nothing to worry about. Steve slips his hand into Louise's and notices her other hand by her mouth biting into her finger nails and feels her tremble, he squeezes it gently.

They enter the camp and pass the former accommodation blocks for the female guards. White buildings all three stories high and with pointed rooves.

"They are now used as youth hostels and a youth meeting centre..." Hans's running commentary continues, "...they used to host the SS canteen and the right one was a German military infirmary."

The main entrance way is a division of two large yellowish beige walls, slightly off centre and to the left is a large entrance way where a large metal gate once stood. On the right hand wall is a doorway which also housed a metal gate and behind the walls stand various sized buildings that guard the front of the camp. They make their way into the first building and visit the museum. Louise begins to absorb the conditions and the lives of the women in the camp as she takes in all the collection of photographs. The sleeping arrangements startle her, each dormitory had a small walkway through the centre of the room and on each side of the room were wooden cubicles in sleeping bunk form and they were three tiered bunks from floor to ceiling. The bunks were made of wooden planks and each bunk was equipped with pillows and a mattress filled with wood shavings. At some points in the camp the overcrowding was so high that women would have to share a single bed all squashed together and actually slept piled on top of one another. Many artefacts display in the museum, a significant one being a wheelbarrow.

Ellia reads the inscription to herself:

'The prisoners had to transfer cobbled stones in these wooden wheelbarrows for road building. The survivors took a wheelbarrow when they were liberated from the camp and then gave it back in 1959 when this memorial was built.'

"An electric fence went around the entire perimeter of the interior walls and many warning signs are still there now. They were sporadically placed along the fences warning of high voltages..." Steve reads aloud "...to prevent the prisoners from leaving or face death by electrocution if they tried."

The layout of the camp had been wooden cabin blocks in two long rows arranged in a grid formation and spread down the entirety of the camp on cinder gravel. The camps kitchen was in the same building as the bath house and the grid layout of the cabin blocks was built in such a way that the women prisoners could always be easily seen. Louise looks out of the window and stares at the markings on the ground where the dormitories once stood.

Steve places his arm around her shoulders "Are you ok?"

She remains silent and a small tear slips down her cheek.

"It's very overwhelming trying to take it all in. 130,000 women Steve..." she responds, "...45,000 lived here at its peak, where did they put them all?" She pauses and lets out a sorrowful sigh "They had been beaten, executed, gassed, starved, poisoned, experimented on or just worked to death. I just read that anything from about 60 thousand died right here, I'm finding it immensely shattering, my mind isn't absorbing this...."

"Go and get some fresh air" Steve responds. She

steps outside and is consumed in her thoughts to all the women passing through or who had died here. She tries hard to understand the complexity of emotions these incredible women had experienced. The bonds and friendships the women must have made just trying to survive one day at a time and the grief at the loss of friendships. Ellia walks slowly towards Louise, grabs her hand and squeezes it.

"Can you even begin to understand their desperation being separated from their husbands and children? The mental trauma?..." she says to Louise sitting herself on the steps and takes a few sips from her bottle of water, "...I can't even begin to think this is where my Grandmother lived she really was one of the lucky ones."

Ellias phone buzzes from her pocket breaking the heaviness of their thoughts. She chats for a few moments and Louise asks "Is everything ok?"

"Oh yes it was just about the arrival of the rest of the team. Come on let's go for a little walk about. I think we've seen and read more than enough." Ellia says and reaches down she pulls Louise up, sympathetically smiles at her and links Louise's arm with hers and they walk along the perfect line of Linden trees at the left side of the camp.

Chapter 17

Hans moves toward Caleb who looks at a collection of stamps made by the German Postal Service commemorating Ravensbrück. The stamps each have pictures on them of various female prisoners that had spent time in the camp.

"Come with me..." Hans says to Caleb "...let me show you the Wall of Nations, it's a long wall containing the graves of 300 prisoners and the crematorium is just the other side of it."

Ellia and Louise approach the far end of the camp, to view the workshops that still exist at Ravensbrück and stare at them. Six rows of long rectangular buildings and all the adjacent walls covered in barbed wire. Louise studies the buildings in detail and absorbs the atmosphere around her. She counts twelve window panes evenly spaced down the length of the beige building block and sees they each have a skylight window in the rooves. Women had been forced to work in the buildings, it was generally extermination through work. Tens of thousands had died of overwork coupled with malnutrition and despair. The huts had been run by four S.S companies. One of the companies was a textile and leather business, the prisoners had to make uniforms for the S.S and another company was a famous telephone production business.

"The thing I'm finding so hard to digest is the incredible beauty of its surroundings," Ellia says as she looks out at the breath taking landscape. She hears a soft shuffling noise behind her, a group of school children in double formation follow their teacher at the front of the line and a teacher at the back.

"They are respectfully well behaved," utters Louise. They pass another statuesque monument and she realises the significance of having so many around the camp, the surreal awareness to grasp and impress upon the number that had been whipped or beaten and how many had been shot or killed.

In the museum Steve is mesmerized at the different fabric patches worn by the prisoners. His mind wanders back to his Grandad and his memory flashes to holding the yellow star in Mikolai's lounge. The yellow stars were notoriously the Jewish prisoners, red triangles were political prisoners, pink triangles were for homosexual men, purple triangles were the Jehovah's Witnesses and the black triangles represented work-shirkers, gypsies and prostitutes. He feels very naïve at the enormous scope and terrors of the Holocaust and stares at the wall of faces, thousands and thousands of photographs documenting the prisoners look back at him. For many this was their last home.

The little group reunite outside the S.S quarters and the five of them sit on the lush green lawn, Hans pours them all a coffee from the flask he's brought with him.

"Let me tell you about the 'Rabbits of Ravensbrück'..." he starts, and hands out cups of coffee

"...some of these wonderful women imprisoned here had discovered that the S.S had made a decision to execute the 'Rabbits'. They were the main subjects of the most horrific and barbaric Nazi experiments on their legs...."

Steve, Louise and Ellia suddenly exchange uncomfortable glances to each other and realise it's only the three of them who know about Viktor's revelations of the child experiments.

"What the Nazi's had done defies all that is human, they sliced the ladies legs open during surgical procedures and then contaminated the wound with soil, glass, puss, splinters of wood, well, anything they could get their hands on and then tested the wounds with various sulphonamide drugs. They would then allow the wounds to heal and repeat the process over and over again..."

Louise heaves the taste puke at the back of her throat.

"...at the end of the war the women of the camp had unravelled a plot amongst the S.S that the Rabbits were to face death the following morning in an attempt to eliminate all evidence of their war crimes. During the night before their impending execution, the women of the camp came up with a daring and extremely audacious plan to grab and hide the 'Rabbits' during the morning roll call right in front of the Nazi's. The real challenge came trying to keep the 63 women hidden and fed within the camp for a whole 3 months. It was beyond bravery what these women did, how they covertly kept them concealed until they were all liberated by the Soviets was improbable, but they overcame the unimaginable. It was one of the most extraordinary rescues in Nazi concentration camps history. Catholic, Protestant and Jewish women from over twenty countries came together to save these very young ladies. It doesn't matter what religion you are or what nationality you are, when true love is shown, humanity flourishes. Despite machine guns, disease and the fear of death these wonderful women had immense courage, love and compassion, they accomplished the impossible and saved all 63 ladies. The doctors that carried out the experiments were all faced by some of these female prisoners at the Nuremburg trials where their wounds were shown to the entire world as evidence and their experiences were shared. Those involved in these experiments all received the death penalty by the International jury."

The group is silent and the air is still, the soft distant chatters of the school children becomes dimmer until the noise falls into a sudden nothingness. Their thoughts consume them and soothed by the meditative qualities of the camps surroundings. The morning is very intense and mentally engulfs Louise. She is finding the complexity of the camps historical details amidst such beautiful exquisite surroundings agonizing in her thoughts and emotions. Tempestuous feelings, she's suddenly scared, the images from the museum impacts into her thoughts, she feels her heart beat like the thrusting wings of a caged bird within her chest and the fine hairs prickle the back of her neck. All her thoughts magnify the smallest of things, tiny movements, slight noises and dark looming shadows created by the camps wall and its electrified wiring.

"Are you ok Lou?" Steve questions.

"Do you believe in ghosts?" she responds with a shiver. He can tell exactly what she's feeling. He puts his arm around her shoulders to give Louise some comfort.

"I have never been to a place like this before," she continues.

"I don't think we ever truly considered the impact this might have on us," he whispers back.

Steve and Caleb head into town to visit the Fürstenberg Brewery which dates back to 1283. Above the ground it proudly stands four stories high and is painted in a salmon pink colour. The centre of the building has 'Fürstenberg' written on its external wall and this grandly rests with an emblem crest above it. In front of the building displays a dignified statue and water fountain. The fountain sits at the statues base which displays a hunter with a bow and arrow and a dog at his feet, making a dramatic welcome to the brewery. The outside seating area is more than ample; plenty of parasols giving the tables shade from the splendid heat.

The two men get to know each other better, chat about their families, jobs, and sample the variety of beer produced at the brewery.

"So, what brings you two gentlemen to Fürstenberg?" asks the waiter as he pours another round of samples for Steve and Caleb to try.

"We're on an expedition," chuckles Caleb as he looks directly at his counterpart.

"In Fürstenberg?..." the waiter laughs. He speaks very good English and has a staunch crisp German accent, "...there's nothing but trees and lakes around here, oh, and a Palace of course."

"Over at Ravensbrück," Caleb continues with a big smile on his face. A loud cough comes from the adjacent table, which seems to coincide sarcastically to Caleb's comment. Steve looks over and sees two old men sitting in the corner. He surmises that the men are in their eighties, tough leathery skin with deep set wrinkles that frame their eyes. Neither of the gentlemen look over at Steve or Caleb.

"You don't want to be snooping around Ravensbrück," the man's tone is cynical and very abrupt.

"Ahh don't mind them..." whispers the waiter as he pretends to clean the table, "...some people around these areas are extremely superstitious about Ravensbrück."

"It's hardly surprising..." Caleb replies kindly "...given its history. I just need to nip to the bathroom."

"Terrible things happened there," the older gentleman says and makes his way over to Steve's table. He grabs onto Steve's arm and leans in towards him.

"It's not safe!"

"What do you mean?" Steve questions as the two

gentlemen loom over him.

Steve notices his deep set wrinkles and wonders what he may have looked like as a young man. His mind takes him back to the photographs in the museum earlier in the day. Some of the women were incredibly beautiful and he wonders if any are still alive today. The old man has very raspy tones to his voice and holds Steve's arm firmly. Steve immediately notices an unusual ring on the man's finger. The band has twisted interlaced flames that wrap appealingly around the crumpled furrow of his finger. The setting is a dark black onyx stone that sits perfectly in the shoulder of the extravagant flames and in the onyx is a beautiful gold symbol. Steve thinks to himself the symbol looks Aramaic or Hebrew.

"You can never out run a bear," the old man continues and turns slowly to walk away. He is supported by a very elegant wood carved walking stick and leaves the brewery with the other gentleman.

Caleb returns to the table to find a very puzzled look on Steve's face.

"Thanks for leaving me when you did..." he laughs in an ironic tone "...the waiter's right about the superstitious people in this town. Are there any bears in this area?"

"Bears?" laughs Caleb "...have another beer mate."

"I suppose it must have been very difficult for the people in this town," Steve says as he picks up the pitcher of beer.

"Oh absolutely it's so close to the town. Creating

memorials like that are a fantastic way to educate society on how not to ever make the same mistakes again. So what do you think about these mysterious tunnels?"

Steve thinks about Viktor. He ponders for a moment on Caleb's question and gathers images of the child 'Rabbits' no one has any knowledge about and how incredibly lucky the 63 women were to escape. He starts to hope that Louise is incorrect about finding several child skeletons in the tunnels.

"It's all very intriguing Caleb, should make an amazing story for our newspaper back home," he responds.

Back at the hotel Louise is very animated about her visit to the Palace and its lustrous beauty; she's a lot calmer in her thoughts than when she was at Ravensbrück earlier that day.

"What time are the new arrivals getting here Ellia?" says Hans.

"I'm collecting them at five o'clock, so we can all meet in the restaurant for dinner later."

In his bedroom Steve starts to think about his journal. He fires up the laptop and begins to document everything he's learnt at Ravensbrück. He uploads a variety of photographs that he's taken and is distracted with his own thoughts. He picks up his phone and calls home to speak to his family.

His brother Robert answers "Oh hello stranger, not heard from you in a while. Mum says you're on vacation in Germany? Are you having a nice time?"

"It's work Bob. Nice area though. I've missed you, not seen you in ages. Let's catch up when I get back yeah?"

"No worries mate, are you ok?"

"Not bad, it's quite a heavy assignment, mentally draining really. Have you seen Grandma and Grandad recently?..." Steve fills his brother in on his past few weeks, "...I spent weeks secretly wishing something exciting would happen – something out of the ordinary, and can honestly say I was never expecting anything like this Bob..."

Robert is very quiet as he listens to his brother's story, he doesn't say anything and knows his brother has changed, "...I was always the type that liked to seek adventures that's why I went into journalism, an experience like this has made me think about my place and appreciate the little things in life."

"Moments like these are few and far between Steve. Experiences of this kind make you realise that families need to stick together, you will always find your way back to where you came from mate, and appreciate the little things in life."

"I'll call you back later Bob, there's somebody knocking at the door."

"I'm sorry to bother you Mr Garrett..." The hotel receptionist passes an envelope to him "...a gentleman dropped this in and asked us to give it to the people doing the research over at Ravensbrück."

Steve notices the paper has an embossed image

pressed into the top right hand corner. Seven flames interlace curving around the outer edge of its circular shape and in its centre is a symbol he's sure he's seen before. The note simply reads...

'PLEASE SHOW RESPECT TO THOSE WHO LOST THEIR LIVES'

Steve takes the note to show the others "I've just been given this..." he hands it to Ellia, "...there is nothing threatening or sinister about it, it's just a bit odd."

"People are very protective over history, especially with very recent events like the war..." Hans looks over Ellia's shoulder to view the letter "...it's to be expected, they don't know what we are looking for and might have concluded all sorts of things. There's a massive difference between being an archaeologist and a grave robber. Small towns like this can have huge superstitions about disturbing the dead; it's incredibly sacred to them."

"Superstitions! That's it! The symbol.....there..." Steve points at the embossing "...I saw it earlier, when Caleb and I were at the brewery. A gentleman had it on his ring."

צוֹפָה

"Mmm, interesting..." Hans slides his bifocals to the bridge of his nose and takes a closer look "...I wonder what it means?" he continues, taking a photograph of it on his phone "I'm not sure, but I think I know somebody who might."

Chapter 18

In the evening Hans, Steve, Caleb and Louise wait for Ellia to arrive with an additional four more to the ever growing team. They sit in the dining room of the Kleine Strandhütte Hotel and Ellia appears with the additions, she introduces them individually.
"This is Logan Adernne; Russo Groves; Reade Nowak and Sabrina Richell."
Sabrina immediately interrupts the introductions and holds out her hand to Caleb, "Everyone calls me Rina."
"Caleb, nice to meet you," he responds.

The group spend the evening getting to know each other and learn about the military backgrounds of the newcomers and everyone's individual professions and their involvement in the expedition.
"Russo has particular experience as an EOD operator," Ellia exclaims.
"Which is?" Louise replies.
"It stands for Explosive Ordnance Disposal," Russo says unable to take his eyes off of Louise.

He stands next to Steve and just a smidgen shorter, so Louise surmises he must be about 6 foot to 6 foot 1. He's incredibly stocky and muscular in appearance, a mountain of pumped muscle. Louise stares at his upper arms and thinks how massive his biceps are.

"I was in the army for many years and went onto work with the Royal Engineers as an Ammunition Technician..." Russo continues, "...I met Ellia a few years back and she invited me to come along for this. I've taken annual leave for this," he laughs loudly looking at Ellia.

"If we find these tunnels we have to consider that they might have been shut and forgotten for 75 years there could be undetonated bombs still there..." Ellia says "...or booby-traps, especially if the Nazi's didn't want the tunnels found."

Steve and Louise stare at each other and exchange uncomfortable glances, they realise they haven't considered the probability of 'live bombs' in any of this.

Russo is brown eyed and has a shaved head. He has stubble on his face, in fact more hair around his jawline than on his head and the whiskers that frame his face have small grey hairs amongst the dark hairs which makes him possibly a lot older than he looks. 'He must weigh about 17 stone' Louise continues to think to herself. The crisp white t-shirt he wears looks three sizes too small for him with all the bulging muscle. Both his arms are decorated in a variety of tattoos, some tribal and Celtic and some that would seem they stand for a significant purpose. She notices he has an array of ink across his collar bone that suggest they're on his entire torso also. His smile is very cheeky and his facial expression looks as though he's up to mischief. All in all, his enigmatic smile and very long eyelashes make him quite a beautiful specimen.

Logan is definitely the quietest of the newbies. Hans is unable to work out if he's arrogant or generally just quiet and shy. He tries several times to draw Logan into conversation but mainly receives responses in one word answers. Logan has very piercing grey eyes and a sharp pointed hooked nose. His hair is a dirty blonde colour and he has a good three inch beard. He is much shorter than Steve and Russo, stands at around 5 foot 7 and is quite slender in build. He's another American, speaks a very impressive four languages, English, French, Polish, and Russian, although they don't learn this from Logan, Ellia is very keen to share this information. He barely makes any eye contact with anyone and spends most of the evening with his earphones in and stares at his phone every few minutes.

Reade is much more sociable, mingles amongst everyone for most of the evening. Reade has the most exquisite olive complexion and his eyes sparkle when he smiles like topaz gemstones. His whole face ignites with radiance as he engages in conversation. His hair is tightly braided and he looks extremely smart in his fitted lemon shirt and dark jeans. He spends a good half an hour sharing photos of his twin boys back home in Brighton, England. Louise and Rina take a great interest in the twins and Reade shares that they've just started preschool.

Rina is a very strong character and has quite a volume in her voice. She's strikingly beautiful, wears no makeup and has very short cropped hair with shaved back and sides. Rina also loves a tattoo; and is also covered in them. She wears cut down frayed denim shorts and a green vest top. She's very slender and toned, Louise contemplates that she definitely wouldn't want to get on the wrong side of her, as lovely as she is; she's highly intimidating. Louise notices that one of Rina's tattoos is a pair of dog-tags. 'The tattoo artist that had penned these is immensely clever' Louise thinks to herself.
"They are incredibly real looking..." she says to Rina and points to the dog-tags "...the shadowing makes them look like they are just sitting on your skin." She's not close enough to Rina to read the names or numbers on the tags.
"I'll tell you about them sometime." Her sassy response is terrifyingly aggressive despite the huge smile.
Steve notices a huge pile of equipment that's now beginning to take over the hotel reception area and see's the very edge of a handgun in Logan's back pack. "What's the gun for?" his highly agitated tone is sharp and snappy. He's very distracted by the awkward atmosphere now filling the room.
He doesn't reply and pushes the gun lower into the backpack, puts his earphones back in and turns his music up.
"Why the hell has he got a gun?" He shouts and turns

to face the rest of the group, his lip curls and his nostrils flare in anger "Seriously...what's with the gun?" He can feel his heart race like a freight train.

"He's military Steve!" Ellia jumps to Logan's defence and senses Steve's sudden 'fight or flight' response.

"It doesn't mean anything mate, we carry guns; it's our jobs. We carry handguns to protect ourselves and being armed we make unarmed citizens safer. In the army, firearms are much more heavily regulated than in civil society, we have extremely strict regulations that go with the military's use of guns. You might be surprised to know that if a soldier cannot qualify with his weapon, he's not actually allowed to carry or shoot it." Reade puts his hand on Steve's arm to calm him down.

"Ok? But why does he need it for finding tunnels and I'm supposed to move on and just ignore this? We went to Ravensbrück today, there's nobody there except tourists and school children, I do not agree that violence is power or that life is dispensable," he replies.

Taking his earphones out Logan utters his only words of the entire evening "Chill out man, I carry it everywhere with me even take it to bed with me." He puts his earphones back in and looks away from the others and stares back at his phone again.

"You're British Steve, seeing a gun must be alarming for you." Reade continues.

"Yeah ok..." Steve's demeanour calms down "...you have a point, it isn't something I'm used to seeing at all and I respect that they are a part of your jobs.

I just have strong opinions that most Americans grow up in a Disney fairy tale that their right to bear arms is without any burden of responsibility, I'm a journalist remember I've heard a hell of a lot of very dumb arguments around gun control."

"It really is just a deterrent, a protection, it's that same old argument that guns don't kill people, people do and if they really wanted to harm someone they would use anything like knives or hammers." Reade acknowledges Steve's opinion and smiles at him.

"Isn't that why the second amendment protects guns and not knives or hammers? Isn't that why mass murderers choose guns and not baseball bats? My opinion is the excuse is lame because you can use anything as a weapon, my grandmother could use her rolling pin," he responds sarcastically.

"Come and have a look at some of the other equipment we've brought," he throws Steve a hard hat with a headlamp on it. A wondrous array of knee and elbow pads, gloves, boots, harnesses, compasses, rope and first aid kits laid out on tables, he hands Ellia some of the overalls that she hangs onto a portable clothes rail.

"Tunnels can be very cold and humid so we must have the right equipment and protective clothing... safety first," Reade continues.

"...and food and water," Ellia smiles at Steve and reassures him.

"We don't know what kind of condition the tunnels may be in..." intrudes Caleb into the conversation and picks up a mask "...it's good to have the proper equipment. I've been caving a lot in my role, I know it's not exactly man made tunnels but exhausting work, with a lot of risks."

"Like?" Louise questions.

"Risks of drowning, rock-falls, lack of oxygen, hypothermia…"

"Gosh! What's this for?" she questions and picks up a very odd looking compass.

"This is an inclinometer; it measures angles, slopes or tilts with respect to the direction of gravity. We probably won't need it as hopefully our tunnels are all on one level, but you never know."

"…and this?" she continues her excitable succession of questions.

"This is a heavy duty hand-held borehole drill."

She giggles and puts on the largest yellow hard hat down over her eyes "Look Steve I'm a Minion."

"You're such a flipping nutcase Lou!"

Rina grabs Louise's hand and drags her to a small area she has now turned into a makeshift dance floor.

"Let's dance," she laughs.

"Come on Ellia," Louise says as she grasps Ellia's hand and pulls her to join them. The three of them dance in a triangle shape and sing very loudly and out of key.

Calm restores itself in the hotel and most have gone to bed except for Steve, Louise and Ellia.

"Quite a little team you've pulled together in such a short space of time," Steve says to Ellia.

"Not really Steve, you have to remember my family and I have been aware of Viktor and my Grandmothers romance for a few years now. We had Grandma's locket, the very unusual stories she told us and then Viktor's sudden jaw dropping revelation."

"I've been thinking a lot about those children, after visiting Ravensbrück today my mind has been full of all kinds of thoughts..." Louise starts "...we've all become so caught up with the excitement of finding mysterious tunnels, we're putting off actually dealing with what we might find."

"Denial is powerful," Steve interrupts.

"You know, seeing as we're the only ones aware of what was happening down there, don't you think we owe it to the victims? Remember Hans's story of the 63 Rabbits, we may not find anything, or some kind of discovery may give closure to family members around the world," Ellia replies, "Have you heard of Yad Vashem?"

"Yes I have, we did a massive article about it in our newspaper..." Louise responds "...isn't that the Jewish International database that has been collecting the names of all the victims from the holocaust?"

"Yes, they've gathered together nearly five million names of the six million Jews murdered in the war. Think about it, these few children may just be the missing links to desperate families that have been waiting eight decades to hear about. Time is rapidly running out now."

Steve thinks of his Great Grandmother and his Great

Aunt, to have that kind of knowledge might possibly bring peace for Mikolai.

"It's all the uncertainty Lou, our brains do not function logically with uncertainty."

"I just don't relish the idea of seeing little child corpses in these tunnels," Louise says staring into her glass.

Chapter 19

"Have you got all the kit Lou?" Steve fumbles through his backpack.

"Camcorder, cameras and body-cams all fully charged and raring to go; these overalls are really scratchy!"

"Well they're tough and waterproof, I don't think they're designed to go clubbing in..." he replies "... definitely fully charged?"

"Yep."

"Spare batteries for all of them?"

"Yep!... stop flapping!"

"We've come all this way we can't afford to cock it up now, you know what Bryan's like..." Steve's very distracted with a gentleman by the trees at the bottom of the driveway. He notices that the man tries very hard not to be inconspicuous and makes a shoddy job of it. Ellia drags an enormous holdall full of equipment along the shingle path and scrapes most of the tiny stones along with it. Steve grabs the end and they lift it into the back of the truck.

"Well you certainly look different out of your power suits and high heels Ellia."

"Very funny!"

"Ignore him Ellia, he's been sarcastic all morning." Louise checks that her backpack definitely has all of the camera equipment as Steve makes her overly paranoid.

Ellia notices the man spying from the trees. She suddenly drops her head and turns away like she's seen a ghost.

"Hey! Do you know that creepy dude over there? Steve puzzles.

"Who?"

"You know exactly who, the weirdo doing a bad job of hiding behind those trees over there. You blatantly looked at him and turned your face away."

"I've never seen him before in my life!"

"Oh my god, seriously Ellia you recognised him! I'm not an idiot..." he laughs "...do you have a mystery stalker or an obsessive ex?"

"Mr Garrett! I don't know who he is. There's nothing creepier to me than a bloke hiding in bushes." She jokes deliberately trying to get Steve off the conversation.

"Have you been here before? I mean Heidi's story is pretty epic I would be surprised if you haven't come with your family?"

"Good morning everybody! Are we all ready for a fun filled day?" Hans bellows, claps his hands and looks up at the sunshine. Ellia's extremely overwhelmed with relief in the sudden change of conversation and Steve whispers to Louise "I reckon he's an ex spying on her."

"Drop it Steve, you're making her very uncomfortable you know."

"Maybe I'll go over and shake his hand."

"Stop it!" she giggles slaps his arm.

"I'm sure that there are laws against hovering

around bushes these days. Actually to be fair the people in this town are pretty peculiar."

"You have one incident to go on you can't say things like that."

"What about the freaky note then?"

"Oh yeah I'd forgotten about that, ok, that is a bit odd, but you can't stereotype the entire town folk as 'odd!' Why the hell are you waving at him you prat?"

"Just being friendly."

"Well he's gone now! Ellia's frowning at you."

"Yep probably."

"Right everyone, so we've literally been given one weeks grace and the permissions to see if we can discover anything..." Ellia begins "...there's no right of access to the public so we won't have any awkward questions to answer."

"Told you, she knew him," he whispers. Louise kicks her boot into the side of his foot to shut him up.

"Morning Lou..." Rina says throwing her backpack into the boot of the truck, "...I slept like a log last night."

"Does he ever take those earphones out?" Steve questions as he looks over at Logan.

"Ignore him this morning Rina, he's clearly in one of his asshole moods."

He watches Logan skulk pass Caleb and Reade, his head bobs as if it's way too heavy for his neck to support. His neck is extremely skinny which makes his Adam's apple protrude prominently. Steve surmised that everyone around him is particularly shifty, but Logan especially seems to drain whatever happy feelings anyone might have. Steve's own cynical brain pulls itself up on being too judgemental and remembers his mother telling him it's ok to have social anxiety. He thinks to himself that he must reign in the sarcasm, that nobody is the same and everyone has their own battles to fight.

"I wonder if he's just socially awkward or he's seen some disturbing things in the Army," he says softly to Louise and Rina.

"Yep, I've known a lot of people with P.T.S.D..." Rina replies "...and I can tell you something for nothing, he's pretty normal. My dad always told us as kids to remind ourselves we're good people, we must do good things and to have a heart for everyone on our tiny planet. That's why I joined up, to look after good people, I have always been a people person and I'm pretty sure at some juncture in his life Logan was too."

They stand outside the Oberfurhers office Ellia grasps the key in her hand and makes her way up two of the steps by its front door. She stops to look back at them all staring keenly at her, she glances at Steve. He grins encouragingly, she's about to walk into her late boss's office. Viktor Otto-Wolff, the enigmatic, elusive ex Nazi who managed to avoid capture, execution or imprisonment his entire life. The events that took place in this room were the structure of his life map and thousands of others at his hands. She holds her breath, draws a deep intake of air, turns to face the door and her hands tremble a little bit as she slightly loses grip of the key. With one swift turn at the lock, the door of the S.S. Oberfurher's office swings open.

They stand in the doorway and stare in. There's not an awful lot to look at apart from an extremely grand desk. A deep brownish red solid mahogany pedestal desk and its statuesque varnish lustre display's a very unique floral pattern in gold. It has a two inch deep boarder that runs itself along the edge of the top and four drawers down each side of the desk. The golden handles match the floral top design and a worn tattered dark brown leather chair sits snuggly behind the desk. On the wall behind sits a five foot by four foot Swastika flag. Louise takes grip of the camera in her hand snaps a photograph of the room, everyone is exceedingly quiet.

They view the fireplace, which in itself doesn't look any more than just that, a fireplace, although an ample black cast iron fireplace. From the ground up it stands a good 6 feet in height and five feet in width and it distinctly has no mantel on its top. There's a six inch depth that pokes out from the walls edge and stands four inches off the floor. The outline of its boarder is a grape pattern with vine leaves that intertwine and inside of its outer iron vine boarder sits beige mosaic tiles with red grapes and green leaves and the grate sits dead centre. Louise steps forward slightly and takes another photo and its flash momentarily lights up the fireplace.

"I wasn't expecting to see the grate full of coal dust and debris..." Ellia says "...I honestly believed it was a fake fireplace to conceal the tunnel."

"Well..." Caleb responds and steps in front of the group "...they would have done anything to make something look functional and real...Help me Russo..." he continues and he grabs onto the iron grate to pull it forward.

Russo takes the other side and drags it forward they lift it off the fireplace base and settle it to one side of the room. Caleb sits himself down and shuffles his bottom backwards into the fireplace, he switches on his torch and looks straight up the chimney shaft.

"It's fake alright, about seven feet up I'm guessing it's solid brick, it's definitely not a real or functioning chimney." He taps the wall directly behind and listens to see how hollow it sounds. The very dense noise that penetrates back is definitely not hopeful. "Well I had my hopes up that it'd be easier than this."

"What did you expect, a big arrow pointing to the fireplace saying 'hidden tunnels here'?" Steve responds.

"Seriously! What the hell is up with you today?.." Louise shouts and slams the camera into his chest and walks to the other side of Viktor's desk, "...you really are such an arrogant pillock sometimes."

"Grandma said the entire fireplace opens up like a door, there has to be some way of opening it." Ellia responds and touches Louise's arm as she walks away from Steve.

Caleb slides himself out of the hole in the fireplace centre and Russo helps to grab tight of it and pulls hard at the ornamental fire surround.

"Jeez that's not shifting let's try the left side..." says Russo. "...the left side is still not budging an inch, are you sure Ellia?"

"Definitely!"

"Emmm well maybe there's a keyhole? Or one of these grapevines is a latch or the mosaic tiles pushes in?" Hans responds and gets onto his knees, he touches, pushes and tries to twist all the iron grapes to see if any turn.

"It's like Indiana Jones." Louise laughs.

"And it's definitely this building and not the one next door?" Hans continues.

"Hundred percent!"

"Well we all need to spread out in the room and look for clues, hang on a minute...." Hans pauses for a moment and notices a very small half circle shape indentation, it's about an inch in size between the depth of the fireplace and the wall behind it.

"That's just where the screws go in to secure it against the wall Hans," Caleb responds. Hans slide his glasses up his nose, thrusts his index finger into the crest shape indentation. Using his finger to feel about, his eyes suddenly light up "Aha! I believe this is a...."

~CLICK~

"...latch."

Hans pulls his finger out, Russo and Caleb rush to try and pull the fireplace again. With a lot of pushes and brute force it moves open in its entirety. They all stare at the solid brick wall behind it.

"Well that's disappointing but not surprising, whatever the Nazi's were hiding they definitely wanted it kept hidden..." Hans says "...they were absolute masters of documenting every tiniest detail and then panicked when their distorted idyllic dreams came crashing down around them trying to destroy all evidence of their sadistic crimes."

"I'll grab the bore-hole drill and tools then," says Reade.

Reade and Russo kneel down each side of the wall and start to chisel away at the fake brick wall. Steve puts the camera down onto the desk and stares at the huge Swastika on the wall.

"What's up today?" Louise says and gently touches his arm.

"I'm sorry..." he sighs "...I dunno, I feel very aggravated, I have a really horrible feeling about all of this."

"Well we know it's not gonna be nice whatever we find down there."

"No, I mean, a really-really bad feeling."

"Has it been since 'unexploded devices' was mentioned?"

"No, I don't think that's it either," he crumples his face. She lays her hand on his shoulder to soothe and wrap him in a duvet of concern.

"Well that's just great..." Reade says in an ironic

tone, looks up at Russo and takes off his eye goggles "...let's get the rest of this outer layer off."
Behind the brick work is a solid concrete mass and the two men continue to chip away at the external layer of bricks.
"You know there actually could be several layers?" Hans says to Caleb and he nods at him,
"Yeah you're right."
After an hour the entire brickwork outer layer is down, the girls, Steve and Logan work hard to shift the chipped bricks in a convoy onto a tarpaulin sheet outside of the building. Hans opens the windows to let the dust filled foggy room settle down.
"Let's go outside and have a drink whilst the dust drops."
"Your Grandmother was certainly right about the fake fireplace leading to something Ellia," Steve says.
"I'm gonna phone her, Steve can you send me a couple of the photographs you've taken please? I want to send them over to my Aunt Leticia so she can show her."
"Pass me the drill," Russo outstretches his hand to Reade.
The suspense deafens, more than the grating roar of the spinning drill.
"I hate the sound of drilling it sets my teeth on edge." Rina grimaces.
"Like the dentist?" Ellia smiles at her.
"That annoying high-pitched whine and the heat from the friction, you can actually smell the burn-

ing as it drills, it's like water torture!"

"We need a longer 'bit'" Russo says to Reade. The bit on the bore-hole drill is now half a meter long, "this block of concrete is very deep..."

"WAIT! Fellas stop!" Caleb shouts and rushes forward "Stop a minute...!"

Reade and Russo stop drilling suddenly and pull their hard hats off.

"Professor Tassin, I think you need to take a look at this."

"Well I'll be?.." He responds in a surprised but baffled tone "...no, no, no, this can't be what I think it is?"

"Worryingly I actually think it might be!"

"What?" Ellia questions.

"Look..." Caleb points to a very small hand chiselled engraving in the bottom right hand corner of the solid cement block, "...I hadn't notice it because of all the rubble lying on the floor in front of it."

Ellia looks at it closely it's a small chiselled triangle with a dot in its centre.

"What does it mean?" She asks.

He looks at Hans and notices their confused faces look at him "I do believe it's a Lily-Code marker."

"A what?" Rina responds.

"What's a Lily-Code marker?" Puzzles Louise.

"During the war an infamous Japanese General called Tomoyuki Yamashita was commissioned to occupy the Philippines with a quarter of a million troops. They built a complex underground city of tunnels in the mountains and hid billions and billions of bullion, treasure and gold there. For nearly seventy years it has attracted treasure hunters from around the entire world on a quest to find it..."

"Told you it was like Indiana Jones!!"

"...the treasure was also disputed in a lawsuit involving the former Philippine President Marcos. The process of finding the gold has resulted into mass murders, pillaging, gang rapes and horrific war crimes. When they were building the tunnels it was named 'Operation Golden Lily' after a poem written by the Japanese Royal Emperor Hirohito. The Lily-Code was a complex treasure map of markers left on rocks, trees, walls....anywhere that would leave hints to the whereabouts of the treasure. Many of the tunnel entrances were blasted with dynamite and sealed and then filled with cement walls to completely block them off from the rest of the world. If there were any men left inside of the tunnels at the time of sealing, well, if they didn't commit suicide they were left to suffocate to death being taunted by all the treasure and gold surrounding them. The Lily-Codes became widely sought after explaining to treasure hunters what might be lying behind a rock or tree etcetera."

"So what does that symbol mean?" Ellia asks and points to the dotted triangle.

"A bomb!" Caleb and Hans say in unison.

"Or booby-traps..." continues Caleb "...we know Yamashita had met Hitler a few times, it's very likely, looking at this that he might have used him to devise something very similar here."

"What...to bury treasure?" Louise asks.

"Oh no I doubt that, not at a concentration camp Miss Randall..." Hans says. "...no, no, using Yamashita's technique to build a network of tunnels at very fast speed and his ability to have them detonate or collapse if need be, Ravensbrück was particularly known for its sadistic experimentation. Under the watchful eye Heinrich Himmler, he assigned his personal physician Dr Karl Gebhardt to perform the ghastly experiments on the women here, some of the documentation has never been found and a laboratory that was described in excruciating detail at the Nuremberg trials was considered to have been destroyed or demolished... I'm thinking it was neither..."

"Neither what?" asks Louise.

"Destroyed or demolished..."

"Tell them..." she continues and looks at Steve and Ellia. Hans glances towards Ellia, with his mouth slightly open and loose and his left eyelid scowling, he responds "Tell us what?"

Chapter 20

"I worked for Viktor Otto-Wolff, as many of you know, his personal assistant..." Ellia starts, she sighs "...I don't know where to begin..."

"This is how Louise and I found out about the tunnels too..." Steve interrupts, "...Ellia already knew about them from her Grandmother Heidi."

"Heidi and Viktor had a relationship after the war..." Louise chips in excitedly as all three of them babble to get it all out at once "...Heidi had been a prisoner here and they met in a market place after the war, she had recognised him as one of the Ravensbrück officers."

"My Grandmother was very reserved at first but Viktor was totally captured by her beauty. She never told him that she had been at Ravensbrück and a very unlikely relationship blossomed between the two of them."

"Louise and I went to interview him after his capture, as he was dying he told us all about his love for Heidi and then explained to us about a Top Secret mission or an experiment they had carried out here. They performed this experiment on a group of children, a serum designed to create the strongest Aryan race." Steve explains.

"My Grandmother had been assigned to provide food for the doctors and officers in the tunnels but had never seen any children down there, she was only allowed to go so far, handover the food and then had to leave."

"Viktor told us that when the war was coming to an end they immediately shut the child human experiment down and sealed the tunnels leaving all evidence of it an abandoned mystery. Until this very day he knew the tunnels had never been discovered," finishes Steve and they all catch their breath staring attentively at the faces looking back at them.

The quietness in the room paralyses deep.

"I don't know what to say," Russo says.

"Sometimes a loss for words says more!" Logan muffles.

In unison they all turn their heads in complete surprise by Logan having actually spoken. His non-committal statement unintentionally fills the awkward void with an eerie appreciation.

"Well, all I can say is that there's even more reason to find out the truth now." Caleb says and smiles at Logan.

"Exactly that Dr Beldman..." agrees Hans, "...I think it's time to get out that G.P.R!"

"Well if there are any structures subsurface, this baby will let us know. We need to gather as much data as possible to minimise any damage to the historical elements." Caleb says and moves the GPR outside the Oberfurhers office, adjacent to where the fireplace is situated.

"Good grief that didn't take long! Come and have a look at this, there's a tunnel alright, a bloody great big mass directly underneath us!"

"How far could it go?" Ellia quizzes.

"Depends; I will walk along and see which directions it goes..." continues Caleb fixated at the GPR readouts "...I think we need to compare the GPR data and the evidence we collected from the boreholes to see what we could possibly be dealing with here. The GPR will help us most importantly minimise any risk of damage or cave-in's to the tunnels."

"What's it processing Dr Beldman?" Hans enquires at the array of grids, lines and dense colours appearing on the screen.

"We're looking at about three inches of asphalt thickness and the depth of the rebar mesh," Caleb states.

"What's rebar mesh?" Louise's inquisitive nature steps swiftly into the conversation.

"Reinforced steel mesh used in structures to support and strengthen the tension of the concrete..." he replies endeared by Louise's enthusiasm "...I think we definitely have some visualised corrosion and I'm beginning to detect some moisture..." he continues and is now about fifty meters away from the Oberfurhers office.

"What does that mean?" Steve asks.

"Possible flooding into various sections of the tunnels and the corrosion could lead to tunnel collapse."

"Do we have the depth of the rebar layer?" Hans asks.

"Yes, and the concrete slab thickness, there's definitely some other underground debris but at the moment it's very difficult to interpret the data I'm receiving, the electromagnetic pulses I'm receiving are a bit uncertain."

"Oh, it's so clever..." Louise smiles "...like a medical CAT scan or MRI slicing through a human body."

"Yep, pretty much that. I'm going to check the real time software with this collection of data we have gathered." Hans nods and agrees with Caleb "I can't progress into that section there; the terrain is covered with too many branches and rocks to clamber over. We won't be able to get the appropriate data, we really do need to get this processed."

"So what other uses are there for GPR?" she continues with her tireless questions.

"Many things Miss Randall..." Hans replies "...absolutely anything that you might need to see underground. Obviously archaeology, but businesses use it to locate water and gas lines; it's used for root crop and a very useful way of identifying and estimating staple food sources."

"It's so clever. Can we not drill downwards directly underneath us and make a big hole into the tunnel?"

"No it wouldn't work at all, that would definitely cause a major collapse. We could bore a man size hole next to the tunnel straight down and then drill across into the side of the tunnel, but it would take a considerable amount of time and manpower to accomplish that. I'm thinking secondary entrances and air shafts Hans, what do you reckon?"

"Completely agree..." Hans says "...there will most definitely be many other exits or entrances that have been hidden, it's about locating them. Keep mapping out what you can with the GPR, I am going to download...."

"What do we need to be looking for?" Reade questions and interrupts Hans.

"....the Lily Code markers. From here on in, these markers will be our bible. We will need to be extremely careful but I'm going to send you all a copy of the kind of things we need to be looking out for."

"There's another man lurking about down there by that statue, I thought you said no access to the public Ellia?" Rina says and points in his direction.

"That's right."

"Maybe he's a groundsman?" Louise says.

"No, I know all the staff that work here, and he's definitely not one of them," Hans responds.

"Well, I one hundred percent don't know who that guy is," Ellia states slipping up.

"So you did know 'Creepy-bush-guy' earlier? I bloody knew it." Steve says shaking his head and rolling his eyes.

"You really do like to push it Steve," she responds.

"Observant I think is the expression you're looking for..." he replies sarcastically "...apart from the fact it was blatantly obvious!"

"Ok well he was an ex-boyfriend of mine, but I haven't been here before!"

"That's a bit freaky Ellia. What is he doing here?"

"GET BACK! GET BACK!" screams Rina and she grabs Louise's arm.

An unusual canister glides majestically through the air hissing in its wake.

"What the....?" Yells Russo and quickly turns to face Logan who grasps his gun and pulls it swiftly out of his back pack pointing it in what he believes to be the direction of the statue, but the air fills rapidly with a deep fog of greenish gas. Everything becomes hazy, panic and disorientation swamps the group.

"My eyes! I can't see..." cries Louise "...Steve, Steve!"

"I'm here Lou, I can't see you, I can't breathe."

"Chlorobenzalmalononitrile, we must exit the area!" screams Hans.

"In English?" shouts Reade on his hands and knees as he gasps for air.

A deafening sound of gunfire envelops the hysteria that encompasses them. Logan blindly fires his gun upwards, their eyes and ears burn and the shots vibrate to confuse their senses of reality further.

"We're being attacked" screams Rina.

"Tear gas" wheezes Hans in response to Reade

"Do not lie down! We need to move...Now!" Reade yells at the rest of them.

Their sense of direction is completely eradicated as they individually scramble to exit the target area from its acidic vinegar stench. The pain in their body's grips intensely, paralyses them to drop involuntarily onto their knees and doubles them over. Steve's hand searches frantically for Louise's but fails. The tightness in his chest is so bad he feels his heart is about to explode and for a few seconds his thoughts flash that he is about to die from the burn in his eyes and throat, it is like a disorganised insane anxiety. The area that surrounds them is completely veiled in an air-filled blanket of pain, it hangs heavily on all of their senses suffocating them and it's excruciating to swallow.

The fog slowly begins to float away with the gentle breeze, its darkness seems to swallow up every object in its wake, trees, buildings and the statues vanish in its enveloping indiscriminate cloud. The pain takes over their bodies distressfully torments them like being burnt alive and a sensation that wraps their internal organs in a vice. The cloud looms as far as Caleb can see and it shrouds everything it touches. They lose their sense of direction, exit one by one and drop to their knees, crying out in agony and gasping for breath, but mainly terrified of the sensations that harrow and punish their bodies. The confusion slowly wanes and it becomes alarmingly apparent this is an attack with calculated precision and the canister landed exactly where it needed to. Steve looks around expeditiously for Louise and notices the platoon of tunnel-hunters lying on the ground, doubled over or perched against the Oberfurhers office wall. He can't find her, his eyes sting and stream. Logan holds Steve's head back and pours water into his eyes.
"Don't rub them, it'll be all over your hands and will just go back into the eye and irritate more."
"I can't see Lou," Steve grimaces.

Steve squints and struggles to focus on a shadowy figure carrying Ellia from the murky smog and lies her down gently on the grass. Steve struggles to focus everything around him is fuzzy and blurry. He looks up at the stranger and barely wheezes out "There's another!"

The outsider signals to Logan to attend to Ellia and hotfoots back into the slow dispersing mist.

"We need to get out of our clothes," Russo chokes.

The utter disorientation and mass confusion dims slightly as the stranger appears with Louise nestled in his arms, she's limp and lifeless. He staggers drops to his knees and she rolls slowly out of his cradle hold onto the ground. He coughs violently and wretches repeatedly until he vomits. He sits next to Louise to recuperate and looks over to Ellia. She signals back barely lifts her hand from the ground to let him know she's ok.

Steve crawls over to Louise "Lou?" he shakes her gently "Lou, honey?" his voice desperate and raspy.

"Get her in the office," splutters Rina.

Logan and Reade clutch hold of Louise's shoulders and Steve drags his pain stricken body off the grass to take her legs. The three men carry her up the stairs into the Oberfurhers office and cough violently.

"On the desk," says Reade and they place Louise's motionless body onto the mahogany pedestal desk. Reade takes Louise's face and feels the warmth of her breath against his hand, "She's breathing," he responds and slumps himself onto the floor, draws his knees in and drops his forehead onto them.

"Lou, sweetheart," whispers Steve. He struggles at the searing pain that grips his throat. Her face a prominent flush red and streaks of black mascara striping her cheek bones. He lifts the back of her head holding it affectionately in his hand and pours water very slowly into her eyes and strokes her cheek with his thumb.

The rest of the group stagger wearily into the building, sounds of coughs, gasps bounce of the walls and tears stream from their bloodshot eyes.

Louise opens her eyes swiftly snatches the water bottle from Steve and gulps fast.

"I'm on fire!.." she whispers "...ahh my eyes feel raw and my chest, something's squashing my rib cage!"

He stares into the blank expression from her crimson eyes but is immediately diverted by the unknown stranger, the immediate hero of the moment, enters into the room.

Ellia speaks very softly but with an offish sharp tone. "Everybody meet Arthur, Arthur meet everybody..." She swings her arm from one side of the room to the other side in a kind of hundred and eighty degrees semi-circle, she really does not care less about his presence and she's way too exhausted to utter individual introductions. "...or as you are currently referred to as 'creepy-bush-guy'. What are you even doing here Arthur?"

"That overwhelming gratitude as ever Ellia!" he responds.

"Oh you do know her quite well then?" retorts

Steve.

"Guys, I think our main priority is to get out of these clothes right now." Repeats Russo harshly.

"Russo is right everybody, this stuff lingers, we need to get out of our clothing and shower or we will just keep causing this burning irritation to ourselves," Caleb says as he looks at the crowd of slumped bodies all desperately try to expel air from their lungs like a pack of wild barking animals.

"Agreed Dr Beldman..." Hans nods in acknowledgment "...if you all want to remain here there is a fully functional shower block in one of the lower entrance buildings used regularly by groundsmen or we can make our way back to the hotel?"

"No disrespect Hans but the thought of showers and concentration camps makes me feel very uncomfortable, if you get my drift. I for one have had enough today, I'm going back to the hotel. I'm taking Louise too, she needs the rest, what the rest of you decide to do is up to you," Steve fields the question to the rest of the party.

Chapter 21

The other members of the faction decide to clean up at the hotel too, they all travel back in total silence, the void only broken with moments of inflicted coughs. Their thoughts twist and suffocate their minds by the confusion of the past hour, the biggest question simply being... Why?

Steve stares out from the hotel bar and gazes at the gentle ripple from the lake. He tries desperately hard not to blink, the lids of his eyes still sting like a slicing razor each time they shut. Totally bewildered by the harrowing event Steve struggles with the situation at hand. Baffled as to how and why anybody would comprehend or perceive storming them with an onslaught of C.S. gas could be acceptable on any level. Slowly in succession the others appear each one silent and reserved; low-pitched inaudible tones as they order a drink at the bar and scatter around the seats in the room. The atmosphere is speechless and soundless, so much to be said but everyone's tight lipped. Ten minutes pass and Louise appears last.
"Would you like a drink Lou?" asks Steve.
"Gin and Tonic please."
Reade looks over at Arthur who seems extremely uncomfortable and out of place amongst them.
"So, you are my knight in shining armour," Louise speaks softly and holds her hand out, Arthur shakes

it gently.

"How are you?"

"I've felt better, but then I suspect you all have. How long does this stinging last?" She replies.

"A while." Hans responds and places his hand affectionately on her shoulder.

"Is anybody going to start?.." blurts Russo "...clearly we weren't welcome!"

Louise stands timidly in front of them all "Firstly thank you everybody for your help today, but I need to apologise for putting you all in that situation."

"What are you apologising for Lou? You did nothing wrong?" responds Ellia quick to defend her.

"It was my fault I was trying to get another camera out to capture what was happening and put myself and my team at great vulnerable risk."

Her voice quivers and her chin trembles as if she's about to burst into tears.

"Honey, I know I said I wanted everything caught on camera, but not at the risk of your life," claims Steve "Bless you."

"Is anyone going to question the elephant in the room?.." quizzes Rina, "...I mean why? Why would anybody even think to gas us? Some kind of perverted sick joke at a concentration camp?"

"No that was calculated for sure. I've been thinking about this all afternoon. First the old boy over at the Fürstenburg brewery, I totally understand the fact when Hans says the local people are superstitious from what happened at Ravensbrück, but then the note handed to reception telling us to show respect for those who lost their lives. We are being watched very closely, our presence is definitely not welcome. Physically attacking us with tear gas is unacceptable..." says Steve "...Hans did you message anyone about the symbol on the embossed paper and the gentleman's ring?"

"In all that pandemonium I hadn't even thought about it Steve. I will forward the photo of the symbol now." He asserts getting out his phone.

צוֹפָה

"I wonder what it means?" whispers Louise gently.

"Well, they probably don't want you all to find the treasure before they do!" Arthur states and glares indignantly at Ellia.

If there is ever a better expression than a chilling 'pin-drop' moment this is the time to use it as the room falls heavy at Arthur's statement. Mouths drop open one by one, the silence is more painful than the dragging searing symptoms that still burn inside their chests and throats. Louise's mouth moves ever so slightly but nothing other than a gasp leaves her lips.

He lingers momentarily "Looking at your expressions I take it...."

"Treasure? As in Treasure – Treasure? Or the tunnels themselves being the treasure?" questions Reade.

Everyone turns and gawks at Ellia. She can feel their eyes burn intently toward her, the irony being that they were burning literally. Steve sits himself onto one of the lounge sofas and folding his arms he looks up at Arthur.

"Oh I think I'm going to love this…"

Arthur is slender and elegant with lush olive skin that is completely offset by the shiny soft flickers of silver in the jet black hair that frames his head and face; Piercing dark brown eyes and beautifully groomed eyebrows for a man. His broad shoulders are particularly prominent considering his slender physique. The others can see that he is very uncomfortable by his sudden intrusion into the group, the circumstances and his blatant resentment towards Ellia.

"I would refer to my earlier question…what are you even doing here?"

"Are you deflecting the conversation Ellia? It's definitely unlike you to withhold information." Steve's voice stings venomously.

She huffs a cynical snort and turns to the bar.

"Err…..treasure?" continues Reade.

"I do have to say Miss Addario this does all seem very unusual I've never known anything about the tunnels and have lectured there for decades…" exclaims Hans "…today I find out about the specific child experiments, your grandmother's involvement, only to discover the location of these tunnels with the GPR, we find Lily-code markers, been attacked with tear gas and now a 'treasure' has been thrown into the mix."

"I feel like I'm on the set of the Goonies," Louise whispers to Rina.

"I'm quite happy to fill them all in?" states Arthur.
Ellia snaps back immediately "Look, I'm not trying to keep this to myself and quite frankly this is the exact reason I have not mentioned it." She waves her hand at Arthur to indicate he's the reason.
"Me?"
"Yes 'this' Arthur...you've completely proven my point. Everyone was happy to do a little dig, a bit of archaeology. Uncover a network of hidden tunnels. If..." she pauses to emphasise her words "...IF... we found any treasure well then I would have told everybody that there may have been a possibility, but then you breeze back..."
"Ellia I knew about the bloody tunnels just like you. You were the one that went on a compassion crusade to try and find out about Heidi's necklace. Did you get the information?"
"No."
"You left me high and dry Ellia, discarded me as soon as you could."
"It wasn't like that!"
"Really? Because the way I remember it you trotted off to the other side of the world before I had the chance to wake up! I went to bed that night with my fiancé in my arms and when I had awoken you were all but obliterated from my life!"
"I ceased a unique opportunity and took it Arthur! He needed an assistant. I wasn't going to let that pass by!"
"Good grief that was seven years ago! Did it really take you seven years to not only 'Not' find out any-

thing about the necklace and key, but to just reiterate that there were tunnels we already knew about anyway?"

"It all became very complicated. The longer I was with him the more obligated I was. It was like an addiction for us both in the end."

"He was a Nazi Ellia!"

"I know! At times when I was snooping through his desk or paperwork I was pretty ashamed of myself, but I couldn't go, he was contagious and addictive. You may believe that I was selfish and it came as a personal cost to yourself, but believe me it came at personal cost to myself too. For the entire time I spent as his P.A I faced abuse and ridicule for just associating with him. But, the reason I stayed for so long, he was incredibly loyal. He knew what the regime did was despicable and atrocious he never denied that, but he was skin and bone too. He had his own views but allowed me to have my own too..." she pauses and softens her pitch "...I loved him Arthur like a Granddad. I could see why my Grandmother loved him; I bet he was charming as a young man. I wasn't just his assistant in the end I was his nurse, maid, cook, confidante, friend and I was like his granddaughter. So no, I never found the right time to ask or drop the Heidi bombshell, so instead I poked and snooped about his business behind his back at every given opportunity. I was deceitful, manipulative and untrustworthy – a femme fatale!"

"Very much Heidi's granddaughter!"

"What do you mean?"

"Oh come on Ellia, I've given it so much thought. She knew that information about the tunnels and the treasure, do you not think for one moment that she truly loved Viktor or was playing him like a fiddle?"

"No I don't! Because if that was the case why go after Viktor? She already knew what was at Ravensbrück, why not just go straight back there? No! They both needed to save each other. She wasn't after vengeance or the desire of self-preservation, she never needed to get involved whatsoever and could have quite easily buried her head in the sand but she didn't, she loved him. Otto-Wolff's guilt would consume him up, he knew that one day the past would catch up on him and he knew that people would make her a target for just being associated with him. This was so much deeper Arthur. I'm sorry I left you, we had planned to do this together but the strategy changed. How long have you been in Germany? What stopped you from searching for yourself these past seven years?"

"You! Like an idiot I still felt this should be something we did together. It didn't feel right to do it without you."

"You act as if my love is owed to you, I know I hurt you. So you never told a soul?" Ellia's pitch is sceptical and mistrustful.

"Never! I knew when I read that he had died you would be on your way here any day. It was so predictable Ellia, your brother is still my best mate it wasn't at all difficult to find out your plans. But that's not to say I haven't been here before because I have! It's like a bitter deja-vu being spied on in this town in fact it seems to be a hobby of theirs."

"So have you been attacked before?" questions Caleb.

"No, but warned off... forcefully at times. I've never been harmed although I have been threatened. I just stayed back observing all of you and I apologise if you all thought that was creepy, it may have been but I had my reasons. I had a gut feeling something was going to occur, but I wasn't certain what it would be until the event."

"Well thank god you were here," responds Caleb and shakes Arthur's hand.

"Everybody..." Ellia says and looks back at the hawk eyes around the room "...Arthur is in the same fields as Professor Tassin and Doctor Beldman. We went through university together. As you have probably gathered he was my fiancé and was there the day at my Grandmothers and all of my family when she saw Viktor's capture on the television."

"Minus one tiny small probably quite insignificant part of the story?.." voices Steve "...why don't you fill us in on the treasure part you seem to be avoiding so well."

Ellia scowls at Arthur who icily shrugs his shoulders withers a slow burning scowl straight back at her. She struts away from them all, holds her chin up slightly, just to allude she has a measure of power and confidence in her brisk dominant stride.

"I'll be back in a moment…"
Arthur knows exactly what she's going to get. Everyone is fixed on him with eagle eyes. He faces them and places his left hand onto Caleb's left shoulder and his right hand onto Hans' right shoulder, beaming he rubbernecks from one to the other "You're gonna love this!"
A couple of minutes pass and Ellia reappears, her demeanour is a lot more mellow than the attitude she exited with. She relaxes her shoulders and her body language is temperate.
She slips her hand into her pocket and in an unimpassioned self-restrained manner pulls a black velvet pouch out with a drawstring tie top. Very gently and composed she tips an orangey object out onto her hand. They cluster around her to see an exquisite rose carving out of a shiny yellow orange stone or glass. The details in its petals are flawless and polished. It's about three inches in diameter and sitting on engraved shoulders of gold leaf.

She smiles at Arthur and looks towards Hans and Caleb "It's Amber."
Hans shakes his head in disbelief and grabs tightly onto Caleb's arm "This can't be?" he cries "No, no, it can't be?"
"Hold it," says Ellia and passes it to Hans.
"I'm taking this is something significant?" Russo exclaims.
Hans continues "My dear man if this is what I think it is we could be looking at what some called the

'Eighth Wonder of the World'."

He slides his glasses up the bridge of his nose and holds it very close to his eyes. Steve looks at the redness in their faces but the sparkle shimmer off the reflection from Hans' glasses is that of excitement and elation. He hands it quickly to Caleb who examines it in much the same way. He looks up at Hans and the two let out an excited cheer, followed by appreciative grins from Arthur and Ellia.

"How on earth have you kept this secret for seven years?" questions Caleb to Arthur.

"I loved her and have an incredible amount of respect for her family and Heidi. I knew she would come I just had to wait."

"What is it?.." asks Logan as the beautiful piece is gently passed along the room, "...what's the eighth wonder of the world?"

"Well this is made out of Amber and this small piece could probably well be a part of an entire room that vanished during world war two from the Catherine Palace in Saint Petersburg, Russia. It was originally made in Berlin in the 1700's for the Charlottenburg Palace and remained in Berlin until it was given by Frederick William I to Tsar Peter the Great, it's affectionately known as The Amber Room," continues Caleb.

"One day when my Grandmother was taking food to the soldiers she had seen hundreds, maybe thousands of crates taken in a convoy through the tunnels. This piece must have fallen from one of the crates and she slipped it beneath her clothing and managed to hide it away. She would have been shot for certain if she'd been seen or caught with it."

"How much is the Amber Room worth now?" inquires Reade.

"Today? I'm not too sure, maybe about five hundred million in US dollars but I think that estimate is several years out of date" extends Hans.

"That's if it's still there!.." responds Steve "...we were attacked today, why? I'm pretty sure we're not the only people that know about it. Like you said Ellia, a lot of soldiers must have known what was in the crates, if any of them survived what's to say they didn't go back?"

"This is very true Steve..." replies Hans "...there's only one way to find out!"

Ellia tips the velvet pouch upside down and two gold coins fall snugly into her palm.

"There's more than just the amber down there," she proclaims grinning confidently.

"So this is what this whole thing has been about?" quizzes Louise "You're Treasure Hunters?"

"Yes and no. If it was just a matter of treasure hunting we could have come here years ago, but my grandmother feels that the key in the locket is a lot more significant, we need to try and exhaust that curiosity first."

Chapter 22

The morning breaks. Fear, excitement, confusion and uncertainty overwhelms the group as they prepare to set back out to Ravensbrück. Louise stares unconsciously at the majestic sunrise that spans its orange and pink calypso colours as a silhouette across the tangerine lake. It's the start of a new day and new hopes.

Hans mumbles to Caleb "I've been thinking a lot more about the Lily-Code markers."

"I agree Hans it would make so much more sense than it did yesterday morning. I couldn't quite grasp the connection of Yamashita and Ravensbrück – but a treasure? Definitely! Hidden caves and complex tunnels are unequivocally his field of expertise. The Amber Room?...One hundred percent that Hitler assigned Yamashita for the job!"

"Undeniably!"

"So what are we going to do if there's another attack?" continues Caleb.

"Well..." Reade reacts and lifts a box into the back of the vehicle "...I'm handing out gas masks for everybody today, hopefully nothing more sinister will occur."

"But you don't know that?" interrupts Steve.

"No we don't at all. This whole situation has been blown out of the water now so you are all going to have to rely on Russo, Logan, Rina and myself. If you don't feel you can cut it down there Steve nobody would think any less of you?"

Steve peers over at Louise who's completely mesmerised by the dazzling sunrise. She looks distant and lost.

"What do you want to do Lou?"

"I wonder if this is destiny?" she responds without taking her eyes off the water's trance.

"How do you mean?"

"Is this my path in life? This means something to those women and children that were experimented on. I have to follow this rising sun Steve. Those women at the camp would have looked out over the exact same beauty and serenity here but suffered in unimaginable ways. We need to open those tunnels up, find out the children's story, what happened to them, we just have to find out. The war may have been decades ago but it is far from over. We need to tackle any adversity that hits us no matter what, it will be nothing compared to what all those women and children went through."

"That's very brave of you Lou."

"Is it? When someone is brave it's because they are intensely afraid, the two things conjoin hand in hand. My instincts are to listen to this electrifying adrenalin that's pounding in my ears by making the right choice…and that's by not walking away. I'm not going to just give up and surrender! I keep thinking about everything an entire generation went through and only a few years ago at that. I visited Anne Franks' house in Amsterdam once…"

"Your point being?"

"Was she always afraid or always brave? You see it's the same thing just two different words to describe an emotion. This isn't about tunnels, treasures or conspiracies; this is about truth and justice. Everyone that suffered deserves their own individual rectitude and virtue it's the decent and moral thing to do. I am scared, very scared but this has suddenly become so much more prodigious than a lunatic with a canister of tear gas."

Steve slips his hand into Louise's and focuses on the bewitching mirror image that glows an apricot sky and water.

"Has anyone seen Logan this morning?" asks Rina.

"No I haven't, is he in his room?" responds Russo.

"Checked there, can't find him anywhere..." Reade says "...try calling him please!"

"He's probably not been here all night! Somebody throws the words five hundred million dollars into the conversation that's enough to make anybody thirsty!" howls Steve. Russo, Reade and Rina exchange sharp glimpsed acknowledgements at each other.

"EVERYBODY GET IN!" screams Reade. He puts his foot down hard on the pedal and everybody thrashes about on the back seats and Russo tries frantically to keep up in the vehicle behind him.

"I hope he's not just in the toilet," whispers Louise into Steve's ear as the acceleration increases even more, so much so the dust off the wheels is so vigorous its causes a temporary visual disturbance against all the windows.

The vehicles screech and come to a sudden halt. Reade and Russo fly out of the cars and they soar up the stairs of the Oberfurhers office.

"I bloody knew it!.." screams Russo "...Don't you dare!"

Logan ignores him which riles a fury inside the normally very placid Reade.

"Logan I'm ordering you to stop! Right! Now!"

"I'm sick of all this messing about....we're getting nowhere and I AM doing this!" he snarls back at Russo.

The team congregate inside the doorway and Logan strategically places sticks of dynamite into the boreholes drilled into the concrete wall behind the fire place yesterday.

"No! You will cause a major cave-in!" screams Caleb "We have no idea how or what bombs are in that concrete or behind it. The tunnels will implode, like a building being demolished. Logan! Please?!"

"Stop now!" Rina screams and pulls a gun from beneath her jacket "I mean it Logan I will have no qualms, take the dynamite out.....Now! This whole thing will be ruined and for nothing!"

"Please?.." begs Ellia "...please Logan we can't risk this there will be other ways."

"Most definitely there will be many ways to get in. A network of tunnels will have many secondary shafts and air vents like we said yesterday, it's just a matter of locating them..." Hans pleads with Logan, "...The Lily codes are treasure map clues! Yamashita always built front and back doors to his tunnels, we just need to find them!"

"And what if another idiot tries to gas us or worse like yesterday hey? What's the point?" yells Logan.

"Logan please you're literally doing this blind, we could all die if there are bombs the other side of that concrete, we're talking World War 2 here not pirates and cannon balls...come on mate..." says Russo in an affable tone, "...the dynamite will cause a shock-wave shattering the concrete and the walls will implode not explode, it will all collapse inwards and have devastating knock on effects mate." Logan sighs and removes the long pillowed tubes out from the boreholes. Russo slowly lowers Rina's arm. She looks over at the stunned onlookers as they realise there's a lot more depth to the military support in this venture and doubtlessly more hand weapons than they originally thought.

Steve steps down out of the building and Louise hurries after him.

"Strange isn't it? How the sudden mention of treasure and millions of pounds sends everyone bat crazy?

"Do you think that's what he's after? To find this so called treasure first?" she quizzes.

"Oh, without doubt! Lou, where there is hunger there will be greed. Greed makes the mind selfish to the detriment of others...like this whole place it exudes a stench for power...even seventy five years later. It absolutely sucks."

"I've just had a reply about that symbol." Hans declares and stares at his phone, it detracts quite nicely from the very strained tense atmosphere. A few gather around him and stare at his phone.

'צוֹפָה - Guardian or Protector and definitely Hebrew'

"Interesting!.." exclaims Hans, "...what do you think?" he says and turns his attention toward Caleb and Arthur.
"Mmmm? Guardians of the tunnels? Guardians of treasure?" replies Arthur.
"Not sure?.." responds Caleb "...we're not even certain if any of this is related but very very interesting. Steve saw this on the ring and then we had the embossed letter..."
"Yeah...not to mention being attacked with canisters of gas!" Steve says and rolls his eyes.
Hans proceeds with his curiosity and ignores Steve "Even more interesting that it's Hebrew though... the original language of the Jews, not German, very intriguing!"
"What's the plan for today?" asks Ellia to the three professors.
"Hans and I have been thinking a lot more about Yamashita and the Golden Lily code..." replies Caleb "...the interesting thing about him was that he liked to build tunnels near to water sources....particularly water in fact..."
"Why?" she questions.
"...he had an intrinsic way of devising water traps

or cleverly devised booby traps. He would build a water reservoir shaft contained securely behind thin walls and if any treasure hunters breeched the wall the water would be released at some power, drowning them or sinking a case of treasure further."

"I'm liking your thoughts..." acknowledges Hans and points over at the lake "...well, we know the tunnel is directly underneath us and heading in that direction."

Hans and Caleb view over to Lake Schwedtsee, the tall memorial steel looks out and protects its vast beauty.

"There's way too much vegetation to hack back..." observes Arthur, "...you'll never get the GPR through all those trees and foliage!"

"Yep, you're absolutely right...how does a couple of metal detectors and a LiDAR sound?" replies Caleb with a big grin on his face.

"You have an actual LiDAR here?" Arthur replies his face lights up in sheer delight.

"I'm taking it that a LiDAR is another piece of prodigious equipment...," laughs Ellia "...and that is precisely why you are here Caleb!"

"And my one..." he says and pulls a large box off the back of the vehicle "...is fixed to a rather marvellous drone."

"It looks like a toy helicopter, well, sort of, but with 6 rotors instead," smiles Louise.

"Very similar concept, this is a hexacopter drone because of its 6 propeller rotor arms. This helps it to have a more stable flight and also much easier to control when the wind is strong..." he replies with all eyes on the drone hovering 2 meters off the ground "...but my main reason for bringing it was it would safely navigate us through the tunnels if they are a good size. It has a 360° sensor mounted underneath."

"Marvellous idea." Responds Hans and places his hand approvingly on Caleb's shoulder.

"So how does this work?" Louise smiles at her own certain conscientious interrogations.

"You do ask a lot of questions Lou." laughs Steve.

"Nothing wrong in learning..." she retorts "...how does it work...again!"

"Well, it uses pulses of laser light to measure the ground and creates a 3D map of the earth. It's extremely accurate, so if we send it over all those trees it's able to completely block them out like they don't even exist, strip it all back without ruffling a single leaf!..."

"Wow that's amazing!"

"...the first LiDAR appeared on the world stage at the Apollo 15 lunar landing mission in 1971 to map the surface of the moon. But this beauty is going to tell us any land elevation changes, rocks, water, tunnels, it can even detect roads and pathways from generations ago," says Caleb.

The screen image feedback is an exotic array of rainbow colours. Caleb momentarily makes a clenched fist and punches it excitedly into the air, which causes a commotion amongst the three men.

"We have gone from the little league soccer to the state championships everybody!" He hears the sound of his heart race and has an electrified giddiness. The colours glow and light up the tunnels beneath them and into the distance they become a cobweb of intricacy. A secret map is directly below them, a treasure map. They stare in awe at the screen and look up to glance over the landscape, then back to the monitor again to compare the physical reality against digital interpretation.

"Amazing!" yells Reade as he grabs a metal detector and beckons them all to head over towards the mini woodland. Caleb continues with the drone maps and they run with enthusiasm as they follow him.

"What do we need to be looking for?" enquires Rina.

"We need to head over to the left, can you see this? There are two pathways that come to dead ends, we can try and find a way into these," replies Caleb.

They hack their way through the overgrown grasses, climb down some rocks at the lakes edge that descends to a much lower ground level and into a tiny creek that's completely hidden from view. Steve turns to assist Louise down over the slippery rocks "Be careful."

"Isn't this beautiful?" she replies and watches the crystal clear water flow calmly through the mini creek with infinite tranquillity. She admires multi-coloured dragonflies dancing backwards and forwards then hover, almost motionless, above the water's diamond sparkle. The sun peeks tiny beams through the leaf canopy above, like miniscule spot lights on the dragonflies dance routines. They paddle in the shallow pool and directly to one side of the creek they spy a pile of large rock boulders all stacked together like nature had played a random game of Jenga. The rock mass spans a good three meters high and each individual rock being a meter in diameter, with many smaller pieces scattered in between.

"This is a very unusual rock formation," puzzles Hans.

"Look!.." points Arthur at a rock about a meter up "...a marker!"

"Grab me some water, I'm struggling to identify it..." he continues, Logan hands him his water flask and he washes the caked on mud off to clear the marker "...there's a definite carving there!"

"There's another!" shrieks Rina.

"...and here!" responds Russo.

Hans moves in closer to view the variety of carvings.

"This is what I believe to be a 'Story Rock'..." he says and cleans more dirt from the markings "...Story rocks and markers are just like treasure maps, we just need to figure out what they are trying to tell us!"

Reade wanders around the banks edge with the metal detector in hand. The entire group turn to view him when a pitchy thudding noise wails from the device. Reade kneels quickly and starts to dig around the dirt.

"It's all go!" squeals Louise and photographs the

rock markers and then snaps a picture of Reade.
"What have you found?" quizzes Ellia.
"A very long thick rusty nail..." he replies as high pitch wailing noises come from the metal detector, "...and another."
"Keep looking!" states Arthur adamantly.
"What for rusty old nails?" Reade wonders.
"Look at the length of them, what would they even be doing here so randomly? I'm guessing it's highly likely they've fallen from or come off wooden crates being taken into the tunnels? Keep looking."
Everything is quiet except for the dull murmur sounds of the hexacopter above and the occasional bleep from the metal detector.
"This place is so beautiful and serene it has quite sedative qualities," whispers Louise to Steve.
"Did you see that?" he whispers back.
"What?"
"I thought I saw movement or a shadow over there." He points.
"I can't see anything?"
"Shhh..." he signals in silence to alert Russo and Logan's attention and points to a small area the other side of the overgrowth. They crouch in unison and both grab their guns. They creep to the water's edge to evade being seen. The lurker spots them and makes chase, which quickly engages Russo and Logan into pursuit. Logan reaches the clearing back at Ravensbrück and just like fleeing prey the mysterious man vanishes. Logan raises his gun, hooks his finger over the trigger and fires it into the air.

"I'm getting Deja-vu" he grunts at Russo and they retreat back down to the creek.

"He's gone!" reassures Russo to the others.

"I really don't get what his problem is..." proclaims Ellia "...we have full permission to be here, he's the trespasser not us!"

"Everybody you need to see this!" shouts Hans. The group tiptoes around the creek and gather towards him.

"This is a 'Giveaway' marker. Look..."

He grabs a piece of chalk from a small tin of bits and pieces from his inside jacket pocket, he starts to colour in the chiselled areas around the high stacked boulders.

"Here...the square chiselled above the small hole."

"Which means?" asks Steve and snaps away with his camera.

"Giveaway markers are to distract treasure hunters with a small or nominal amount of treasure. The intention was to completely deflect them from a much larger quantity as a deterrent. It's usual that very close by there will be a small deposit and then a greater amount either below it or extremely close by...pass me a twig please Steve."

Steve pulls a brittle dry piece of twig off a branch that hangs nearby and passes it to Hans. Hans holds it in a pincer grip and places the twig directly into the hole beneath the square marker. He pushes it as far as it will go and uses his chalk to mark where it sticks out from the rock.

"The Japanese used the Shaku measurement system;

one shaku is about thirty and a half centimetres give or take a millimetre. This twig marking measures about ten centimetres so we're looking at approximately three and a half to four meters from this point..." he says "...Reade, move the detector in proximity to this marker."

"Does it work ok in water?" asks Ellia.

"Yes. These ones are waterproof..." responds Reade "...salt water can sometimes affect the mechanism, but we're in fresh water so technically it should be ok."

Reade scans the area and the soft vibrating noise of the hexacopter above bounces off the acoustics of the creek. Hans continues to chalk in the odd carved shapes around the story rock to make them more pronounced whilst the others wade through the water to look for clues and markings. Hans halts after shading in a triangular shape and swiftly pirouettes to scan his eyes over the dazzling brook.

"Reade! Go there!" he says to denote to a scant range in front of him. "We have a triangulation marker on this rock. See that other rock over there and that one across there?" he continues and spans his arms outwards in a large 'V' shape.

"Triangulation markers are an accepted technique to reclaim treasure in the future, three fixed points intentionally placed." He wades gracefully to the central point in between where Hans stands and the two shapely formations that sit regally out of the water. Instantly an orchestral array of high pitched beeps, thumps, blips and squeaks radiate beneath

Reade's feet. A moment of silence follows and echoed gasps, the group splashes zealously towards him, the slimy rocks beneath them cause them to slip. Ellia loses her footing lands on her bottom and the very capricious Logan holds out his hand to stand her up.

"Thank you," she whispers and he nods silently in acknowledgement.

Russo unclips the folding shovel attached to his backpack.

"Lou! Get the camera!" shouts Steve.

Russo digs purposely and after ten minutes he stops "It's no good the water and silt fill back in as quickly as I'm shifting it."

"Use the borehole drill," says Rina and passes it to him. The three minutes of drilling feels like twenty as the heightened exhilaration through the group becomes intensely contagious. They transfix on the drill until suddenly they hear a dense thud, a whining spinning sound followed by a cascade of bubbles being released from the cavity. Russo rushes forward and uses the drill to make numerous more holes with the same enthusiasm.

"Reade....crow bar!" he says.

With multiple efforts large splinters of wood crack and split, they pull hard at the pieces to dislodge them from the crate and throws them behind.

"I can't see its way to murky where we've disrupted the area," says Russo as he drops onto his knees and lunges his hand downward into the expanse.

The tension is excruciating and he pulls up a solid

gold bar. Elation and cheers fill them as they shake hands and hug.

"Let me see it please..." says Arthur "...look, the inscriptions here are from the Deutsche Reichsbank and hallmarked with the Nazi eagle and Swastika!"

Russo continues to pass the gold bars up and shares them amongst the others. Everyone's pumped with excitement and examine them scrupulously with trembling hands. They all seem to forget the traumatic events of the previous day and feel an intense buzz of euphoric electricity run through their veins.

"That's all of them, how many are there?" Russo says and gets back onto his feet.

"Eighteen!" Ellia cheers and washes the dirt off the two bars she holds down into the water.

Steve is distracted by Caleb who's across the other side of the creek with his back to them all. The LiDAR is on the floor beside him, no one has even noticed the silence of its propellers in all the pandemonium.

"Caleb?.." says Steve "...isn't this incredible? Can you even believe it?"

But Caleb doesn't answer, he pulls apart two overhanging branches and stares in complete silence through the parted clearing. Steve steps up to look over Caleb's shoulder. Behind all the dense vegetation is a strategically placed stack of rock boulders. Unlike the story rock at the creek these are not smooth, but pointed shards of rock maybe from an explosion. Some of them had fallen from the upper part of the stack to expose the top of a man-made cement archway.

Chapter 23

One by one the others all come over to see what Caleb and Steve are looking at. If all the fan-fair of finding the gold bars wasn't exhilarating enough they are all faced with a definite doorway. Ellia has dreamed of this moment for seven years and her Grandmother for about seventy five years. They clamber through the overgrowth and hack back branches to remove the immediate restrictive rubble in their path. They make a convoy and pass the blasted pieces of rock that blocks the entrance. Two hours pass of hard labour, they find old lamps and relics of potato masher grenades, but nobody notices the time that passes, the euphoria is beyond stimulating. The doorway arches majestically and spans three meters in width and a good two meters high.

"It looks a lot like Mussolini's super bunker in Monte Soratte," exclaims Arthur.

The formation of the arch is solid concrete and in the centre an iron double doorway, a crest shape and covered in rust. The double doors display a four pointed star mid-point and the rust from it stains the sides of its concrete structure like splashes of naturally formed graffiti. They admire the impressive architecture in its state of neglect. On the right door is a square bolt with a long armed lever. Hans steps forward with an adjustable spanner and screws it tight onto the square.

"Hans wait!.." shouts Arthur "...what if there's explosives or traps here too?"

"We need to get in, we have to try at least or we can keep procrastinating the same way at every point we arrive at. It's a risk, but we need to start somewhere."

"I'll do it!" interrupts Reade "Everybody... stand back."

"Are you sure?" questions Rina and he nods with an insincere smile.

He takes hold of the spanner and turns the square bolt and lifts the lever. Reade pulls very slowly and the heavy door swings towards him, the rust on the large hinges screech with each tug. A peaceful stillness swamps the party temporarily. Hushed placidity envelops them and they calmly survey the condensed obscure interior corridor.

"I can't believe it," mumbles Ellia in her melodic Italian tone.

"Everyone needs to put their hard hats and goggles on, also get your torches out..." expresses Caleb "...we have no idea how secure this structure is."

Logan and Reade light up their torches and shine them down the length of the passageway and scan up and down the bunker walls.

"There!" Logan says and points at about two meters up on the left hand wall "A fuse box."

"Surely it won't work?" quizzes Steve.

Logan hovers his light over the switches and on his tip-toes he flicks them upwards. A dull whir and

hum echoes around them and bounces off the concrete walls. In succession multiple staggered lights fizz and illuminate the bulbs all the way along lighting up the entire bunker. Exuberant joy engulfs the troupe and they say nothing, in awe they gawk at the vast formation in front of them. Louise loses temporary grip of the camera.
"You ok?" asks Steve.
"This is unbelievable," she replies and steadies her hold.
"We've just made history everyone!" declares Ellia in high pitched emotion.
"Astonishing!" responds Arthur.

They guess the walls span into a length of about a kilometre that decline into a small scope in the far distance.
"This is huge!" declares Rina.
On each side of the main tunnel are multiple doors all the way along it. Some of the walls host drawings made by soldiers that spent their time down there, in an attempt to try and make it look more homely than a cold grey cell. Some of the drawings are very appealing despite the occasional Swaztika. Old beer bottles and corroding tins of food are scattered along the floor. Various cables run along the upper edge of the walls and pieces of furniture, chairs, tables all lie in disarray as if it had been abandoned in a panic.
"We're going to have to be just as cautious opening each door as we were at the start..." says Caleb "...if

any are already open we should be ok, but we must stick together. I'm thinking the best thing to do is walk this passageway, if any of the doors are open we can scout those areas and rooms. Any doors that are shut we leave for later in the week, we need to assess what maybe behind before accessing them... safety is paramount!"

"Carry on using the detector Reade and we need to go back to the creek and excavate it in meticulous detail later this week too..." responds Hans "...I still haven't highlighted all the markings."

Ellia touches his arm to calm him "It's not going anywhere Professor Tassin, look at all of this." She reassures him with encouragement.

"I suppose I had pictured the tunnels in my head as dank, claustrophobic and murky, I hadn't really considered these elaborately arched and vast hallways," Louise says and looks at a small glass dish still full of old decaying cigarette butts.

The air smelt of a stagnant stale moistness. Steve reads the names engraved into the top of a wooden table and messages to other soldiers, he doesn't understand them they're all in German but he smiles at the cartoon characters of Hitler and Churchill etched and drawn in several areas. The first open door to their right is a small oval room, it resembles a giant chimney shaft that ascends straight up about ten metres. On the ground are four cylinder tubed iron rods that stick vertically out of the solid concrete floor. Arthur shines his torch up the enormous vent.

"I think this may have been an observation post, look at these cylinder rods down here," he says.

"Yep, I think you're right," replies Russo.

"What are they for?" questions Steve. His query makes Louise giggle as it's usually herself with the exhausting inquiries.

"Those rods would have hosted a platform that elevated on turrets up to the observation slits around the top there..." Arthur answers and shines his torch back up the vent "...can you see those thin rectangular sheets of metal drilled into the walls around the top? Originally they would have been observation slits."

"I wonder why they covered them over and removed the platform?.." questions Louise "...well, seeing as they seemed to have left everything else in a panic, it would be very strange to remove them?"

"Well maybe Miss Randall, unless they moved them along to use in another post where the mechanism may have failed," replies Hans.

Slowly they wander along the gloomy cylindrical man-made complex. Its oppressive horizontal featureless arches amaze Ellia.

"Why are all the corridors and passageways arched like that?" she asks.

"They were built this way in case there was a shock-wave impact. The arch is usually strong enough to hold the impact and avoid collapse," replies Arthur. The next ten rooms they arrive at are large sleeping dormitories, five dorms on each side of the tunnel and span some considerable length. Each dormitory hosts twenty five sets of bunk beds where the soldiers spent their nights. Every bunk is wooden built, metal sprung and the mouldy decaying mattresses are only about three inches deep.

"It's hard to believe soldiers actually occupied these lifeless concrete shells," says Ellia.

Louise thinks at how much nicer the sleeping arrangements were compared to what was in the ladies camp behind them and how many of the female prisoners had to share just one bed. Beside each bunk is a double unit for the soldiers to keep their personal effects.

"Come and see this!.." Reade calls out and opens one of the cabinets, "...some of their personal pieces are still in here!"

"Really?" responds Caleb and opens a drawer to see for himself "'Feldwebel Schmidt 17.09.1925' this is a Soldbuch. The soldiers handed these in to each administration unit. They contained information about their assignments, battles, injuries or illnesses. Feldwebel, I believe, was an Army Technical Sergeant?"

"Yes it was," agrees Hans.

"Oh my goodness, check out this perfectly preserved bar of chocolate!" Steve says and holds it up, "Peter's Schokolade..."

"NO!" scream Hans, Caleb and Arthur, the unison is so together and dramatic it is as if it had been rehearsed.

"It's ok guys... I'm not going to actually eat it! Jeez!" Steve laughs and shakes his head in disbelief.

"You don't understand Steve," Caleb rushes forward and meticulously takes the chocolate bar out of Steve's hand and slowly lowers it onto the floor, very gently as if it is made of porcelain. They all watch and think the professors have completely lost their minds with their overly zealous theatrics.
"Reade, run the detector over the chocolate bar!" beckons Caleb.
He hover's the device over the chocolate and it makes very pronounced noises that sends confusion amongst them all.
"Ok...explain?.." stresses Steve feeling very humbled "...is it the internal wrapping?"
"No. This is a bomb," replies Caleb.
"In a chocolate bar?" laughs Ellia, but her laughs more of a nervous impulse than actually finding the situation funny.
"One of the most ingenious booby traps by the Germans during World War 2..." continues Caleb "...Peter's chocolate bars were definitely a candy to die for – quite literally. They coated the steel with a dusting of real chocolate to make It look like an authentic confection, but as soon as the unsuspecting victim breaks off the end strip of chocolate it pulled on a canvas primer that's directly connected to the explosive...seven seconds later this little candy trap...BOOM!"
"For real?"
"Oh yes Steve, for real. The Nazi's found many ways to hide bombs in inanimate objects. Food sources were brilliant because the entire world was hun-

gry and on rations, tins of food and bars of chocolate were excellent ways...ingenious in all honesty. Baron Rothschild once defused a booby trap bomb in a consignment of onions."

"German spies landed on the southern coast of Ireland," interrupts Arthur "with apparently four tins of peas they hoped to sneak into Buckingham Palace..."

"Yes these weren't the brightest of men!" laughs Caleb.

"...the very first gentleman they ran into they asked him if he could take them to the I.R.A..." Arthur laughs and pauses for a moment "...of course he took them straight to the local Garda Police instead."

"Well, it takes on a whole new meaning to 'Death by Chocolate'" says Steve.

"There is so much here! We're going to be cataloguing all of this for a very long time," Hans observes as he looks at the vast extent of items.

"We can worry about all of that later, but you're right, so much work to be done..." agrees Caleb "...and many more rooms to look in yet," he smiles.

The group continues to venture along the main passageway and stop occasionally to stare at an object or artefact. Arthur and Louise lag behind the others,

"Some of the archways span slightly higher in places," she observes.

The corridor midway is airless and would be particularly featureless if it wasn't for the debris decorating its gritty floor.

"There's so much junk everywhere!" she continues.

"Not junk Louise, every piece is history. I would like to say 'messy & discarded' but definitely not junk!.." responds Arthur "...do you know, some people will pay a fortune for the tiniest of war relics, this is literally an Aladdin's Cave."

"Even without the real treasure..." she grins, "...what are those wires going up the wall there?" She questions and uses her camera lens to zoom in on them. Arthur moves in closer to inspect a bundle of cables that enter another area with a viewing window directly into the room. He wipes dust off the glass to see an office full of communication equipment on two long wooden desks, radio devices, high & low-band receivers which allowed the soldiers to listen and transmit information. Arthur momentarily admires all the antennas, wires, dials and machinery and shouts in an excited tone up the tunnel to the other Professors, his voice bounces like springy elastic off the sides of the tunnel walls,

"Hans! Caleb!"

He grabs hold of the handle, Louise steps back to film Arthur's sheer delight but she feels her feet propel off of the floor and her whole body being launched at high speed backwards. Disorganised confusion ignites amongst them all as they all involuntarily dive face-down onto the floor. The explosion in the passage way deafens, a pain howls in their ears that makes them hold the side of their heads tightly in an effort to stifle and block the griping discomfort. Smoke and dust shoots quickly along the corridor and forces them to remove their hands from their ears to frantically put on their gas masks. The flash of instant smoky pollution causes a foreboding panic and fear. In the haze of thick cloud Steve hears a lot of crashes, terrified and unsettled he thinks the tunnel is collapsing. He shifts himself backwards and sits up against the wall. He isn't sure if this is the right thing to do; he thinks if the tunnel collapses did it really matter anyway. Commotion and bemusement restrains them all in a helpless turmoil, they can't see each other the smoke cloud renders them in a veiled trap of utter blindness. They stay completely still and motionless for what seems like ages. Slowly the smog of dust gently descends with gravity. Reade and Logan switch on their torches and flash it back up the corridor. The passage is shrouded in a veil of powdered fragments that hinder the view. Sounds of the last few blasted crumbles of cement roll onto the floor and all is totally silent. They battle to focus all muted and voiceless and try to take in and discern what just happened. Gradually one at a time they stand up and gaze back along the way they had come. An accumulation of cement and rubble now blocks the tunnel and completely seals the original entrance.

"Louise!" Steve screams and runs back to her as the enormity and panic hits him.

"Arthur?" shrieks Ellia, her voice muffles through her mask.

In unison they battle against the settling dust and blindly work their way back. Steve finds Louise lying unconscious and covered in a thick layer of dust. He spots a large boulder a matter of inches away from her head, he thinks to himself she's lucky it would have flattened her skull for sure.

"Lou? Lou?" he says and gently shakes her shoulders. She groans and moves her head and very slowly opens her eyes.

Steve uses his hand to wipe the dust off her face,

"I've definitely had better weeks!" she coughs and winces in pain as she tries to sit. Logan kneels down beside her and gives her his water flask.

"Oh my body hurts and my head...!" she whines.

Steve turns to view the others as they slowly remove their masks in total silence. They stare in disbelief at Arthur. Ellia wails, drops to her knees and sobs.

"Get him out...get him out!" screams Rina. She clambers over large fragments of rubble and begins to frantically throw clusters of the concrete. Arthur's lifeless warm body is buried from his chest down under the lumber, only his face and left arm are all that is visible. Caleb crouches beside him to feel for a pulse or breathing, he shakes his head sadly to the others and doesn't say a word.

"Help me!" wails Rina anxiously "Help me please-.....please."

She sits onto the debris and places her head into her hands. She caresses the dog-tag tattoo affectionately and lets out a mournful whimper and rocks herself to alleviate her pain. Ellia holds Arthur's face in her hands, cries out in despair "Sono cosi dispiaciuto" she lifts his hand up to her cheek and nestles her face affectionately into it. Her tears stain miniscule little tracks down her dusty skin. The hexacopter is remotely visible under the debris.

"It's completely crushed. Were we attacked again?" quizzes Rina quietly and tries to absorb the surroundings.

"No I don't think so?.." replies Russo. He investigates the doorway to the communication room, which is now completely destroyed "...a trip wire. Sadly I think it detonated when the door was opened."

They sit in silence, sip water, wash their faces and throw sporadic sympathetic glances to Ellia, she's very distressed and cradles Arthurs face in her lap.

"Has anyone got phone signal?.." questions Steve "...we need to get help."

They all look at their phones, but all shake their heads in the negative.

Rina sighs

"We can't go back this way now we have to find another way out to get help and alert the authorities about Arthur."

"We can't just leave him here!" wails Ellia. Caleb crouches down next to her gently places his hand onto her back

"What else can we do Ellia? You can stay with him whilst we try to find another way out nobody would blame you."

"It's all my fault," she sobs.

"Arthur was a very intelligent man Ellia, he waited all this time for you to experience all of this because he wanted it as much as the rest of us."

They crouch and tap Arthur's shoulder gently in succession.

"I'm coming back for you Arthur," whispers Ellia.

Chapter 24

"Are you ok to walk?" Steve asks and helps Louise to her feet.

She wobbles unsteadily to regain her balance.

"I'm sure I'll be ok. My back and head hurt a bit. Steve, I'm so sorry but I think I broke the video camera," she responds nervously.

"Lou, like I said yesterday it's your health that's more important."

He checks the SD card and places it in his wallet, "we'll chuck this camera away...we have more," his voice encourages and is sincere, he smiles and helps her to step over the rubble.

"I think everyone should keep checking now and then for phone signal. Please do not open any closed doors, I'll have to get a specialist team down here to sift through and find any further exploding devices and bombs..." says Russo "...in the meantime we really do need to stay safe!"

"I agree..." replies Hans "...these buildings were made with air shafts and multiple exists, we just have to keep our wits about us."

"I'm glad the electrics didn't fail with the blast..." whispers Rina to Reade "...I feel completely shut in and claustrophobic now."

The past hour and losing Arthur begins to take its toll. The fear of being trapped amplifies in their minds but nobody addresses the issue. If this isn't enough mental drama already to battle, the next room causes a gut wrenching quietness amongst them. It's the largest room they have embarked upon, bigger than all the dormitories. The walls, floor and ceiling are all painted white. The space is sterile, the room is a laboratory. Its appearance resembles an old fashioned hospital ward, a few beds down one end and long reclining couches similar to antique dentistry chairs. In the centre of the room, two surgical operating tables adjacent to each other with an approximate 2 meter gap between. The tables both host overhead surgical theatre lights and there are lots of trolleys with various implements and clinical tools. There's a large fridge still with many vials and bottles inside it, stethoscopes and sphygmomanometers lying in various points around the laboratory.

"What's that huge device?.." gasps Louise.

The contraption stands with two long steel supports both about ten centimetres in diameter, approximately two meters in length and a metre apart from each other. The steel supports stand majestically up from the floor and a large screen sits squarely in between them. From the centre of the supports are large bolted arms that face directly forward and holds a smaller square plate at about chest height. The smaller screen plate seems to move with the variety of lever and pulleys "...it looks like some type of crushing torture machine?" She whispers.

"It's an old x-ray machine," Hans reassures her and points to the very rudimentary radiograph of leg bones clipped on the vintage x-ray light.

Steve feels a chill go through his body, he turns to Ellia and Louise, an anxiety fills his torso with the sudden recognition this could be the exact room Viktor Otto-Wolff had told them about. In the left hand corner is a large desk and a swivel chair. The desk has a set of three locked drawers down its right hand side. Lots of handwritten documents and notes scatter its top and numerous files. Next to the desk stands four metal filing cabinets, each cabinet has six deep drawers. Hans pulls out one of the drawers and removes a brown cardboard file. On the front is a sepia black and white photograph of a young lady.

"Helga Morallheff 07.10.1927 aged 16," he reads aloud.

They gaze into the open drawer of the filing cabinet "There's got to be about two hundred files in this drawer, if these are all full..." exclaims Steve looking in disbelief at the twenty four drawers.

"It's going to be in the thousands Steve," replies Ellia.

"What does it say about her Hans?" Louise enquires, she doesn't understand the written German.

He clears his throat "she was Polish, arrived in 1941. She was a twin; her twins name was Heike..."

Reade immediately stares at Hans, his thoughts are soon consumed with his twin boys back home, he looks in the drawer and the very next file is Heike's. Various photos of the two teenagers had been taken in varying stages of confinement.

"...sadly twins were of immense interest in experimentation."

"This is what we came here for everyone. Well, Louise and myself anyway. Not treasures or relics. We came to find out what happened to the children. This is our part in this journey, so do we continue looking for an exit or at least look through the lab for evidence or any information about the children?.." questions Steve, "...I can't read German, so could really do with your help please Hans."

He looks at Ellia's puffy eyes, the sore red eyes seem to be a daily occurrence. She nods at Steve to explore the laboratory and stay for a while.

"You know what doesn't make any sense?.." starts Louise "...Viktor said they just shut the door on the experiment and left when the allied forces liberated the camp. I haven't seen anything in the tunnels that would make me suspect any children lived here? It's completely abandoned, as if it was vacated in a hurry by the German soldiers."

"This is very true Lou, but there are doors we haven't opened..." replies Steve.

"For obvious reasons!" interrupts Rina.

"...yes, I mean that maybe their story lies behind another door?"

"Well, after poor Arthur was taken by a booby-trap we need to be highly meticulous about opening any closed doors. The reality is Steve, you may not get the exact answers you initially came for, but a lot more answers than you started out with," replies Reade.

"Intriguing!" Caleb interrupts and thumbs through an old book scattered with another on the operating table.

"What is it?" asks Logan.

"Very unusual it's the 'Book of Enoch' and this one here is the 'Book of Giants'" Caleb replies, his face looks baffled as he holds them up and gestures to Hans.

"What are they? Like books from the Bible?" quizzes Louise.

"Well sort of, yes and no to that question. These texts are not in the final Bible Canon as we have it today; but it's very intriguing as to why they would be in here like this," says Caleb.

"No...no..no.., something's amiss, look at these..." Hans says and points to tiny pieces of parchment secured tightly behind two pieces of glass. Each glass display hangs along the wall like decorative artwork. Nine of these designs sit simultaneously along the laboratory wall. Very warily Hans removes one of them off its hook and places it onto the surgical table.

"Do you think these lights will work?" he smiles to Steve.

Steve follows the wires from the overhead surgical light across the ceiling and down the wall to a set of sockets. He flicks it up and an intense operating light shines brightly which illuminates the entire laboratory. Lights inside the glass-front refrigerators flicker and the whole room glows. Caleb looks directly opposite to the other side of surgical table at Hans "Do you think it is?"

"It can't be they weren't discovered until two or three years after the war ended. Ravensbrück had already been liberated and closed by then?"

"I agree this absolutely makes no sense... but then again, nothing about anything that's been happening here makes any sense."

"What are they?" questions Reade.

"No, this really doesn't add up," Hans reiterates.

"It could only mean that these tunnels haven't been shut since the end of the war at all! Even if these are fake copies, how would anyone have known to duplicate them and bring them down here years after the war?" states Caleb.

"Hey, Professors, what are they?" Reade repeats.

"They appear to be some of the fragments found in the Dead Sea Scrolls near Qumran," says Hans in a heightened confused tone.

"But they shouldn't be here I take it?"

"The timeline is wrong..." replies Caleb "...the Dead Sea Scrolls were found sometime between 1946 & 47 and the other caves were discovered during the decade that followed that."

"I thought all the manuscripts and pieces of parchments from the caves and Qumran, are in Jerusalem?" says Steve, and his mind flashes back to his dear neighbour Mrs Sanders. He has quite a bit of knowledge about the Qumran site as her husband had been an archaeologist's assistant there.

"...Another treasure hunt story Steve. The first parchment was found by a Bedouin looking for his lost goat. As soon as archaeologists realised the significant implication of the Bedouin's discovery it was a mass treasure hunt to find more scrolls amongst the locals, scientists and the Bedouin tribe. They were the first writings discovered on parchments for a long time. A lot of the writings they found were about the teachings of a Jewish civilisation called the Essenes who lived at Qumran, their rules, beliefs, prayers and some Biblical texts. How they are here in this lab is a total mystery, but the locals in Israel may have sold pieces of the writings to private collectors rather than declaring them, a lot of smuggling goes on in artefacts" Caleb replies.

"The curious thing was that the Book of Giants and Enoch were found amongst the Dead Sea Scrolls and also at the excavation site of Qumran, where it is believed all of the scrolls were originally written before being hidden away in the caves," expands Hans.

"I've never heard of the Book of Enoch or the Book of Giants?.." puzzles Ellia "...they're not in the Bible?"

"They didn't have to be..." continues Hans, "...many writings are not all considered as 'inspired'. They are ancient writings from an ancient civilisation. The Jews wrote many tales, teachings, beliefs that never made it into the Bible...or the Canon as its known."

"Canon?"

"The final accepted writings that make up the Old and New Testaments. The Bible was written by various people over a period of more than a 1000 years between 1200 B.C.E and the first century C.E. The Essenes esteemed Enoch as a very special man of God. These two books are comprehensive narratives expanding on the story in Genesis...in a lot more detail. The book of Enoch was extremely revered by many Jews, and others disputed it because it is about the reign of the one thousand year Messianic kingdom and a book specifically written for 'The Last Days'. A lot of the Jews rejected Christ and this book prophesied about him in great detail. It's like anything in history, many humans can write about a version or story of an event, each story is similar but each one will be from the writer's perspective making it just a little bit different to another person writing about it."

"But why aren't these two books in the Bible if they are so significant to Genesis?" asks Louise.

"Well Emperor Constantine was very worried about the extreme religious conflicts and utter disorder within his empire, it had been going on for hundreds of years..." says Hans "...so he gathered a council of men together to try and unite them together called the Council of Nicea..."

"Oh! I know this story! Ian McKellen tells it in The Da Vinci Code movie!" she responds very impressed that her movie knowledge has some credence.

"...yes..." Hans chuckles "...although it caused a lot of arguing about merging beliefs together and gave birth to Christianity which Emperor Constantine allowed to further his own political ends, pretty much the same as politicians today! Anyway, I digress...these men argued in detail about which writings were to be acknowledged in the Bible and which writings were to be disputed. The movie credits the Council of Nicea as to which books made it into the Bible but that there's more to embellish on that story. Christian Bishops agreed which writings would be included into the Bible that we know it today. The church reformer Martin Luther was the one who published his own German translation of the Bible and from his 'picky' version we pretty much have that rendition today. He really didn't like many writings and deemed them heretical and tailored his translation of the Bible to ratify his own doctrines. He had issues with the book of James, and stuck James, Hebrews, Jude and Revelation at the back of his translation because he thought them to be very 'questionable'. The Book of Enoch and the Book of Giants were not included amongst the accepted writings because many men believed the content would be too terrifying for people to read and comprehend. Many people believe that the Book of Enoch was supposed to be found by a very distant 'future' generation to understand and unlock its secrets."

"Did that future generation ever transpire and who gave these men the authority to cherry pick and choose what writings should make the cut?" Louise continues enthusiastically.

"Not as far as I know and exactly that Miss Randall. A lot of people believe that the future generation are the ones living in the 'Last Days' that will be able to unlock its secrets. When the scrolls were discovered by the Dead Sea an eruption of terror and fear broke out in the Roman Catholic Church by what the archaeologists might discover, they had covered it all up and called it apocryphal. People won't accept the books out of fear. Look how many women throughout history were burnt or drowned for being witches? They were just intelligent ladies, the men feared that and destroyed them. The Council of Nicea & Luther twisted so many truths, removing Biblical teachings and sacred books. The book of Enoch didn't fit in at all well with the invention of the Trinity, so they couldn't possibly include it in their version of the Bible. Out of complete fear a lot of other religions have followed the Church in their decision to exclude it calling it Apocrypha..." Hans exclaims.

"What's that?" She asks.

"...the word apocrypha comes from the Greek for 'secret' or 'hidden'. The strangest thing is this German priest Luther also expressed an opposing and violent outlook towards Jews and requested the destruction of their synagogues and their deaths, just like Hitler. Yet Christ was a Jew, what gave Luther the right to decide which Jewish writings were 'inspired' and which ones were not is ridiculous. I've heard many argue that if God would want these texts in his sacred book he would make it happen, but can you imagine it? Someone trying to put the writings back that Luther removed. People wouldn't accept the correction, they can tend to be a naive or frightened."

"But why did the Essenes and other scribes write so many copies of these two specific books found at Qumran and in the Dead Sea Caves?" asks Ellia.

"Basically because they didn't have printing presses back in those days; we can pop down to a book shop, in ancient times they duplicated every single book multiple times by hand so the people could read the teachings and practices," replies Steve.

"That's right, scribes were very important people..." continues Hans "...but they may have also written so many copies because maybe they knew it's prophesies were so incredibly precious people would try to abolish it. The Book of Enoch may not have been written by Enoch himself no one actually knows, but by inspired men prophesying his story and expanding on what happened in Enoch's day and what's to occur in the Last Days. The Qumran community considered the Enochic texts as extremely precious and so important that they retained many copies of it and buried the others in the caves by the Dead Sea, the scrolls were the original Time-Capsules. In fact they were so meaningful to the Essenes they had more copies' of the Book of Enoch in comparison to all the other texts the archaeologists found there..." replies Hans, "...many people reject the Enochic texts found amongst the Dead Sea Scrolls purely out of fear. They argue that it may not have been written by Enoch so cannot be authentic, but Genesis happened many centuries before Moses walked the earth and he wrote that. You also have to consider that the argument of the Enoch books' unknown author is incredibly weak. People rant 'it wasn't written by Enoch, we don't know who wrote it!' The reason this is a profoundly controversial and shaky argument is because there are many Bible books whose authors were unknown....so who knows?"

"What do you mean by that, which books?" Ellia interrupts again.

"Ok, well Moses wrote all about the creations beginnings, the first humans, the flood, Abraham, Isaac, Joseph and his technicoloured coat and many many other characters..."

"I love that musical!" whispers Lou.

"...but he wrote all about these characters many centuries later. So why couldn't it be possible that someone wrote about Enoch centuries later too? We don't know who wrote the books of Kings or Samuel. Judges, Joshua and Ruth also have mysterious unknown authors. It is believed that the book of Isaiah may have been partially written by his loyal followers long after his death, many years in fact - exactly like Enoch's followers. One thing we do know for sure is the Apostles clearly revered the writings in the book Enoch because Matthew, Mark, Luke and John all quote word for word direct passages exactly how they were written in Enoch. In the Bible book of Jude he quotes from the written passage and prophesy of Enoch and credits Enoch directly. Jude actually states that Enoch had prophesied, his words specifically state this and quotes the Enochic scripture word for word. But Enoch certainly hadn't done this anywhere in the Genesis account, Moses just wrote about Enoch's existence and definitely not any prophesy, so where was Jude quoting it from? Was he reciting from the same writings his Qumran neighbours were meticulously duplicating multiple copies of? Jude's book almost didn't make it into the Canon as well, Luther considered his book as dubious and the Early Church disputed it being able to make the cut of their very calculated choices. There was a lot of discussion surrounding the Book of Enoch being included in the Canon by a few people from the Early Church but they didn't put it in the Bible, well not our common day diluted version, there are many faiths around the world that have kept it in their version of the Canon. He removed many other texts like the book of Maccabees and Esdras...actually to be completely honest, there are quite a few missing."

Caleb picks up the book and gently fans its aging pages with his thumb. He nods at Hans' exceptional knowledge with sincere appreciation and responds zealously.

"We do know that the Qumran community perished at the hands of the Romans in or around 68AD, just a couple of years earlier in 66AD the Jewish population had rebelled against the Roman Empire. Fast forward a further two years after the slaughter and extermination in Qumran the Romans marched onto Jerusalem and destroyed the temple in 70AD. The destruction was beyond catastrophic, but the annihilation of this eclectic little society in Qumran proved conclusively that they co-existed alongside the time Jesus and his followers were causing dissent amongst the people a few decades earlier. So bearing this fact in mind is the very intriguing Biblical passages quoting Enoch's book word for word by the Apostles throughout the New Testament. People really shouldn't worry about what secrets the scrolls could reveal but consider them as very precious gifts from our ancestors." The enthusiasm in Caleb's words are deeply passionate.

"But this doesn't explain why these ancient pieces of parchment are here?" wonders Russo.

"You're right…" responds Caleb "…but somebody seems to think they are significant enough to bring them all the way down here in this bunker. The only way we can confirm if they are from the Dead Sea is to get the pieces examined."

"How can we do that?" asks Ellia.

"Clever equipment is able to carbon date the fragments to confirm if they are from the Dead Sea caves. Even if they are digital copies it still means somebody has been here since the war," replies Caleb.

Hans places one of the glass encased fragments into this back pack, "We need to keep looking in this laboratory there might be clues as to how they got here."

Reade, Russo and Rina take to the filing cabinets and look through all the files that documented the experiments performed on the female prisoners. The others spread out around the laboratory to examine documents and photographs. Steve opens the large refrigeration unit that contains an extensive stack of bottles, vials and ampoules. He holds one up and stares into the crystallised mixture. Louise sits on the swivel chair and tries to open the set of three drawers under the desk, but they're locked securely. Logan takes a crowbar from his bag.

"Is there anything you don't have in there?" she giggles.

"We didn't know if we needed to crank open any doors," he answers wedges it into the drawer, forcefully breaking the latch. She pulls out some tatty green files, all stamped in red ink with the words 'STRENG GEHEIM' on them.

"Professor Tassin what does this mean?" she asks holding them up to him.

"Top Secret," he replies and takes hold of the top file and starts to read its content. Louise pulls out the files from the other two drawers and stacks them all onto the desk. Logan is instantly distracted by the now empty bottom drawer and taps it with his knuckle.

"What's the matter?" inquires Louise.

"The depth of this drawer is shallower than the other two..." he says and pulls it completely out "... it's heavy."

He shakes it and he hears something move below the base of the drawer. He grabs the crowbar tears into the base severing the wood, it splits as he wrenches the bar back and extracts a black metal box. They all gather beside him to survey his find. The box is rectangular about twenty five centimetres in width and thirty five centimetres in length, together with a depth of ten centimetres. It's apparent the box opens into two pieces with hinges at its back and a small keyhole on the front. On its top is a raised circular dial with a heart shaped indentation hosting a pattern imprinted in its centre.

"It's extremely fastened..." he asserts and tries to move the dial "...nope, completely jammed!"

Ellia comes forward to examine the dial and turns to acknowledge Steve and Louise. Endorsing her expression Louise recognizes Ellia's speculation without a word. Louise nods in agreement. She removes Heidi's locket from around her neck and takes out the small key inside. Her hands shake in impatient agitation as she places it into the small lock. It fits perfectly and the lock clicks as it turns but the lid doesn't lift. She ponders the dial on its top, places the front of the locket into it the pearl cherubs that sits comfortably within the indentation. She feels the anxious moistness in her hands and rotates the round dial with a swift twist. The box unfastens and cautiously Ellia uncovers the top of the box to unveil its contents. More files although this time the covers are marked with the title 'DNA1333'.

Ellia picks up a notebook that contains a multitude of numbers and equations and flicks its pages. On the front are the words 'DAS NEPHILIM ASSIGNMENT'.

"Well...that's what the DNA stands for then," she declares and passes it to Hans.

Each filed docket is individual to every child. It contains a photograph of the children, all from different nationalities and backgrounds, their ages, limb and various body measurements. The measurements are recorded onto a graph that catalogued their growth. Caleb counts twenty six files. Ten of which were considered to have been failed attempts at creating the perfect serum and the other sixteen were successful. Hans reads a diary record from a file about a six year old boy named Elijah.

"Elijah has grown five inches in four months. He is crying all the time complaining of severe headaches and has extreme mood changes, tiredness, fatigue and apparent vision problems. The 1333 growth hormone is producing excessive growth in the soft tissues and bones significantly increasing his blood pressure; Along with a rapid heart rate and irritability. Adrenocorticotropic hormone has caused weight-gain; he's bruising easily and definitive stretch marks on arms and legs; thickening of his skull and jaw denoting Acromegaly along with Gigantism.'"

Steve becomes distracted by a small piece of paper that sticks out of the Book of Giants on the surgical table. He wanders over to take a look whilst the others pass around various files of the children. He pulls it out of the book, it's folded into four and he unravels it. Steve realises it's been ripped in half and its contents are a collection of letters and numbers.

"What is somatotropin?" he asks.

"It's a growth hormone..." answers Caleb and he takes the piece of paper "...this is the growth formula!" he shouts.

"It's incomplete," replies Steve.

"They discovered a way to induce tumours into the pituitary gland!"

"That's precisely what Viktor told us," responds Ellia.

"Where are the children?" Steve says and walks out of the lab.

Chapter 25

They all follow Steve in succession and exit the laboratory.
"Do you think Viktor lied to us about never coming back here?" wonders Louise.
"Who knows Lou? Lying is the least of his crimes!" snaps Steve.
"But why did he give the locket to Heidi? 'The key to his heart'... Maybe he did love the children and hoped they would be found."
"Narcissist! If he loved them he'd have come back himself!"
They ramble along the passageway and arrive at an end with two separate tunnels that split from it, one to the left and one to the right.
"Which way now? We need to get out, has anyone got any phone signal yet?" asks Reade.
"Nothing!" answers Rina "Let's toss a coin, heads to the right and tails to the left."
She flips a coin into the air "Right!"
A reasonable five minutes pass into their disheartened hike along the dank hallway and they arrive to a large unlocked metal gate that leads to an Officer's Mess Hall. Rows upon rows of long tables all edged with multiple chairs. The tables present with the odd pieces of crockery, trays, cutlery, the odd cruet set and extremely old newspapers. It's not long until they hit another dead end although this time

the end of the tunnel Russo holds his arms out each side to prevent them going any further. The wall in front of them is solid concrete with a variety of wires exiting it to an explosion device.

"If my calculations are correct this is the other side of the fireplace in the Oberfurhers office," announces Caleb "...well luckily for us we made the right call!"

They exchange glances to Logan who appears to ignore them, he shrugs his shoulders and walks back down the tunnel.

"Are we actually going to get out of this place?" demands Steve.

"Let's go back to the Mess Hall and have something to eat," acknowledges Rina.

They gather their thoughts with some nourishment and refreshments they've brought with them, everyone is deathly quiet.

"This must be the gate where my Grandmother was forbidden to pass when she came to feed the soldiers..." states Ellia and cracks the silence. She takes a photograph of the room, "...I can't believe she was here, it's surreal I'm eating in the place she brought food to the soldiers."

"Are you ok?" Louise mutters softly to Rina, "...you were so distressed about Arthur."

"Brought back haunting memories Lou...but I'm ok," she replies stroking the tattoo.

Louise doesn't push the conversation, but grabs Rina's hand and squeezes it purposely.

They saunter back towards the alternative route and tread in the new room-less walkway.

"This is desolate," says Rina disheartened.

"It has to lead somewhere?" replies Logan.

"What's to say that there's an air shaft or exit in one of the closed doors we've already passed?" she continues.

"Rina, you might be right and we can exhaust that option if we have to later, but after Arthur we should at least give this a crack first."

"I can see the end!" declares Russo.

The tunnel ahead has an elaborately decorated cast iron door that arches on its top. The door has been painted with seven golden flames that interlace exquisitely along the curvature of its structure. Hans runs his hands over the lavish intricate artwork. From the base of the third flame displays a gilded aurous lettering that quotes the Bible text Job 38:9-11.

"What does the scripture say?" asks Louise.

"I don't know, but there has to be something significant with the 7 flames?..." he replies, "...the Jewish Menorah lampstand was made of pure gold and had exactly 7 branches that burnt flames of pure olive oil. The Menorah from the Jewish temple stood over 5ft in height!"

Rising up from the intricate flames adorning the top left corner is the Hebrew inscription which Steve had seen on the gentleman's ring at Fürstenburg brewery and embossed into the letter handed to him at the hotel.

"So, somebody has been here?.." he realises "...whatever's behind this barricade is what these people are trying their best to prevent anybody from knowing about"

"It might explain the strange items we found in the lab?" replies Caleb.

"Nothing in all of these tunnels, have been as prolific and as lavish as this," responds Hans.

"Do you think the treasure is behind this wall?" asks Logan.

"It's not going to be here Logan...look at all this... someone's already been here and evidently why they didn't appreciate our presence," snaps Steve.

Logan smacks his hand firmly against the fastened opening that echoes a vibration along the underpass.

"The writing means 'Guardian' Steve, maybe they don't want us to locate what they are guarding in there," states Hans.

"Oh come on, reality check Hans, the Amber room, treasure or whatever? It's long gone! Wake up people!" howls Logan.

"So what do we do now?" Steve's exclamation is full of trepidation.

"There's no lock, this beauty is completely sealed," Reade states and knocks his fist on the impenetrable portal.

"Right, so what if there's some kind of booby trap or tripwire ambush the other side?" worries Ellia.

"The way I see it we have several options, open this

gateway, take a risk opening one of the other sealed doors back up the tunnel or shift the explosion wreckage in the main passage and go out the way we came in. All of our choices are hazardous and risky. The other option is to wait and hope for someone to come and rescue us, every avenue is fraught with danger. We need to evaluate which dilemma is less treacherous," asserts Reade.

"I vote to blast the concrete perimeter around this door and figure out if we can penetrate this gateway. Use the dynamite to pulverize it..." acknowledges Russo, "...we can secure ourselves back up the passageway, it's not ideal, it's going to have to be a total plunge of faith."

"We have to get out of here," exclaims Steve.

The other's signal acceptance and Logan removes the borehole drill from his backpack. He drills along both sides of the door he places the dynamite into the holes and attaches the wires and they stroll back to the T-Junction. Rina advises everybody to put on their protective ear-defenders. Ellia crouches behind the wall and glances back along the first corridor to focus on Arthur, Louise holds her hand gives it a sympathetic squeeze. They huddle together anxious & scared, Ellia clenches onto her Grandmothers locket tightly.

Russo lingers for a moment to defer the task "Is everyone ok?" he asks gently.

Steve removes his phone from his trouser pocket and taps out a text message 'I don't know if you'll get this mum, but if you do, I just want to tell every-

one that I love you all. Tell Grandad he's my hero'.
Russo presses the switch and a fleeting time lapse blankets the uncertainty. Louise cowers and grimaces in dread, she clutches firmly onto Steve's hand. A smoke filled vapour bellows at high speed that engulfs the aisle, the sound of the canopy above them cracks and groans. Momentary peace hushes around the iron doorway and Russo glimpses back. Amidst the haze, sudden bursts fracture the concrete releases the hefty ironclad fixture and it plunges in slow motion onto the ground. Dust granules that float majestically descend into a smooth carpet along the floor until all is still. They stir gently as they stand up and position themselves securely behind Russo. The doorway lies motionless and exposes a dark void at its rear. Obscure blackness girdles the expanse and the dust shrouds the view as Rina shines her torch down the corridor. The others all switch on their torches, tiny illuminated beams that dance rhythmically from one side of the room to the other. It's about ten metres wide and double its length. Reade treads softly over the iron door.
"Be careful!" expresses Rina.
He floats his light around the floor and looks cautiously for any trip wires. Along the length of each side are bunked shelves four tiers high to the tunnels roof. Each shelf hosts long oblong wooden crates. Individually the crates measure eight to nine feet in length, three feet wide and two feet in height.
The dust settles from the explosion and Reade

walks the length of the space "It's safe!" he declares.
A total of twenty nine wooden boxes on the shelves all the same size except one carton that's six feet in length.

"This one's smaller?" Louise exclaims and shines her torch on it, "it's about three feet shorter than all of the others.

At the furthest end of the room is another door.

"These must be the crates my Grandmother watched the soldiers carrying?" Ellia wonders.

"We've done it!" hails Logan and grasps his crowbar tightly to wrench open the lid of a crate. He locks the tool into its lid and levers it in a downwards motion and cranks the top up. Hans takes one end and Logan grasps the other to ascend the lid. Excitedly Caleb positions his torch directly into the carton...

"Son of a...."

The horror and gasps encircle them all in unison.

"It's a SKELETON!" cries Rina.

"This is a crypt!" Hans howls and shines his torch around the whole area of the room.

"A crypt? As in graveyard?" cries Louise.

"This skeleton is enormous!..." continues Hans "...look at the size of its skull! It's almost double the size of an average human!"

"Are all these boxes skeletons?" she shrieks.

"Its frame has to be eight feet long!.." declares Caleb "...so their experiment worked?...and they lived a long time, this has to be an adult surely?"

"Viktor told us they were all children between 5 & 10 years old!" announces Steve.

Louise crosses the coffin and kneels at its head.

"So how did they get in here? Someone had to have built these coffins and rest them in the caskets," reacts Hans.

"Yeah the towns folk!.." retorts Steve "...their freaky cult insignia on the door!"

"They can't all be skeletons?" furies Logan & he randomly opens up two more chests.

"It's all about the bloody treasure for you," Steve shouts and thrusts his hand to nudge Logan's shoulder and grasps onto the crowbar to prevent him from desecrating another casket.

Logan yanks it away from Steve's clench aggressively and pushes his face up against him shooting a sharp glance.

"Enough!.." screams Ellia forcing her way between them, "...think about Arthur! No treasure is worth dying for. Yes, it would be nice to find it...but NOT from a hospital bed!"

"Everyone look!" screeches Louise and points to a miniscule niche toward the end of the chamber. She rambles hurriedly to it observe a slight diminutive glow from the crevice. She presses her nose firmly on the door, positions her eye directly over the aperture. She inhales a sharp aghast of breath and rotates to look at her team horrified.

"What Lou?" Steve expresses.

The confusion and puzzlement in her facial expression is outstanding.

"I...I..."

"What?" he repeats to her and he moves in to scru-

tinize the crack with his own eyes.
"I think I've just seen Hagrid!" she announces.

Chapter 26

Each of them take turns to spy through the small crack and they see a man attending to vegetable crop. Next to him is technically a young boy facially, but has the stature of a six foot man. He's a good three feet shorter than the nine foot gentleman teaching him how to tend to the produce. Muted, the team stare in disbelief at each other.
"They survived!.." whispers Steve "...not once did I even conceive that concept could possibly be a reality."
"Me too," replies Louise and places her face against the hole repeatedly.
"The hypothesis is reasonable. In theory the children found a way to endure and procreate. As humans we've found ways to exist for thousands of years," says Hans.
"Survival of the fittest!.." announces Reade "...where do we go with this?"
"They've been isolated here for almost 8 decades, if we go storming in we might terrify them. Look at the size of him, he'd destroy us!" replies Russo.
"I agree they've isolated themselves for a reason," says Rina.
"Err, yes, the reason is they're giants Rina, how on earth would they have fared in our society?" replies Steve "...but ...we still need to get out of here, that's the first daylight we've seen since this morning!"

Louise grabs her water bottle to stifle a cough, but the irritation in her throat takes grip and seizes her into an uncontrollable coughing fit.

"I'm sorry it's the tear gas..." she barks "...it keeps catching me."

Caleb stares out of the hole and views the man and child halt their work to glance back at the crypt door. He swiftly picks his son up and rushes off.

"They heard us!" exclaims Caleb.

"Well what now? They could come back and we get ambushed!" whispers Ellia "...we don't know how many of them there are?"

"We only have one choice now, take a leap of faith and go through the door. They might be just as frightened of us as we are of them..." says Caleb "...take off your hard hats and put all tools away...DO NOT get your guns out!" he snarls at the military faction of the group.

Caleb hesitates and lifts the latch on the door but its locked "It's bolted from the outside."

Logan pushes them all to one side and he kicks the door vigorously but it doesn't open. Reade and Logan take a run up and forcefully thrust the sides of their bodies against it, the bolt on the outside rips away from the frame and it swings open. Very tentatively they step out into an immense enclosed range.

It's a colossal area with a walled perimeter that disappears into the distance. The wall is marginally visible behind the trees and vegetation grows along its boundaries. The circumference is humongous in size and impossible for them to even fathom a guess at its range. In the distance to their left is a tower so large it seems to touch the clouds visually. The tower is lavish in vegetation that climbs up its sides and it's circular in shape.

"I think it's a Flak Tower?" wonders Hans looking at Caleb for confirmation and he nods in agreement.

"What's a Flak Tower?" asks Ellia.

"They were blockhouse towers built by the Nazi's to defend against air attacks, on the tops they used to host multilevel guns to fire against the R.A.F and U.S.A.A.F bombers. They were big enough to shelter thousands of civilians..." replies Hans, "...Hitler had an obsession with great architectural constructions like the Roman Colosseum. These Flak towers are fortresses similar to the siege towers Titus used on the Roman siege against Jerusalem...They're pretty much impenetrable."

"When you say sheltered thousands of people, how many?" she replies realising the enormity of the construction.

"...anything in between ten to thirty thousand," he answers. Behind the flak tower is a collection of large rounded grass top huts scattered about this unique camp. It appears to resemble a quaint Austrian street with cobbled pathways. Calmly they tread in unison towards the inhabited stretch and from the huts and from various points around the compound appears an imposing audience gathering to survey their unexpected guests. They stand in a long line grasping tightly onto their children's hands.

"How many are there?" says Ellia in a soft tone.

Steve swiftly counts along the line of unique human specimens, "About twenty eight and there's one, two, three…twelve children."

Two of the men step forward cautiously from the gawping crowd and they hold their arms out to the others to stay back. They advance several meters to slowly view their intruders and stop.

"Hold your hands open…" Russo tells them quietly "…let them know we mean them no harm."

They breach the gap between the two groups which seems to take forever and the eerie silence is formidable.

"I'm scared," hushes Louise.

Caleb holds his hand out to the older of the two men, he takes Caleb's hand & makes him feel an uneasy anxiety as he towers over him. The span of his palm engulfs Caleb's. Hans repeats this process with the younger of the two men.

"Guten tag," says Hans.

The two titan men glance at each other and reply "Guten tag."

Their voices are deep, masculine and exquisitely dynamic.

"Bist du Deutscher?" asks the younger of the two.

"Ich bin, aber die anderen sind verschiedene Nationalitaten," says Hans. (I am, but the others are different nationalities.)

"Sprichst du Englisch?"

"Yes…" he responds "…hello, my name is Abraham,

this is my father Gustaw."
"I am Hans and this is Caleb, pleased to meet you."
He turns to face the others "This is Ellia, Steve, Russo, Rina, Louise, Reade and Logan."

Abraham is very slender in physique and towered a good four inches above his father. Both men have exotic brownish-orange eyes that sparkle similar to Carnelian stones, alien and hypnotically alluring. The captivating charm is their hair colour has almost identical chromaticity as their eyes. Lush warm complexion, unlike more pale skinned redheads, their skin has a sun-kissed glow. Gustaw inquisitively questions Caleb "Have the Guardians sent you?"
"No!.." screeches Louise thrusting herself forward "...we came here to find you! Hello, my name is Lou!"
"To find us?" questions Gustaw and embraces Louise "...how do you know about us?"
"I think we all have a lot of questions," smiles Steve as he looks up at the two men.
A commotion from the collective of giants erupts as a young girl runs towards them.
"Ada! ... Ada!" screams her mother and tries to catch her.
"Hello I'm Ada..." she beams and throws her arms tightly around Louise, "...I'm six!"
She touches Louise's blonde hair, "...how old are you?"
She's only a couple of inches shorter than Louise making her about five foot and eight inches.

She holds Louise's hand tightly and smiles back at Gustaw and Abraham.

"This is my daddy and granddad," she announces proudly.

Her anxious mother plunges forward maternally protective for her daughter "...and this is my mummy!"

"Hello..." she whispers and doesn't take her eyes off of her daughter "...Stefanie," she says softly.

"My wife," states Abraham, his voice is distinguishable from the others, much deeper and commanding with a mellow calm undertone.

"I'm twenty nine," Louise replies to the excited vivacious Ada.

Ada giggles "...you're so tiny!"

"Gustaw, Mala Sroka wants to meet our sudden guests," snaps a slightly intimidating woman.

Gustaw looks at Caleb "This is my sister Aleksja. My Grandmother wants to meet you all."

They follow Abraham and Gustaw into one of the enormous huts. Louise looks up at the colossal entrance as they enter,

"Why are the rooftops covered in grass?" she asks.

"To hide from your satellites!.." responds Aleksja, "...we pray that they look like little hills from up there."

"You know a lot about the outside world?" questions Louise.

"The Guardians tell us all we need to know."

The round hut is one level with numerous rooms

that lead off from the main entrance. A frail elderly lady sits in the corner, giant in size but as with most aging humans the discs in her compressed vertebrae stoop her posture. She looks fragile and weathered.
"Mala Sroka..." murmurs Gustaw and holds her hand "...we have special visitors."
"Mala Sroka means little magpie in Polish?" questions Logan.
She chortles a crackly snigger at Logan's declaration "Yes young man, yes it does. It was a nickname I was given by the German officers. I was often caught stealing shiny things and food!" she laughs "...come here let me see you all my sight fails me these days."
They all step forward and sit on the floor in front of her. She views them all individually smiles and nods, she stops when she inspects Steve. Mala Sroka scrutinizes his face and contemplates it in detail.
"Amazing..." she says "...you remind me so much of someone I used to know."
He reciprocates her sweet gesture and touches the back of her hand and she taps his with her other hand.
"How is it you are all here?" she asks.
"Mala Sroka, we have not come here to harm any of you, we came here to find you," replies Ellia.
"To find us? Why? Who knows about us?" her face screws across her brow quizzically which enhances the wrinkles deep set in its skin.
"We learned of your existence and the experiments from my late boss he was one of the soldiers here," continues Ellia.

"I often wondered if this day may ever come. If any of those soldiers had ever told anyone about us," she replies.

"To be honest ma'am we didn't expect anybody to be alive, if anyone had survived the ordeal. We only found out about what these monsters did a few weeks ago and we needed to close a chapter," answers Steve.

"Close a chapter?.." Mala Sroka replies "...as you can see the chapter is far from closed," waving her hand around the room.

Steve looks behind him to an intensely quiet audience of amazing humans. Everyone's silent and hangs onto every word of the conversation. Ada jumps up excitedly and waves at him.

"Haha, I see you've met my great great granddaughter, quite the feisty little angel."

"She's lovely," grins Louise.

"Yes she is. So you can all see, we coped, we lived and we carried on despite our unique appearances."

"Please tell us your story..." begs Louise sincerely "... we will tell you how we came to find you..."

Mala Sroka caresses the side of Louise's chin. She feels no threat from the sudden newcomers. She knows they are more scared of the impressive humans that surround them.

"I was only seven years old when the Nazi soldiers moved into my town. My mother and I were separated from our family and we were brought to Ravensbrück. My mother didn't fare very well & became sick within a month in the camp. They

worked her for sixteen hours a day building transistors for radios with little food or water. She fell ill with a high fever and died. I never found out what she died off, although I think exhaustion and heartbreak were huge factors. I was all alone and very scared, but being a feisty child..." she pauses and glances over at Ada with a loving smile "...I had to adapt. I was lucky enough to have met a lot of women who were more than happy to adopt me like aunties. They protected me, fed me and made sure I was always ok. I used to get into a lot of trouble with the soldiers, always stealing food whenever I could for the other women in the camp. They would make them work for hours every day, handing them the little scraps I could salvage would always make them protect me more. I made a couple of extra special 'aunties' who cherished me, I still see their faces when I go to sleep. One day a group of soldiers walked into morning roll call to inspect all of the children, but the children they gathered together were very healthy, scrawny, but healthier than the other sickly children amongst us. I can remember them pulling me out of the line-up and my aunties protesting and sobbing. With seven other children I was ushered down some tunnels to a laboratory, it looked a bit like a hospital. We were all stripped naked and every part of us was measured in meticulous detail. We were then subjected to a series of injections and then twice daily for another month."
"The DNA13 33 serum" interrupts Louise.

"I never knew what it was called..." replies Mala Sroka "...we were put here in this place we call Ziemia Obiecana."

"Promised Land?" asks Logan.

"Yes, Promised Land...or home. This is our home," she continues.

"Why Promised Land?" asks Reade.

"It was promised to us as children to keep us safe after the war and all we had suffered at the hands of our oppressors, just like the Israelites in the book of Exodus, they were given their promised land when they were freed by the Egyptians. It was a nice name to call our home. Poetic don't you think?"

"Why have you never left here? Integrated with the rest of the human race?" quizzes Steve.

"Your world is not forgiving or accepting, we would be considered freaks or monsters and persecuted for that. A genetic mutation created by Nazi's. We would have been banished for sure."

"It's different now, equality for every race, religion, sexuality..." he continues.

"Yes...maybe? Humans take a long time to accept change and will fight it at every corner. Look how long it took for the Americans to accept humans based on the colour of their skin? Can you possibly imagine how they would react to the rest of us? It happened amongst us many years ago..."

"What do you mean happened amongst you?" asks Rina.

Chapter 27

Mala Sroka unsteadily stands up with the help of Aleksja, "Stay...stay with us for a while. You have many questions, as have we."

"We came all this way to find you all, we will stay," Louise says and strokes the dry weathered coarseness of Mala Sroka's arm.

"Then let's eat, you must be starving," she smiles and cups Louise's face in her giant hands.

The small community of impressive mortals nervously accept their guests, but are very reserved. The children are much more big-eyed, inquisitive and peer at the arrivals they're definitely not as frightened as the adults. Ellia's team are given water to wash and bathe their dusty coated clothes from the various blasts earlier in the tunnels. They are given some of the children's clothing to wear whilst theirs are washed lovingly by a few of the women.

Ada sits herself directly in front of Louise whilst food is being prepared. Louise plaits Ada's hair into pretty French braid pigtails. Two other very jealous little girls line up for Louise to do their hair too. They have never had their hair look so pretty before, Stefanie sits beside Louise and is eager to learn the braiding technique.

"Have you ever left this camp?" ask Louise.

"Never! We mustn't!"

The food is prepared outside of the huts. A long

bricked oven with metal grates and logs burn beneath roasting vegetables on a mammoth sized barbeque. Konrad, Joshua and Aleksja's husband Joseph take Reade, Russo and Logan on a small tour of the area.

"They remind me of the Amish..." whispers Reade "...simple living."

In the camp everyone sits around in a large circle eating and talking.

"Mala Sroka, Konrad told us earlier that you all speak many languages, how is this?" puzzles Russo.

"When we first came here as children we were from many different nationalities. There were ten children before us already here, but they did not make it and died as young children. Our Oma told us they were the first experiment but it was unsuccessful. They grew large but suffered extreme headaches, had strokes and heart attacks."

"Oma? As In Grandmother?" asks Steve.

"Yes, Oma Mary. She was a Nazi SS Officer assigned to look after us children. There was eight of us that the next serum was successful, myself, Mordecai, Abigail, Rachel, Asher, Daniel, Deborah and Elijah."

"Are you..." he hesitates "...are you the only survivor of the original children?"

"No, Elijah is still alive..."

"We read about Elijah in the laboratory." Hans interrupts.

"...he's very weak and he wanders a lot very confused. He calls out sometimes for his mother and sisters. His mind takes him to distant memories these days."

"It sounds like a dementia or Alzheimers?" responds Steve.

"We do not know about these things. We call it brain failure. If your heart gives up its called heart failure, if you kidneys give up its kidney failure, when your brain doesn't work the way it used to, it's simply brain failure."

"That's actually a really nice way of putting it than giving it misunderstood titles," agrees Rina.

Joseph takes them to meet Elijah "Grandfather... grandfather.., we have guests..." he whispers "...he's actually sleeping, probably just as well. Sometimes he's with us and other days he's not. We're never quite sure how he's going to react when the Guardians are here, sometimes he's alright and copes very well and then other times their smaller frames terrify him."

"Who are these guardians we keep hearing about?.." says Steve "...I got a letter from them... well...we believe it might be them? With this symbol on it and the same symbol was on the door in the tunnel when we came into the crypt."

"Not forgetting they attacked us!" shouts Logan.

"Attacked you?" replies Gustaw "...they are peaceable people, they would never harm anyone!"

"They are Gustaw, but they will do anything to protect us..." responds Mala Sroka, "...unless the Watchers know we could be exposed by these people and it was them that attacked you?"

Gasps and glances exchange sharply around the

camp.

"Oma Mary was a very special woman. When the war was happening she was one of the many who looked after us children and we were treated by her as extremely precious, not because the Nazi's really wanted to succeed in this experiment, but because she genuinely loved us. But when the war was coming to an end it caused extreme panic and fear. The Soviets arrived at Ravensbrück and the officers decided to abandon the camp quickly. The Third Reich had no time to dispose of their laboratory or us children. One man wanted to execute us and obliterate any evidence of our existence but Oma Mary and an Oberfurher named Otto-Wolff mastered a scheme to hide us in a special place until the liberation was over..."

Ellia, Steve and Louise exchange sharp glances to each other but remain intently silent listening to her every word.

"...Oma Mary told Otto-Wolff that she loved us children as her own and would raise us away from the judgemental eyes of the world. She had lost her husband and son during the First World War so we were all that she had. We learned to speak each other's languages, she taught us to farm and how to build. We taught ourselves carpentry, sewing and many useful things to survive. The love she gave us was amazing. After a couple of months when the war was over we were awoken one night, we could hear Oma Mary crying, there were many men in our camp arguing and shouting at each other. It transpired that some of the soldiers that worked at Ravensbrück had told some people of our existence. The disputes and arguing lasted for two days. Oma Mary was very scared keeping us children occupied and as far away from these men as possible. The one man who truly cared for us was Otto-Wolff, he promised Oma Mary that he would do everything he could to keep us safe. The Watchers called us a perverse abomination, mutants and a disgrace to the creation of God. They said that the last time the Nephilim were on the earth God destroyed them and that they should do the same with us. But Otto-Wolff had brought with him a very special group of men, we know as the Guardians. This elite small unity of men promised to keep us safe and away from the knowledge of the rest of the world. The Watchers would only be happy with this outcome telling the Guardians that they would always be keeping their eyes on them as well as us. They would stop at nothing, including violence to make sure our secret never got out. The Guardians keep us safe and pass their unique task down to their own children, who realise themselves they are a part of a secret society. Once a year the Guardians come into our camp with supplies and fabrics..."

"... AND we get to see movies on a BIG SCREEN! They bring a projector!.." shrieks Ada "...it's my favourite time of the year!"

Mala Sroka smiles and the crowd laughs, their mellow voices chuckle like an orchestra of baritone instruments.

"What movies have you seen Ada?" delights Louise "Movies are my favourite thing."

"I've seen The Little Mermaid and Aladdin and Tangled and Snow White, but my favourite, my most favourite is Beauty And The Beast because Belle falls in love with him even though he's different. I like that one a lot! Have you seen them Louise?"

"I have Ada and do you know what? Beauty And The Beast is my most favourite too!"

"Who are these 'Watchers'?" enquires Hans "...are they German?"

"We're not sure..." begins Abraham "...they call themselves 'The Osservatore' a unique society. All we know is that they keep our secret from the rest of the world and will do anything to keep it that way. We don't know who they are or why they insist we stay hidden away, other than they think we are freaks, but we have to accept that we would be objects of extreme dislike, shameful nuisances artificially created from a despised regime."

"We heard them referred to as 'The Osservatore' so we named them the Watchers after the Book of Enoch, the Watchers were the evil fallen angels watching the human females. But unlike their offspring we mean no one any harm," states Mala Sroka.

"That's so weird because we found that book in the tunnels," says Steve.

"Oma Mary and Otto-Wolff wanted us to understand how special and precious we are, how we inhabited the earth once before and how we will always be rejected. They brought us books and writings of our existence long ago."

"But you were artificially medically enhanced, not conceived from celestial beings?" he replies.

"This is true, but we would still face severe adversity, we could dispute this concept for an eternity..." she smiles and taps Steve's hand "...all we know is the Guardians keep our secret safe and the Osservatore check to make sure it never ever gets out. We have everything we need here."

"What about our technologies? You know a lot about them but seem extremely reluctant to adopt them here, such simple living?" asks Russo.

"A lot of your gadgets transmit signals and data. We have electricity, but no radios or television. We cannot allow any information being tracked to us. The children enjoy watching a movie on the big pop-up screen the Guardians bring them once a year. We don't use anything that might be traceable or raise suspicion. The most modern gadget I think we possess is an instant Polaroid camera. The Guardians bring us refill film for it each time they're here. Come, see our photos," encourages Abraham.

"We lead a simple lifestyle; it's hard work because all of our means are what we have here. This is our small family and our whole world, we're a plain people, we don't shun your technologies, it simply holds no place amongst us without exposing ourselves to the risk of being discovered," he says passing them around photographs.

"How many of you are there here?" questions Hans.

"Forty six adults and twelve children... five generations we have been very blessed," responds Gustaw.

"Oma Mary explained that as we physically developed the serum would affect our growth and some of the females had irregularities to their menstrual cycles and the pituitary gland tumours were consistent with elevated infertility amongst many of us. Pregnancy has been a struggle amidst us all," explains Mala Sroka.

The love in this small simple community flourishes, their gentle acceptance of the outside world intimidates and daunts them as much as it does for the little group of explorers. They feast and indulge in the unique company, meat rotates on the spits, enormous platters full of vegetables and fruits, bread and cakes, fresh strawberries and cream, a variety of cheeses all made from their simple lifestyle.

The sun slowly sets and gives off the same sumptuous cast of colour Louise had esteemed at the start of the very same day.

"It's amazing how your entire life can alter in just one single day," she says to Steve.

"This has by far, been the most bizarre and remarkable day of my entire life Lou."

"Steve..." she continues "...how are we going to write about this? They don't want the world to know of their existence."

"I've been thinking about that too. We did the right

thing putting the cameras away Lou."

"I was thinking about Viktor, you know, maybe he wasn't so bad after all...he did know the children were safe and he almost took it to the grave with him. I wonder why he told us?"

"We can't pretend this never happened..." responds Steve "...I just don't know which way to take it, withholding a secret can hurt but revealing it could destroy lives."

"Some secrets are generations old..." Abraham overhears and interrupts "...it's not about pretending we don't exist it's about the consequences if the world knows that we do. Keeping the secret is not the main problem; the issue is learning to live with the knowledge of the secret all alone in your thoughts. Your world would destroy us Steve."

The evening is joyous, flames flicker and dance in the breeze from the large fire pit. They sing and clap to the entertaining percussion music their hosts perform.

"What do you call yourselves...As a group I mean?" Rina asks Aleskja.

"What do you mean?"

"Well I don't want to call you giants and the Nephilim isn't a particularly attractive label either."

"We call ourselves Rodzina...it means 'Family'. Simply that."

Rina smiles at her and claps along to the music. The children tower above them as they dance and sing.

"So..." announces Mala Sroka "...tell us how you

came to know about us and to find us," she smiles.

Chapter 28

"It really started with me..." smiles Ellia "...I put together this team after the gentleman I represented told us about the child experiments. The soldiers name was Viktor Otto-Wolff!"

Mala Sroka's hands shake and she loses grasp of her drink. The Rodzina stop the music and everyone is motionless.

"You knew him? We haven't seen him for seventy years and we never knew what had happened to him!"

"Mala Sroka, Viktor was on the run, he'd been hiding for decades trying to avoid prosecution for war crimes. He probably never returned in fear of getting caught and exposing your identity or existence. He took your secret with him until he was dying, you, the children from the experiment and my Grandmother were his last thoughts, his conscience and his last loves. He obviously felt he needed to share this, he told us that he didn't know what had happened to you all, but I think... I believe... he said that so curiosity would get the better of us. He secretly knew we would come to find you knowing that he was dying, this big confession, with him out of way, it would be easier for you all ... maybe?"

"I don't think we would be any better off our secret getting out."

"Maybe he wanted us to find you so we could protect you too?" wonders Louise and grabs Mala Sroka's hand.

"My Grandmother Heidi Babik was a prisoner here, she had been in love with him for a time after the war..." continues Ellia.

"I don't believe it!" shrieks Mala Sroka astounded "...Heidi Babik is your Grandmother? Is she still alive?"

"Yes?" Ellia replies confused "...did you know her?"

"Oh yes, yes, yes..." she claps "...Heidi, your Grandmother, was one of my special aunties who looked after me when my mother died. She fed me and kept me safe, I saw her once after I had been chosen for the experiment. I watched her in the bunker bringing food on a trolley. I called out to her, I called and called. She waved calling my name back but the guards grabbed her arms and marched her away. I never saw her again after that."

Mala Sroka wipes a tear from her eye and kisses Ellia on her head "I still see Heidi's face when I go to sleep, she's really still alive?"

"Yes, we came here with a necklace Otto-Wolff had given to her to unlock the secret files we found about you all," Ellia says and pulls the locket up from around her neck to place it into Mala Sroka's weathered palm.

"How did Heidi get this?" Mala Sroka questions with a confused tone flowing off her tongue.

"Otto-Wolff had given it to her, they met many years after the war and fell in love. Sadly their time together didn't last very long. He loved her so much he didn't want to bring shame or disaster open her." Mala Sroka's expression is blank and motionless, she glares at the necklace as if she has seen a ghost. A glint of acknowledgement shines in her pupil, a recognition she does her best to hinder. Her eyes slowly lift from the locket and transfix deep into Ellia's stare, she places its chain back over Ellia's lustrous hair and sits the locket back on her chest.

"I'm tired now, we should all sleep," she says gently, Gustaw and Joseph assist her to stand. Nobody speaks as she exits the small camp fire.

"Good night," she acknowledges the crowd.

Morning breaks and the explorers take their time to exit the various huts they'd spent the night.

"Did you notice how quiet Mala Sroka became when she held your Grandmothers locket?" whispers Steve. Ellia agrees with a firm nod.

"Maybe she'd seen it before?"

"I don't know? I was thinking that maybe she recognised it maybe when the experiments started and she saw them using it opening the box with their files in? But it did put an abrupt end to the evening for sure."

"Good morning..." smiles Abraham "...did you all sleep well?"

Ellia and Louise help three of the women prepare breakfast; Gustaw's wife Yonah, her sister Ingrid and their mother Zofia. Hans and Caleb go for an early trip to explore the overgrown Flak Tower in the centre of the Rodzina compound with their very keen tour guides Abraham, Joseph and Aleksja's son Aaron, Isaac and Thomas. The titans stoop as they enter the doorway into a large auditorium. The assembly hall is displayed similar to an amphitheatre and the chairs are laid out to view the small stage.

"This is our gathering hall and where we worship..." says Isaac "...our Grandfathers took a floor level out to accommodate our height. The upper floors we don't really enter, we use them for supply storage the Guardians bring us."

"May we go up?" asks Hans.

"Of course," they all respond.

Hans and Caleb climb the stairs and ascend height of the tower, at the top is a hatch that leads onto its rooftop, they push it hard to free it but the overgrowth has barricaded the exit.

"Pass me a pen knife," says Hans. He slides it back and forth in a haphazard motion and cuts away around the tiny crevice to unblock the clearing until he's able to push the hatch upwards. He climbs out onto the roof and they admire the view for miles around. The vast compound expands into the distance, completely enclosed by walls that are camouflaged by nature. In the far corner they see the top of a grand building hidden behind trees and directly in the centre of the tower roof is a bricked receptacle. It's rectangular in shape and has also surrendered itself to greenery and flora.

"Do you think it's in there?" questions Caleb.

"I do...yes...if they abandoned the site in a hurry the quickest way would have been to brick it up than trying to dismantle it and hide it."

"I agree!"

"Morning gentlemen!" says Russo and climbs out onto the roof followed by Reade and Logan, "...we wondered if you would want to check out this tower. Shall we take a look then?" he says grabbing the crowbar off of Logan and plunges into the brickwork to pull at it.

He loosens many of the blocks and the others pull them onto the floor.

"I knew it was still here!" exclaims Hans.

"Wow, it's pretty impressive!.." gasps Caleb "...the ammunition is still boxed here too!"

"It's a beauty for sure!" responds Logan.

The 3.7cm flak anti-aircraft gun sits soberly in its picturesque surroundings.

"These beasts had a two mile projectile range and shot one hundred and twenty rounds per minute!" Reade says as he runs this hand along the two metre barrel.

Caleb looks over the edge and waves to the women preparing breakfast below.

"We would like to show you something," announces Isaac as they descend the stairs from the rooftop.

Abraham and Aaron stack up the chairs along the middle bleacher in the meeting gallery. Abraham slides along a small piece of wooden flooring to reveal a bolt and it releases the entire mid intersection of the bleacher lifting it up and exposes a dark passageway beneath. They all focus attentively at Abraham.

"This is the tunnel entrance the Guardians use to annually check in on us. The tunnel leads to a concealed vestibule by the side of the lake. Once a year they adorn the skyline with a wondrous firework display to signal they are on their way."

"Abraham, haven't any of you ever decided to leave here?" questions Russo.

"Yes once. It is something we don't talk of. Mala Sroka forbids it."

"...it was her son..." says Thomas.

Aaron and Isaac poke him hard disapprovingly.

Ada and two of the other Rodzina children, Daisy and Willow, watch in awe at every single move that Ellia, Louise and Rina make. They are transfixed and mesmerised by their alien grace and mannerisms. Louise smiles at the curious trio spying on her from the grass topped houses. It momentarily dawns on her that the appearance of the houses resemble those of a children's pre-school television program and she chuckles quietly to herself. Louise listens to the mumbling hum of chatter travel in the warm morning's air. The aura amongst this unique community is almost enchanting. She senses intense calm and an inner peace with the exceptional surroundings. These unbelievable mortals epitomize all that is love and unity. Ada confidently strides towards Louise with the other two shyly creeping behind and still touching their beautiful French plaits.

"Good morning Louise!" She bellows in a bossy manner.

"Good morning Ada...and what are your friends names? I never did find that out yesterday." Louise's tender expression towards the shy children is soft and loving.

"This is Willow and this is Daisy."

"I love my hair," whispers Willow timidly.

"I'm glad you like it," replies Louise and strokes Willow's cheek affectionately.

"Would you like to see my foal?" Ada exclaims proudly.

"I'd love to Ada."

Rina jumps to her feet "I would quite like to come along for that as well if that's ok?"

Daisy slips her hand snuggly into Rina's and the girls lead them across the compound and through to a fenced boundary protected with lush green saplings and shrubbery. Unlike the inhabited area the grass is longer and wild.

"This is our farm. Over there we keep our chickens. In that barn there are the pigs..."

Louise and Rina freeze unsettled.

"...and over there are the stables," announces Ada enthusiastically.

She looks at the two astounded women, neither of them move and both display the same overwhelming expression of disbelief.

"Are you ok Lou, you both look a little bit worried, is there something wrong?" Ada questions.

A small convoy of placid cattle trudge slowly through the grass.

"I hadn't even thought about animals?" Rina shivers. "Ellia told us that her grandmother had seen an exceptionally large rabbit being carried in the concentration camp," Louise responds transfixed on the cows.

"I suppose I was being a bit ignorant to think they wouldn't have tested or experimented on animals as well."

Daisy squeezes Rina's hand reassuringly, "They won't hurt you."

The herd, each the size of elephants, chew at the grass as if in slow motion.

"Where's the bull?" Rina whispers to Daisy, not shifting her stare.

"Over there in the other field."

"It happens you know…" Louise begins.

"What?"

"Hormone anomalies in animals too. My Uncles cat was huge. We always thought it was just over fed and super furry but it had feline acromegaly."

They trail past the coop.

"The chickens are normal size?" questions Rina.

"I don't think it would be correct to use the phrase 'normal size' anymore."

Rina nods. Willow skips on ahead towards the barns and opens the stable door. The horses are grandiose and majestic. Their superb stature is imposing. Sublime flowing manes makes their phenomenal tallness magnificent and regal.

"Incredible!" Rina utters as she strokes the mare's mahogany bay coat.

"The stallions are kept in the other stable..." Ada exclaims, "...this is my foal Maximus."
"From Repunzel?" laughs Louise.
"Yes!.." claps Ada. "...I couldn't call him anything else with that colouring could I?" she laughs.
"...and Maximus is just a foal?" Louise questions.
"He's only one. Do you ride?"
"I used to all the time but I haven't for a few years now, he's absolutely beautiful Ada."
"Would you like to ride him? He's very gentle, his personality is nothing like Repunzel's Mazimus!"
"Thank goodness for that..." laughs Louise loudly "...Ada, I would love to, thank you."
Louise and Maximus canter the perimeter of the farm. The temperate breeze wafts through her hair as it bounces with each stride. She thinks to herself how peculiar a couple of days can unravel, from being blown unconscious off her feet to gliding through a beautiful green carpet on nothing but an equine baby, a colt so magnificent in size. She listens to the rhythmic pounding of his hooves and watches his mane bounce with every powerful stride. She gazes at the three girls waving to her in the distance. 'I'm never going to leave here' she tells herself.

Rina pulls out a long piece of straw from the bale she's sprawled herself on and Louise perches herself against the stable wall.
"I don't think I want to leave." She announces to

Rina.

"It's easy to fall in love with a place like this. I know, I have many times in my career."

"But Rina, I'm not disregarding the places you have been or the things you have experienced. I expect you have met many incredible people and communities; but put your hand on your heart, have you ever met an entire civilisation unknown from the rest of the world and not just regular sapiens, but a race from an experiment that literally went incredibly - right?"

"I totally agree Lou, I just don't know how we move forward, knowing what we know. It's not like we can just come and go, visiting whenever we please."

"Why not? The Guardians do?"

"Very secretly though. The slightest error will expose and endanger their lives - their whole world - their entire existence."

Rina looks down at her tattoo and sighs. Louise reads her pain something she's seen several times over the past few days, the tensing together of Rina's eyebrows causes little scrunched lines to appear at the top of her nose.

"You touch it a lot - that tattoo." Louise says and sits herself on the hay bale beside Rina.

"We had been deployed to Afghanistan, nothing unusual really as we'd already done two other tours there..."

"We?"

"...my platoon. Amell and I were very close..."

"Lovers?"

"Friends. He was my best friend, we went through military school together."

"Amell, that's a unique name?"

"It means 'Power of an Eagle'. He was definitely that, strong, intelligent and fierce, a true leader. He had a way about him that inspired people. We had been sent to a small village south of Kabul to aid with water, supplies and medication. The villagers welcomed us with great affection. We'd been there for a couple of weeks and just like you I felt a great sense of peace, never wanted to leave, they were like family. They taught us many things, more than we taught them and then one day the village was encircled and besieged. If it was because of our presence there we never found out. I'd known Amell for ten years, knew his family, knew everything about him..." Rina pauses and swallows hard "...we had no warning of the attack. It had taken us completely by surprise and it was absolute carnage. I can't describe it to you, it was complete mayhem. The destruction was catastrophic. I still hear the screams."

She pauses and wipes a tear off her cheekbone quickly. Louise and Rina sit in silence for a while and watch the girls feeding the horses.

"The children of the village were in school. It was only a school of about 12 children. Amell had screamed at the teacher to keep them inside and safe. We couldn't see anything, everywhere was shrouded in a cloak of dust. We aimed to get the villagers into the vehicles we had used to convoy the aid supplies when the Taliban turned their attention to the school. I was getting the villagers onto the trucks and Amell went back to assist the children. He managed to save every single one of them before the building collapsed on top of him. We couldn't save him...I couldn't save him."

Louise places her hand on Rina's arm.

"He was a true hero - you all are."

"I just couldn't help him, he'd rescued me so many times and on so many different levels. I let him down. Two colleagues dragged me away and we were forced to leave him there."

"It's such a sad story Rina, but you have to focus on all those lives Amell saved...and you."

"It's hard to let go. I should never have left him behind, but would have risked everyone's lives if I had stayed to pull him out. The Rodzina are so precious Lou, so very very precious. I owe it to Amell to protect them."

Everyone gathers together for breakfast, eating quietly, there is a sombre atmosphere that ripples through the party.

"I have been troubled all night," Mala Sroka announces and breaks the awkward silence.

"We honestly mean you no harm...we understand our intrusion must have been an incredible shock," Louise panics and rushes forward to embrace her.

"No, sweet child..." she responds "...your company is very pleasant and decades overdue. My trouble is Ellia's locket I honestly never thought we would ever see it again."

They look at her puzzled and mystified.

"Mala Sroka, I don't understand?.." Ellia replies "...we opened the box with your documentation in, why would this trouble you?"

"Let me tell you a little story. When our injections or the 'experiments' begun a lot of construction was underway in the tunnels, building the passages and bunkers, developing this architectural framework, erecting the tower and a vast secret private area that was completely classified. The children were forbidden anywhere near it and this prohibited area was built over there behind those trees, we call it Picollo Petra..."

An uneasy disturbance erupts amongst the Rodzina, murmurs and hushed voices ripple the community, with looks of apprehension and perplexity carry in their facial expressions. Mala Sroka motions soothingly to calm their anguish.

"...Oma Mary told us we must never enter the area and we built an outer wall like the temple at Petra. It's our forbidden cave. She told us we must never try to enter it forcefully and that there was only one way we could access it without facing its traps and destruction. Oma Mary was given a locket by Otto-Wolff. The locket was half of two identical pieces and when fitted with its twin would safely unlock the prohibited area, she said we would perish the same way the Nephilim did in the Bible..."

"The flood?" asks Caleb.

"Yes, the flood. We could only assume a surge of overwhelming water would destroy us. We don't know how or why that would happen, so Piccollo Petra is a sacred place. We never comprehended we would ever see the other half of the locket, so we have never dared to enter it... until Ellia showed it to me last night."

"Where's the other half to the locket now?" questions Ellia.

"With Oma Mary...when she died it was placed into the coffin with her and has been there since the end of the fifties!"

"What do you think they were hiding in there?" asks Hans.

"All I know is large boxes were shuttled there when we were still very small children. I remember a man, he was Japanese I think, heading the construction and lots of boxes, it took several weeks to take them all there. Mordecai, Asher and Daniel were all playing outdoors in this enclosure when the door to it was fixed and completely sealed. It gave them nightmares for years because they heard the screams of men they had locked in there and left behind."

"That's terrible!.." gasps Rina "...buried alive!"

"Yes they were!"

"We have a suspicion the man you saw was a Japanese General Yamashita, we saw markers that he's well known for, before finding the bunker entrance..." says Hans "...his speciality was building complex tunnels with traps and hiding treasures.

Your Oma Mary maybe right, he was infamous for water traps in his tunnel constructions."

Reade takes the gold bar out of his bag and shows it to them all "...we found these in a creek but believe there's a bigger treasure hidden here somewhere, it could well be in your Petra?"

"The greed of mankind," she responds.

"Do you think the Watchers know about this Mala Sroka?" asks Abraham.

"I don't know, but I would doubt it, man is excessive and selfish. They crave indulgence and power, money gives them power...they will murder for the abundance of riches. If the Watchers knew there was a possibility of wealth they would have ripped this place into shreds to find it."

"What did you think may have been in the boxes?" wonders Steve.

"We were never sure, it was the height of the war we assumed it may have been ammunitions or weapons?" Mala Sroka gathers the crowd in closely "We have an unexpected chance to put to rest some of the nightmares of your ancestors. We've lived isolated in this community shackled by fear I think it's the time to break some chains."

"I agree..." announces Gustaw and stands beside her "...we might be hidden from the world, but we should no longer be held captive by dread in our home!"

United cheers and claps surge almost comparable to a burst of thunder, "...step forward if anyone would like to volunteer in joining our guests on this mission."

"Father I would like to submit myself," declares Abraham.

"Me too," announces Thomas. Micah and Luca the twins step to the front enlisting for the task.

"Grandmother, what about the necklace?" asks Gustaw.

"It's not a pleasant assignment Gustaw, this is your choice."

They trek the enclosure back to the crypt, Abraham places his hand on top of Oma Mary's coffin and mouths a little prayer.

"Well…that answers the smaller casket," whispers Louise.

Logan offers Abraham the crowbar but he requests that Logan opens it. Very gently he removes the necklace from the skeleton. Abraham places his hand respectively on Oma Mary's skull and strokes it affectionately

"I wish I had met you."

He shuts the lid and Aaron nails it securely.

Two men enter the reception at the Kleine Stranhütte Hotel and the receptionist politely greets them.

'We've come to see the people excavating over at Ravensbrück," the shorter of the two states abruptly.

"I'm very sorry sir but we haven't seen any of them since they left yesterday morning."

They glare at each other and exit the hotel swiftly and he grabs his mobile phone "They haven't come back!"

Chapter 29

The Rodzina and Ellias small team make their way to the furthest point of the enclosure, hidden behind trees and the climbing ivy they can just about see the top of the monumental building they saw from the Flak Tower. They pull hard at the brambles that climb the walls of Picollo Petra. They all stand in awe at its majestic design and architecture, spans a height of eight metres and covers a width of five metres. It's ornately identical to Petra in Jordan with six grand pillars, exquisite in carvings and detail.
"You built this?.." asks Hans "...it's incredible."
"Our grandfathers did," Abraham replies.
"What prompted them to replicate this structure?"
"I don't know?"
They climb the steps of the grand entrance to the immense doorway. Directly in its centre is a large dial similar to the one on the black box in the laboratory, but four arches where the hearts of the locket conjoin. Ellia opens her locket and holds the key, Abraham opens Oma Mary's and they place them into the indentation on the dial, "...it doesn't quite fit?" she responds and tries to push them in "...what are these four levers for underneath?"
"It's a puzzle..." exclaims Caleb and moves in to take a closer look, "...similar to the lock safe."
Each iron lever is fixed next to a set of numbers from

zero to nine, all the lever-arms are positioned upwards sitting above the zero.

"That's ridiculous there could be thousands of combinations," moans Rina.

"Let me see the lockets," requests Caleb.

He holds them in his hand "Look at this..." he says to Hans "...they are perfect mirror images of each other. The cherubs on this one faces to the left and the other one to the right with the fasteners on the opposite sides to each other."

Caleb opens the lockets again, "They're entirely symmetrical! But this one has a tiny slit here..."

He plays with them and after a few seconds they slot together to become one solid piece. A tiny magnet within the locket releases the internal base of the hearts and flips them upwards.

"There's an inscription underneath!" he shouts excitedly.

"An inscription? I didn't know the inside even had a secret layer?" shrieks Ellia and grabs them to examine the pieces.

"Pragmatic sufficiency – a little means 'solution'" Hans grins enthusiastically.

"What does it say?" asks Steve.

"It's in German, can you translate it?" Caleb asks and passes it to Hans.

"'Will we do what so ever we are disposed to do. For we have amassed silver, our barns are full like overflowing water your falsehoods pass away, for your wealth will not be permanent because you have obtained it iniqui-

tously' – Enoch 96:7-8"

"That's distastefully ironic...'obtained it iniquitously'...the Nazi's ransacked the whole of Europe pillaging riches!.." snaps Steve "...inscribing that is obnoxiously offensive!"

"Morals definitely weren't crucial to their consciences," replies Logan.

Caleb places the connected hearts into the dial "It won't move; we need to manoeuvre these levers to turn it. Let's try the numerals in the inscription."

He pulls the first lever down to the number nine, the second to the six, the third lever to the seven and the last to the eight.

"Ahh this dial really won't budge at all!"

"Great...so where do we go from here? You heard what Mala Sroka said about this place, we can't force our way in...I'm not even going to risk blowing this door off," says Russo.

"Every juncture of this adventure has been fraught with risk Russo. There will be a way..." Hans' enthusiasm ripples through the team "...tackle every task responsibly and gather riches amongst mankind."

"Who said that?" Russo smiles.

"Me!" Hans responds patting Russo on the back.

"It's in the Numbers..." whispers Louise.

"Huh?" responds Russo.

"It's in the Numbers!.." she says louder "...Viktor told me it was in the Numbers!"

"Which are?"

"Try 13 - 33!"

Caleb pulls the first lever down to the number one and a click sound echoes from beyond the door. He pulls the next lever to the number three another snap parallels the first. He tugs the third and fourth levers also to the number three and clunk resounds and reverberates.

"Push the door!" exclaims Abraham.

"No, it's not budging," replies Russo.

Caleb meticulously rotates the dial and a vehement crack vibrates and cautiously Caleb and Russo push the doorway open. They all hesitate anxiously that something harrowing is about to materialize ... but all is completely still.

"I have a really unpleasant feeling in the pit of my stomach," Steve says softly.

It's dark and suffocating. They shine their torches around to explore the crevices, wooden pillars that support the space, they appear to look like the props in a mine. The Rodzina crouch and try desperately not to bang their heads. The dark area is cramped and foul air drifts in the obscurity that makes the atmosphere moist, humid and muggy. Rina steps back and knocks against a stool that falls and crashes around her feet followed by a clattering smash. She moves her torch onto it "Oh my god!" she shouts.

A skeleton crumples in a heap onto her feet dressed in SS uniform. Hans stoops down to inspect the bony structure.

"He was shot in the head the bullet is lodged into his skull."

"There's another one!" shrieks Louise as she moves her light onto a second body.

"They were locked in here for sure!.." exclaims Reade "...I reckon this one took his own life, the bullet chipped through his jaw and escalated through the top of his head."

Reade removes the gun held securely in the skeletons curled bony finger.

"He probably shot this man first and then turned the gun on himself. They would've known there was no way out."

"Oh that's disgusting!" whimpers Louise.

"More than likely a merciful killing. Yamashita was renowned for killing people who knew of where treasures were hidden, once the project was finished he would seal or blast all the exit points leaving the workers entombed, tormented and with no escape..." responds Hans "...we may find more!"

"Come on..." Russo says and takes the lead "...I'll go ahead we need to watch out for trip wires!"

He creeps along peeping in all directions and the rest of the team scramble behind him keeping very close. Steve scowls and follows with a lot less confidence, the presence of skeletons makes him extremely uneasy. He reaches out to grab Louise's hand and squeezes it firmly. He struggles to decide if the foul air is the stench of death scattered around them and wipes small beads of sweat off his brow. They huddle shoulder to shoulder in a line formation and watch Russo closely.

"There's a ridge here be careful."

The floor is a pathway of loose gravel stones that twist and shift under their feet that resonate in crunching sounds.

"Ssh!.." hushes Russo and halts them all "...can you hear that?"

"What?" Logan replies.

"Wait…" he says and holds up his hand "…just wait…" he whispers again. "There! Did you hear that drip? Ssh!..."

Ten seconds pass and a single droplet of water patters on the ground, it lingers as they mentally count the gap until they hear the next onomatopoeia plink.

"Yes!" whispers Rina.

"This tunnel would lead directly underneath the Schwedtsee Lake…" acknowledges Caleb "…it feels dampish in here there's a stale stagnant wet smell."

"I agree Professor Beldman!" responds Hans.

Russo halts and shines his torch frantically in front of him "No? It's a dead end! Have we passed something I've missed?"

Hectically beams of light examine the blockage in front of them similar to a laser light-show. They turn back on themselves and the torches go berserk as they span the walls up and down in a helter-skelter pattern.

"Here!" thunders Abraham's distinctive tone.

A meagre square cavity comparable to a vent is discernible from the floor located in the side tunnel wall.

"What is it a mouse hole? How are we going to get in

there?" sighs Logan.

"I think it's doable..." states Rina and shines her light directly inside "...it's going to be cramped but we could do it," she continues.

Steve glimpses morosely at Abraham, Micah, Luca and Thomas already contorted and hunched over in the restrictive space.

Luca gestures his head and beckons the others to continue "We'll wait for you my brothers," he acknowledges; and in that single juncture Luca gives them a fondness, an appreciation, recognition and acceptance. Steve clutches his arm "Rodzina my friend!"

"Rodzina," he smiles.

Ellia wipes a runaway tear from her cheekbone, Micah grabs her hand and kisses the salty wetness from her finger tip. They stare deeply into each other's eyes and she hugs his titan arm affectionately. Russo crouches and slides his body into the miniscule tunnel.

"It's about twenty meters and looks clear, are you sure you want to do this?"

They remove their back packs and leave them with the giants. Russo moves along in a moderate army crawl, his arms and legs propel his body along the surface and he grips firmly onto his torch. Caleb pursues him, followed closely by Reade, Logan, Louise, Steve, Ellia, Rina and lastly Hans. The cramped cavity is sealed at the far end blocking any further way to continue. On the right hand side of the blockage features a rectangular block which protrudes two inches outwards.

"It has the double hearts carved into it" Russo shouts back at the human train behind him. Ellia fumbles and manoeuvres her body to retrieve the two lockets from her trouser pocket and shifts herself to pass it along to Steve. They all squeeze and wriggle in succession to deliver the lockets to Russo. He grapples the two pieces in the confined space, connects them and embeds them securely into the block. A snapping sound releases from the entrance.

"It doesn't turn?" he calls back.

"Try sliding the block like you would a latch," responds Caleb. With a firm hand Russo slides the block to the left which reveals a small key hole.

"Ellia! Pass the key along," he hollers back.

The same squirms and twists of bodies replay along the queue. Louise holds it momentarily and thinks of Viktor "The key to my heart..." and she passes it to Logan. Russo twists the key in one graceful movement and the door swings open to reveal a gargantuan grotto. He crawls his way out and his mouth dumbfounded.

"What can you see?" calls Caleb but Russo is tight-lipped. Caleb slithers through the door and drags himself onto his feet he's just as muted and voiceless as Russo. In sequence the others stand alongside Russo and Caleb, altogether speechless and flabbergasted. The area is colossal, stacked wall to wall with hundreds upon hundreds of wooden crates all piled on top of each other. The floor all around is under five inches of water. Hans points his light to the top left corner from the ceiling. The droplets splash onto a metal vessel too high up on the crates to recognise what the vessel is and the droplets continue with their irritating echo of intermittent plopping sounds.

"There must be a thousand crates in here," Rina says softly.

"Do you want to do the honours?" Caleb says and grins at Ellia. She takes his pen knife and prizes it along the width of its nailed down lid, Caleb pulls at the side of the wooden crate and rips it into an uneven splinter. Thousands and thousands of gold coins tumble furiously from the crate and splash powerfully onto the water around their feet.

"Oh my goodness!.." squeals Ellia "...we found it! We actually found it!"

An eruption of hugs, handshakes and whoops of excitement, as they cup the coins in their hands. Louise stoops down to gather some of the coins in her cupped hands and throws them enthusiastically animated into the air. Roused and charged they begin to rip feverishly into the other crates, jewels, necklaces, candle holders and many wealthy valuables tumble out. Ellia moves eagerly towards a large box which stands several feet high, there's several of them stacked together against the wall.

"What is it?" asks Steve.

"Please..." she says softly.

Logan cuts firmly along the edge to make a large square in the container and yanks the portion away.

Unique mixtures of yellow, orange amber panels, gemstones, mirrors, gold leaf carvings gleam and bedazzle that irradiate from their torch lights.

"We've just altered history!" she exclaims and strokes the exquisite architecture of Amber.

"What have you found down there?" yells Abraham, his voice echos and carries along the passage. "Treasure!.." Caleb calls back "...lots and lots of treasure!"

"All these crates...it must be worth billions," says Reade as he views the gallery of boxes.

"There's artwork over here!" Steve yells and holds up a painting.

"Let me see that...!" shrieks Hans "...this piece, do you know what you're holding?"

"No idea?"

"This is the missing Raphael painted in the 16th century. Its title is Portrait of a Young Man and it was stolen from Poland...DON'T GET IT WET!"

"What's that large wall over there with the chains?.." Logan wonders out loud and wades through the water, "...I believe it might be a sluice gate?"

The width of the metal gate spans about 6 meters and rises up a good 10 meters in height. It sits grand and overlooks a deep 15 meter chamber directly below it and either side of the chamber is the gate's mechanism with two sets of vast chained pulleys.

"We're directly underneath Schwedtsee..." Russo says and moves in next to Logan, "...that's some doorway," he continues and spans his light up and down the breadth of the closed duct, "...looks like this was used as an entrance to either bring the treasure in or the way they had planned to get this enormous haul out. That chamber would fill up to an equal water level as the river itself allowing the vessels in and out. It kinda works like the canal sluice gates."

The impressive gates mechanism is rusting but appears to resemble the hypnotic cog innards of an antique wrist-watch.

"Look at this tiara," Rina smiles and hands it to Ellia. "Exquisite, look at the intricate detail..." she replies.

Logan takes a step and feels his foot click down onto a small trigger pressure and he freezes.

He suddenly fills with a petrified affliction "...Russo," he whispers "...can you see what I've just trodden on?"

Russo sees the fear in Logan's eyes and plunges to his knees to examine his colleague's feet in the shallow water.

"OH CRAP MATE DON'T MOVE!"

Everyone stops and exchange frantic, chaotic glances.

"He's stepped on a landmine," Russo's tone panicky and distracted.

Reade and Rina bumble towards Logan.

"We need to get something heavy to slide onto the trigger!" Russo shouts.

Panic erupts as they all rummage furiously to find an item of suitable weight and balance. Logan's stomach tightens and his breathing speeds up rapidly causing him to feel dizzy. He feels his heart thumping adrenaline and he's utterly paralyzed with fear.

"Don't move mate," Reade states sympathetically but firmly.

Logan struggles to regulate his breath, the dizziness increases rapidly into a panic attack and he gasps to take in gulps of the stagnant damp air. His brain becomes hazy and scattered, in a turbulent overdrive and his concentration is now completely held hostage by his own foot.

Steve lunges towards them clenching a solid gold bar.

"Is this any good?"

"Perfect! We need more!.." Reade bursts "...go! Get more!"

Bedlam envelops them as they frantically bring more gold bars forward. Steve feels a shameful humility overwhelm him, he hasn't particularly jelled well with Logan, finding him selfish, entitled and arrogant, but he certainly wouldn't wish this scenario on anyone. Steve has always maintained that compassion isn't something taught in school, but that it develops within every human – a natural desire to show concern for a complete stranger. He places his hand softly onto Logan's shoulder as a momentary distraction and to soothe him, Logan's profoundly affected by Steve's warm hearted calming action and is comfortable with the familiarity.

"I'm terrified," Logan whispers and Steve responds

with a silent nod in appreciation.

"Ok...you need to listen carefully mate," Reade begins, "...you know you can NOT take your foot off, not even a millimetre! We need to slide this onto the trigger to keep it weighted and I will push your foot slowly as we slither this brick on."

"... I know..." he responds nervously.

"Right ok? I'm just repeating this...we're going to apply the pressure and weight to keep it secure and then slide your foot away. I'm not going to lie mate we're in darkness down here! The torch lights are reflecting back off the water and totally inadequate, we can't see clearly it's too dark and murky. Right everyone, you have to keep completely still once you've moved back, we can't create any ripples or water movement, we have one stab at this we cannot get it wrong." Reade continues.

Terror washes through Logan. His fingernails pierce into his palm as he clenches his fist to steady the shaking. His stomach churns, he can feel himself wobbling trying desperately not to let his leg buckle underneath him. He holds the position for a prolonged period, his muscles tense causing him to overthink the cramp now developing in his calf and foot. Rina apprehensively edges back slowly from the group and trembles timidly. Louise notices Rina's disposition is the same as when they lost Arthur, her story about Amell, her body language is so transparent that something horrific has happened to her.

"I want the rest of you to move aside carefully"

Russo says.

Backing away they paddle softly through the water. Physical reactions provoke fear amongst them as they face the danger of not being able to see clearly beneath their steps for any further bombs.

"I'm staying with Logan," Steve replies and squeezes tighter onto Logan's shoulder.

"I can't do this!" Logan panics.

They wait for the ripples in the water to still and Reade shines his light down for Russo to slowly slide the gold bar on the trigger to keep the pressure on it. Logan's quakes cause little ripples in the water around him.

"Very slowly mate........you know the drill," he says looking up at Logan.

Logan slithers his foot gently as Russo veers the weight of the auric brick onto the mechanism. Reade promptly places the other blocks on top. Logan treads his foot forward and feels a small tug around his ankle. His shoe lace is caged between the strategically balanced stacked gold blocks, it pulls at the bars and they tumble from the trigger pressure. In an instant Logan's face fills with fear and his brain races for a way out. Adrenaline rapidly surges throughout his body, his temples throb and he stares back at the team, a momentary serenity of silence.... they know.

Chapter 30

Uproarious thunder shrills bouncing off the walls, the entire room jolts and shakes. Instantly an overwhelming wave of heat and blinding light engulfs the treasure hunters. The noise is deafening. Ear-splitting raucous pressure throws their bodies in sporadic directions hitting and crushing themselves against the falling crates. The blast ricochets along the walls, cracks climb through the brickwork and concrete with such ease and speed, like a rocket launch slicing its way through the atmosphere at orbital speed. Steve's lying face down in the water, his ears ring as he tries to decipher the muffled screams around him. His eyes are blurry, the room is a haze as he tries to focus and interpret the pandemonium encircling him and fumbles all over for his torch but doesn't find it.
"....Steve...come on....!"
Steve isn't able to interpret whose voice it is, everything is obscure and disorientated. He scrambles in the water, treasures fall around him like a shower of diamond and ruby hailstones. Cartons tumble and descend from the towers they'd been stacked, each one making explosive bursts of their glorious contents. Abraham and Thomas yell hysterically through the tunnel, the support beams strain splitting under the pressure of the blast.
Coins splash around Ellias feet littering the floor

and the fear that this golden rain will detonate another land mine creates hysteria. She feels the coins shift underfoot and twists her ankle in the panic; losing her balance she crawls along on her hands and knees blindly following the bellowing cries from the Rodzina. Hans manages to pull himself back into the small passageway and he sees Abraham calling to him from the other end.
"GO! GET OUT!" Hans pleads with him.

The bridge overlooking the Schwedtsee Lake wobbles from the blast and sways the people on it. Onlookers sharply draw in their breath in shock and cling tightly onto its barrier rail. Schwedtsee had been very calm and relaxed that morning and now moves in unusual patterns beneath them. Eyewitnesses grab their mobile phones speedily to video the sudden spectacular occurrence manifesting itself.
The walls around the team grouse and groan as small materialising cracks start to spurt and spray from hundreds of separate locations. Overwhelming volumes of dust and rubble lingers, shrouding the group in a blanket of darkness.
"We have to get out!" the same voice echoes, muffled and inaudible in Steve's ears.
"Come on Steve!" and Caleb pulls Steve firmly.

The surrounding support of the sluice gate bulges. Rina wades hurriedly towards Louise who's sitting directly below a tower of wooden cases rhythmically swaying from side to side. She heaves Louise away just as they tumble into a frenzied chaos around them. Fragments of lumber burst into splinters and a piece embeds itself into Rina's thigh. She cries out in agony and without a seconds thought yanks it frenetically from her body. Louise places Rina's arm around her shoulders and supports her back towards the passageway.

"Ellia get in...Move!" Louise screams.

Louise cups her hands and lifts Rina's foot pushing her into the narrow passage and hauls herself in behind. Rina's wound leaves a trail of blood as she manoeuvres along. Micah and Luca hold the weight of the straining load-bearing beam while Abraham and Thomas pull each team member out of the tunnel.

"It's going to collapse!" Luca grimaces.

Russo staggers bewildered and covered in blood gushing from his forehead. Caleb and Steve assist him into the tight ingress.

"Where's Reade and Logan?" Steve hollers as he examines the percussion of anarchy surrounding him.

"Steve COME ON!" Caleb yells and thrusts him forcefully into the cavity.

They wriggle in a frenzied pattern towards the others all screaming anxiously beckoning them at the other end. The force of the water bellows into the tunnel and shows them no mercy. Caleb and Steve propel at speed fully immersed in the water; Terrified and being taken at the incredible velocity and dominance of the lake. Panic envelops as they

are compelled to move with the flow and no access to oxygen. The team at the end rush for the exit, Steve and Caleb's bodies are jetted out of the tunnel like ammunition firing from a canon. Steve scrambles to his feet choking and gulping the air, he pulls Caleb from the direct flow of the angry white water bellowing around them and they clamber to follow the others. Luca carries Rina cradled in his arms and she's losing a lot of blood. Abraham is close behind holding Russo who drifts in and out of consciousness. Hans falls onto his knees tripping over the submerged crumpled skeleton on the floor. Joseph and Aaron rush towards Piccolo Petra after hearing the succession of blasts.
"Go Back!" Abraham screams to them and he passes Russo to Aaron. Panic erupts amongst the Rodzina.
The sluice door bursts inundating the treasure room with a tsunami from Schwedtsee, it floods every crevice at avalanche force. The torrent consumes everything in its path and sets off another dormant landmine. The load bearing beam snaps as easy as a scrawny twig and the entire structure caves-in on itself. The detonation blows out the roof of the fragile infrastructure propelling a geyser of dramatic measurement above the surface of Schwedtsee. A white water cloud twinkles with a display of gold bullion – it's an exquisite masterpiece.

The townsfolk at Fürstenberg spectate the bizarre events developing. Crowds swarm to Schwedtsee and very rapidly their internet videos become sensationally viral. Two men stand outside their bakery witnessing the locals stampede towards the lake.

"What do you think's happening?" Says the younger of the two. Günter, is the baker's son. He's exceptionally intelligent with a high I.Q but he's happy with the simpler vocation in life.

"I'm not sure?.." his father replies "...but we can't take any risks!"

He's warmly known in the village as Opa Brot (Grandad bread) and inherited the business that's been in his family for the past 100 years. They remove their aprons "...we'll be back later Helga," Opa says to his wife and they head to the back of the bakery rushing out of the backdoor. Günter holds his father's arm discreetly indicating towards two suited gentlemen driving their way through the growing crowd. These had been the same two gentlemen asking questions around the village in search of Ellia's team.

Günter talks quietly on his phone "You need to come! Something's happening near Ravensbrück."

Opa and Günter dash about their family home pulling a hidden box from behind a wooden panel in the back of the wardrobe. Opa brushes the dust off the box, it's full of various combat weapons of bygone days. They descend into the wine cellar and push a large barrel revealing a trap-door.

"What do we do now father?" Günter questions.

"We wait," Opa replies and kisses the onyx ring he's

wearing.

"Do they know how to find the entrance if they make it across the lake?"

"It was always a risk son, it wasn't a practice evacuation we could ever undertake."

The two suited gentlemen get out of their car and push their way through the human horde at the lakeside. A television news crew arrives and starts interviewing some of the locals broadcasting their spectacular video uploads internationally. The men view the depth of the river decreasing rapidly just as a further explosion roars its way through the water and they exit the crowd quickly. The lakeside congregation go wild and the explosion is caught on live television.

Gustaw signals to everyone to get to the Flak Tower. The Rodzina and the team surge their way to get to higher ground as the lake engulfs the giant's encampment. It eliminates the area under a powerful unforgiving tide. The children whimper terrified in their parent's arms as everyone is ushered into the tower. Elijah is extremely confused as the younger Rodzina try to gently assist him towards the Flak Tower. He starts to shout and pushes them away aggressively. Frightened and disorientated he wanders back out of the tower door.

"Elijah come on please?..." Stefanie begs him.

"They're coming! They're coming!" He cries.

Mala Sroka takes his hand "It's ok it's not real, it's just another nightmare, it will all be gone in the morning."

She sings him a little lullaby song in Polish and Elijah calms down.

Ada holds tightly onto his hand and distracts him with a cake "Let's go and find more cakes before they eat them all!"

Elijah smiles at her affectionately and is appropriately distracted as he follows Ada's cake inside.

Mala Sroka addresses the elder men of the Rodzina.

"We need to find the Guardians."

"How do we do that?" Gustaw questions.

"We exit through the way they come to us," Mala Sroka responds.

"We could go and find them for you?" Caleb says looking at his team.

"There's no time, you don't know who they are." She replies.

"Caleb and I are sure we met two of them at the brewery we could try there?" Steve says.

"That's right!" Caleb agrees.

"It'll take too long our whole world is flooding out there..." Abraham states "...we will go grandmother." He continues and beckons Micah and Luca. "When you get to the concealed vestibule there will be a boat hidden in the bulrushes, take it across the lake. The guardians say that you will see a large sculpture jetting out into the waters. Dive down under her foundations there is a doorway that will lead you to the Guardians. Be sure to secure the door behind you."

Gustaw grabs his son and hugs him tightly. Stefanie

places her head onto his chest and cuddles him "it will all be ok!" Abraham whispers into her ear and kisses her tenderly on the forehead.

The Rodzina remove the chairs in the great meeting gallery. Micah slides the bolt to lift up the entire middle bleacher.

Mala Sroka touches Luca's arm affectionately "When we look back at where we came from, how this all started, how far our journey has progressed, we have achieved so much. We were just an experiment and now we are so much more. We are human, we have love and forgiveness inside of us and we are a family."

Abraham, Micah and Luca each kiss the back of her hand and descend into the passage.

Hans pulls his team to one side, "We need to salvage us much of the documentation from the laboratory as we can. If the tunnels flood we could lose everything about these people's extraordinary existence. We need to get the paperwork and serum files!"

"I totally agree Hans…" Caleb replies "…we have no idea what impact this is going to have outside of these walls! We have to protect the Rodzina!"

Ellia looks to Steve and Louise "We'll go! Hans, Caleb you need to help Rina and Russo!"

"It's extremely dangerous!" Hans responds and he remembers Arthur trapped in the passageway.

"Ellia's right!" Louise proclaims.

"No Lou! You stay here and look after the Rodzina, they are terrified! Help them with Rina and Russo!" Steve protests.

"We've got this!.." Ellia encourages her, "...keep the others safe! We'll be back soon."

News Anchor:

"We are broadcasting live from the small town of Furstenburg Germany, where the locals have been witnessing some very unusual events developing over the Schwedstee Lake. Several 'blasts' have accumulated in the decline of the lake's water levels. As you can see over the other side of the water is a grand sculpture called 'Mahnmal Tregende' or 'Supporting' in English designed by Will Lammert. It was placed here in 1959 at the Ravensbrück concentration camp during World War 2 which is just beyond those trees. The sculpture is of two female prisoners and to symbolise their unity. Visitors throw flowers from this bridge into the lake in memory of the thousands of victims whose ashes were thrown into these waters..."

Madness erupts around the crowd as gold coins begin to appear around the banks.

"...it appears as though the lake is giving up its wealth!" The anchor continues.

Another explosion has the gathering around the lakeside screaming. The plinth brickwork supporting Mahnmal Tragende crumbles and the sculpture leans over to one side. Large portions of its base slide into the Lake. A helicopter flies over the crowd towards Ravensbrück which appears to be full of army personnel.

"Does anybody know what military faction they are?" The news anchor questions her crew.

Chapter 31

Ellia and Steve splash through the water that's progressively submerging the camp.

"It's getting deeper!" Ellia yells out to Steve.

Ada watches them heading towards the crypt and she slyly sneaks out of the Flak Tower to follow them. Nobody notices her slip away in all the uproar.

"Can you hear a helicopter?" Steve says scouring the skies and sees it approaching from the distance.

"Do you think they are Watchers or Guardians or Army?" Ellia says.

"We can't take the risk...come on!"

"Ellia. Steve!" Ada screams from behind them.

They turn to see her paddle furiously through the water.

"Ada you have to go back!" Ellia states "...why are you here?"

"I'm coming with you!" she replies.

"It's too dangerous Ada! We lost a dear friend in those tunnels beyond your crypt and we've lost Logan and Reade today too. You have to go back!" Ellia pleads with her.

The helicopter hovers above the compound and makes shallow whirlpools in the water from the spinning rotors. A young man wearing camouflage holds a gun and looks down at Steve.

"Shoot to frighten them – DO NOT AIM AT THEM!

There are too many people around, this is out of hand and now the world is watching it live! It's creating way too much public attention!" One of the suited gentlemen orders.

Ellia and Steve instantly recognise one of the men as the tear gas attacker.

The young man fires his weapon, the bullets slow their speed as they hit the water but he creates enough terror to instil into Ellia and Steve that they are genuinely about to be shot. He fires again which startles Ada and causes her to slip in the panic, she loses her footing and hits her head hard onto floating debris.

"Steve!" Ellia screams and points to Ada. She's face down on the water, her head bleeding and she's completely out cold.

Steve scoops the unconscious Ada up into his arms. She's a very big girl for a 6 year old.

"Come on!" he yells splashing frantically towards the crypt door, "...keep moving the water's coming into the tunnels," he continues.

"We need to wake Ada!" Ellia says hysterically.

"Let's get to the laboratory, we can lie her on the operating table or we lie her on top of these coffins, it's your choice?"

They race pass the entombed Rodzina. The structure around them was already weakened from the team blasting through the flame decorated doorway and the tunnel collapse triggered by Arthur. With 75 years lack of maintenance to the tunnels, the vibrations from various explosions are beginning to strain on the supports. The water bellows in, liquefying the grounds surface and deep into the foundations below. The soil begins to lose it rigidity and now flows with the violent current. The earth shifts beneath the foundations. Cracks zig-zag along the masonry walls unsettling their balance and causes rapid subsidence.

"Is she breathing Steve?" Ellia pants.

"She's whimpering," he replies charging along the crumbling aisle.

Ellia shoves all the paperwork, files and the ancient writings haphazardly onto the floor and Steve lies Ada down onto the surgical table.

"Ada? Ada?" Ellia shakes her arm gently and teases the hair off her face.

Ada groans and softly opens her eyes "Where am I?" she whispers.

It's a poignant moment for Steve, Ada's impacting words *'where am I?'* The precise location where all these culminating events began nearly eight decades earlier. An enormous deafening rumble echoes along the tunnels. Steve runs back and watches the concrete perimeter crash into large boulders where the dynamite had been situated to blast into the crypt. Their initial escape route has now caved-in and disintegrated their entire access to the Rodzina and the outside world. They are completely barricaded from both ends of the tunnel. The lights flicker in the laboratory.

"Steve!" Ellia cries.

He rushes back to Ada and Ellia, "The tunnel's gone

the other end! We're completely sealed off at both ends!"

"I think the electricity is failing," Ellia responds.

"The blockade may reduce the water flow but this bunker framework isn't going to hold out for much longer, we don't want to be crushed! Do you have any phone signal yet?"

"I haven't checked for days Steve!"

"Nothing? Dammit!"

"What about the dormitories? We could push the solid metal frame beds together and take shelter underneath, it's what we do when we have earthquakes in Italy." Ellia replies.

"Good idea I'll follow your lead, it's not exactly anything I have any knowledge in!" Steve replies.

He bends down to gather up the documents and files that Hans and Caleb sent them to retrieve. Various medical and personal files scattered across the laboratory floor. He picks up a file with a small piece of paper held on securely with a rusting paper-clip.

The name on the note reads *'Mala-Sroka' Alter 9 Jahre 26.Juli 1942'*

"I think I've found Mala Sroka's file Ellia!"

"Brilliant," she replies giving Ada sips of water.

Steve pulls the rusty paper-clip off and opens the file. Something is extremely familiar about the sepia photograph of the little girl. Steve contemplates that very old photographs are all similar by comparison but something memorable and eye-catching mesmerises him about 'Little Magpie'. He glares at it very confused for a few seconds and slowly draws his eyes to her personal details.

Der Name: *Hannetta Borowski*
Das Alter: *9 Jahre*
Die Nationalitat: *Polen*
Der Geburtstag: *11. Oktober 1933*
Bekannt als Spitzname – Mala Sroka

Steve topples backwards dazed and horrified. He has no time to react as his stomach launches a giant knot into his throat. He struggles to breathe, his hands tremor disturbing his focus on the words. He feels a burning sensation in his chest flushing its way around his neck and forehead.
"Steve?" Ellia questions.
His ears pound from his own heartbeat and he shakes trembling uncontrollably.
"Steve?" She repeats.
"Her real name!"
"Who's?"
"Mala Sroka's, it means little magpie remember?"
"What about it?.." Ellia says trying to calm the anguish in Steve's body language, "…we need to get Ada to the dormitories she needs a blanket. She's wet and cold. I need to find something to put on her head…"
"Her name…"
"Yes you said, Mala Sroka was her nickname. Steve, come and help me Ada's shivering!"
Steve places all the files onto the end of the operating table. He lifts Ada and carries her along the

corridor back to one of the dormitories. He struggles with his thoughts as he makes his way into one of the long bunked sleeping quarters and conceals Ada's face from spotting Arthur in the distance.

"Come on sweetheart, let me get you out of these wet clothes and sort this nasty cut on your head..." Ellia says, "...we need to get out of here Steve, the whole bunker is going to give any minute! You need to try and find another way out..."

Steve doesn't respond, he's not hearing Ellia's words.

"...I know Russo told us not to open any closed doors after Arthur, but we have to take a risk. We have to get out...Steve?...Steve!"

"Her name Ellia!" Steve snorts.

"What?"

"Her name is Hannetta Borowski!"

Ellia squirms her body uncomfortably, "Well Mala Sroka was going to have an official birth name Steve!"

"Ellia stop!.." Steve grabs her forearm "...Mikolai Borowski is my grandfather. After Viktor's funeral I went to see him. He told me about his sister, someone I had never heard of...her name was Hannetta Borowski...she's my Great Aunt!"

Steve feels the knot in his throat do a somersault as the words leave his lips.

"You think this is all one big coincidence don't you Mr Garrett?" Ellia screams escaping his hold.

"Are you my cousin?" Ada puzzles and stares into Steve's eyes.

Steve hasn't even contemplated all of Mala Sroka's children and grandchildren. The Rodzina are literally his 'family'.

"What do you mean a big coincidence Ellia? What the hell!"

Ellia ignores him, she feels Steve and Ada's eyes pierce through her.

"Addario! You tell me right now what you mean by 'coincidence'!" Steve bellows and slams his fist against a wardrobe, "...TALK!"

Ellia sighs, she looks deep at Ada and strokes her chin, "Did you not think it was all extremely strange from the start Steve? The invitation to interview Viktor at the Royal Brompton? You asked me why you had been targeted for the interview and I told you I'd read an article of yours?..."

Steve doesn't respond he gawks at Ellia, reminiscing how he and Bryan had thought it was all completely strange, that the 'Biguns' had been left out. Steve remembers Bryan telling him that he'd been asked for by name.

"...well I hadn't read your work, but I knew you were a journalist."

"How?"

The total void and stillness of sound between them is temporarily interrupted with a flickering of the lights in the barracks.

"You need to start talking and fast!...How Ellia?"

"My Grandmother."

"Heidi knew I was a reporter?"

"Yes! Ok, but before I tell you, you have to know

that I did not know Hannetta had a nickname or that she was Mala Sroka...how would I have known that? My grandmother had met Hannetta the day she was brought into Ravensbruck with her mother. Hannetta's mother died sometime later so my grandmother and other prisoners looked after the orphaned children feeding them and protecting them. Heidi and Hannetta had a very special bond and they became very close. One day Hannetta vanished along with some other children. My grandmother searched for her for weeks and had assumed that she was either taken out of the camp or had been killed. During the time when they had grown very close Hannetta and Heidi had memorised each other's addresses so they could find each other if they were ever separated and vowed to search for each other if the war ever ended. Heidi kept her word and searched for Hannetta after the war and went to the family home in Poland and found Mikolai's note on the door that he'd left for his family with the forwarding address in England. She visited Mikolai's house several times but never found the courage to knock on the door, until one day she plucked up the confidence. A young girl called Adalene answered the door. Heidi told her that she was looking for a Hannetta Borroski but Adalene told her she'd never heard of her and probably wasn't a relative. It made my grandmother very sad and she assumed Hannetta had died, she didn't want to make life uncomfortable or awkward for your grandfather Mikolai and she left without seeing him. Some decades later she sees Viktor on the television, arrested and facing trial. We wanted to somehow get the story of the locket and the mysterious tunnels out of him. She always took an interest in your grandfather, his children and grandchildren. She checked in at a distance from time to time as she wanted to know how everyone in Mikolai's family were doing..."

"You mean she stalked or spied on him?"

"...we knew the press would swarm like bee's making honey and we really didn't want that level of media chaos, because the time was running out. She knew Mikolai's grandson was a small time reporter. You were the perfect solution and my grandmother desired to give you that big break, for Mikolai, for Hannetta. If we'd had that level of mania from paparazzi we would never have got to the significance of the key, but we were not bargaining on discovering an entirely secluded human race, and we got so much more with you than we'd ever bargained for!."

"How?"

"Viktor, that's how. He really did like you, in that short time you spent together he was quite fond of you. When you went home after your first meeting with him he did nothing else but talk about you all evening. You were the only person he ever told about the child experiments! In all these years, all these decades - YOU!"

"But why did Heidi want Louise and I on this entire circus of a trip?"

"When I told my grandmother of Viktor's revela-

tion regarding the DNA1333 serum and the child experiments, she thought you might be able to find something about Hannetta in some paperwork if we ever found the tunnels. Heidi had been back to Ravensbrück several times looking for documentation on Hannetta, what happened to her, if she had been transferred, death certificates…anything, she was just hoping you would discover a file and at least give your Grandfather some closure in his life too. She hadn't known about the child experiments Steve, but I think she needed the peace for herself and wanted that for Mikolai too. It wasn't all about finding any treasure, her necklace, the mysterious crates and tunnels, it was so very much more Steve." Ada flings her arms around Steve's neck tightly "You are my cousin Steve!"
"I need to get back to her Ellia! They need protecting! She's my aunt. She's my family! MY RODZINA!"

"Good morning Mr Nash, how did you sleep? Shall we get you washed and shaved before breakfast?"
He sits up in bed sips his coffee and looks out over the lawns of the Washington DC nursing home. He is very frail and never really speaks much. He stares blankly as the nursing assistant busies and fusses about gratifying him, he hates all the coddling. His legs no longer work and he sits all day in a wheelchair reliant on the staff.
"What are your plans today Mr Nash?.." she questions "…I think the Activities Coordinator is com-

ing in today to play Bingo or I believe there's some young singers from the local college attending later with their guitars..."

Mr Nash tries to block her chatter out and concentrates on the television.

'...the unusual events at the Schwedtsee Lake have taken a dramatic turn. Explosions have resulted in the decline of water levels. As you can see in the distance the elegant memorial sculpture that guards the Ravensbrück Concentration Camp has tilted as a result of these events. Locals have been...'

"...or the other thing you could do Mr Nash is get one of the girls to take you for a stroll around the garden, it's a lovely day..."

Mr Nash clears his throat, his voice is gravelly and raspy "I'm going to the White House."

"Haha how lovely..." she laughs.

"I am extremely serious! You must take me to the White House!"

The White House chief of staff runs along the corridor to the Oval Office.

"Sorry for the sudden intrusion Mr President but we have a General Nash from the Roosevelt and Truman administrations here to see you. He has been extremely insistent and saying that it's an urgent matter of International Security?"

"Roosevelt and Truman...How old is General Nash?"

"He'll be turning 100 on his next birthday Mr President. Apparently he's created quite a disruption at the nursing home he resides, he went crazy at the staff until they brought him here."

The very nervous nursing assistant guides his wheel chair into the Oval Office. She's very anxious and confused.

"Good Morning General Nash."

The President says and shakes his hand.

"Leave us. I need to talk to the President alone!" He says to the apprehensive nurse.

In her panic and confusion she impulsively bends her knee and performs a nervous curtsy at the President and exits the room.

"So I understand you worked here before General Nash, under Roosevelt and Truman, amazing it's an absolute honour to meet you and I hear you have some important information to tell me?"

"Mr President, I have always lived close to the White House for a very specific purpose in my old age, just in case I needed to get to you quickly. Well, that day has come."

"How can I be of assistance General Nash?" The President says endearingly.

"The Nephilim have been breached!"

"The who?..."

General Nash points at the muted television set on the office wall rolling the breaking news story from Ravensbrück and the Schwedtsee Lake. The President unmutes it and the entire world witnesses Abraham, Micah and Luca crawl out of the concealed vestibule among the bulrush grasses and in unison each of them stand up 9 feet tall.

To be continued………..

Part 2 - 'DELUGE'

References and Research:

The British Library -
www.bl.uk

The International Museum of World War 2 –
www.museumofwwii.org

Gigantism and Acromegaly
- www.pituitary.org.uk
- Eugster, Erica A.; Pescovitz, Ora H. (1999-12-01). "Gigantism". The Journal of Clinical Endocrinology & Metabolism. 84

(12): 4379-4384
- www.nhs.uk
- Goldenberg, Naila; Racine, Michael S.; Thomas, Pamela; Degnan, Bernard; Chandler, William; Barkan, Ariel (2008-08-01). "Treatment of Pituitary Gigantism with the Growth Hormone Receptor Antagonist Pegvisomant". The Journal of Clinical Endocrinology & Metabolism. 93 (8): 2953-2956
- In a Giant's Story, a New Chapter writ by his DNA - Gina Kolata - The New York Times January 5th 2011
- Andrė The Giant Official Website - www.andrethegiant.com
- Salenave S, Boyce AM, Collins MT, Chanson P (June 2014). "Acromegaly and McCune-Albright syndrome". The Journal of Clinical Endocrinology and Metabolism. 99 (6): 1955-69
- www.rarediseases.org
- Lugo G, Pena L, Cordido F (2012). "Clinical manifestations and diagnosis of acromegaly". International Journal of Endocrinology. 2012: 540398
- www.msdmanual.com
- www.en.wikipedia.org

The Israel Museum, Jerusalem –
www.imj.org.il

Ravensbrück Memorial Museum –
www.ravensbrueck-sbg.de
- Will Lammert – Mahnmal Tregende
- The Rabbits
- The International Ravensbrück Committee (IRC)

Frédéric Chopin's Piano Sonata No.2

The Savoy Hotel –
www.thesavoylondon.com

YouTube –
www.youtube.com

Kensal Green Cemetery –
www.kensalgreencemetery.com

Yad Vashem –
The World Holocaust Remembrance Center –
www.yadvashem.org

The Dead Sea Scrolls –
www.deadseascrolls.org.il
- Thiering Barbara, Jesus and the Riddle of the Dead Sea Scrolls   ISBN: 0-06-067782-1, New York: Harper Collins,

1992
- Sanders, James A., ed. Dead Sea scrolls: The Psalms scroll of Qumrân Cave 11 (11QPsa), (1965) Oxford, Clarendon Press
- Jodi Magness - The Archaeology of Qumran and the Dead Sea Scrolls, Grand Rapids: Eerdmans, 2002
- www.en.wikipedia.org
- Fitzmyer, Joseph A. (2008). A Guide to the Dead Sea Scrolls and Related Literature. Grand Rapids, MI: William B. Eerdmans Publishing Company. ISBN: 9780802862419
- Burrows, Millar (1958). More Light on the Dead Sea Scrolls; New Scrolls and New Interpretations, with Translations of Important Recent Discoveries. New York: Viking

Emperor Constantine The Great
- Abogado, Jannel N. "The Anti-Arian Theology of the Council of Nicea of 325." Angelicum 94, no. 2 (2017): 255-86.
- Golgotha – Insight on the Scriptures, Volume 1 p.983-984 www.jw.org
- The Encyclopædia Britannica – www.britannica.com
- www.en.wikipedia.org
- Armstrong, Gregory T. "Church and State

Relations: The Changes Wrought by Constantine." Journal of Bible and Religion 32, no. 1 (1964): 1-7.
- Jones, Christopher P. "Constantine." In Between Pagan and Christian, 9-22. Cambridge, Massachusetts; London, England: Harvard University Press, 2014.
- Bowersock, G. W. "From Emperor to Bishop: The Self-Conscious Transformation of Political Power in the Fourth Century A.D." Classical Philology 81, no. 4 (1986): 298-307.
- The Apocrypha –
- www.britannica.com

Martin Luther
- Cargill Thompson, W. D. J., 1969, "The 'Two Kingdoms' and the 'Two Regiments': Some Problems of Luther's Zwei-Reiche-Lehre", The Journal of Theological Studies, 20(1): 164–185.
- Saarinen, Risto, 2005, "Ethics in Luther's Theology: The Three Orders", in Moral Philosophy on the Threshold of Modernity, Jill Kraye and Risto Saarinen (eds.), Dordrecht: Springer, pp. 195–215
- Massing, Michael, 2018, Fatal Discord: Erasmus, Luther, and the Fight for the Western Mind. ISBN: 9780060517601 New York:

HarperOne
- www.en.wikipedia.org
- Martin Luther The Jews and their lies – www.jewishvirtuallibrary.org
- Edwards, Mark U. "Martin Luther and the Jews: Is There A Holocaust Connection?" Shofar 1, no. 4 (1983): 14-16.

Petra – Jordan –
www.whc.unesco.org

Simon Wiesenthal Center, Los Angeles –
www.weisenthal.com

Religious and Biblical References:
- www.kingjamesbibleonline.org
- www.britannica.com
- www.christianity.com
- www.jw.org
- www.sacred-texts.com
- www.catholic.com
- www.jewishmuseum.com
- www.protestantism.co.uk
- www.en.wikipedia.org
- www.gotquestions.org
- www.biblicalarchaeology.org
- www.answersgenesis.org

www.en.wikipedia.org:

- Qumran Caves – Israel
- Deutsche Reichsbank
- Gold Bullion
- Polaroid Corporation
- Mussolini Monte Soratte Bunker – Italy
- Fürstenberg/Havel – Germany
- The Royal Brompton Hospital – London
- Bicêtre Hospital – France
- Fürstenberg Palace
- Mecklenburg Lake District
- Schwedtsee Lake
- DMC DeLorean

The Da Vinci Code Movie – (Ian McKellan – credit) – Dan Brown Ron Howard/Columbia Pictures/Imagine Entertainment/Skylark Productions

J.K.Rowling – The Harry Potter Series – www.thewizardingworld.com

John Lennon – www.johnlennon.com

Marilyn Monroe – www.britannica.com

Despicable Me – Illumination/Universal Pictures

Little Mermaid/Aladdin/Tangled/Beauty and the Beast - Walt Disney Animation Studios.

The Goonies – Richard Donner/Chris Columbus/Amblin Entertainment

Louis Vuitton –
www.uk.louisvuitton.com

Southwark Police Station – Metropolitan Police - Borough High Street London SE1 1JL

Google Earth –
www.earth.google.com

Portrait of a Young Man - Raphael –
www.nationalgallery.org.uk
Barbie Girl – Aqua
Comedy Central Channel UK –
www.comedycentral.co.uk

Facebook –
www.facebook.com

iPad –
www.apple.com

Michael Kors –
www.michaelkors.com

Heineken –
www.theheinekencompany.com

Friends (TV) Series – Bright/Kauffman/Crane in assoc. Warner Bros. Television

Taxi (TV) Series – (Danny DeVito – credit) – NBC

Boer War 1899–1902 – www.history.com

Clark Kent/Superman – DC Comics – Jerry Siegal/Joe Shuster

Joseph & The Amazing Technicolor Dreamcoat – Tim Rice

Indiana Jones – James Mongold/Steven Spielberg/Paramount Pictures/Amblin Entertainment/Lucasfilm

Busted – James Bourne/Matt Willis/Charlie Simpson

Tomoyuki Yamashita and The Lily-Codes
- Yoji, Akashi. "General Yamashita Tomoyuki: Commander of the 25th Army", in Sixty Years On: The Fall of Singapore Revisited. Eastern Universities Press, 2002
- www.en.wikipedia.com
- John Toland, The Rising Sun: The Decline and Fall of the Japanese Empire 1936–1945, Random House, 1970, p. 677
- www.spartacus-educational.com/2WWyamashita.htm
- "The Golden Lily Conspiracy: My Journey of Discovery". Andrew Gough 1 March 2020 www.andrewgough.co.uk
- The Legend of the Golden Lily Operation –

- www.pacificatrocities.org
- Yamashita's Treasure - Billions of Dollars in Gold still waiting – www.alifeofadventure.com
- Water and Sand Traps – www.treasure.net
- General Yamashita's Dream Book: How to successfully find hidden treasure in the Philippines – Aquila Chrysaetos ISBN: 1909740292

The Amber Room
- Khatri, Vikas (2012). World Famous Treasures Lost and Found. ISBN: 9788122312744 Pustak Mahal Publishing
- www.en.wikipedia.org
- The Amber Room: Long Lost Treasure www.uk.askmen.com
- "Treasure Hunters Claim They Have Found the Long Lost Nazi Amber Room". Jun 23, 2017 www.thehistorycollection.com

·

Back To The Future – (Christopher Lloyd – Credit) Robert Zemeckis/Bob Gale/Universal Pictures/Amblin Entertainment

The Nuremberg Legacy – How the Nazi War Crimes Trials Changed The Course Of History – Norbert Ehrenfreund ISBN: 0230610781, 978023610781 New York: Palgrave Macmillan

The Nuremberg Trials – The Nazi's & Their

Crimes Against Humanity – Paul Roland ISBN: 1848589468/9781848589469 London: Arcturus Publishing Limited

If This Is A Woman: Inside Ravensbrück Concentration Camp for Women – Sarah Helm ISBN: 9781408701072 London: Little, Brown

Printed in Great Britain
by Amazon